A DECEITFUL DENIAL

Hawkes's mouth came down to brush Sarah's with a gentle tenderness that startled her as much as the fact that he dared kiss her. Her gasp of astonishment was smothered by the second, more demanding descent of his lips.

Liquid desire welled up within Sarah like a thirst whetted but not quenched. She could not stop from responding to the dangerous matching of their mouths with a little moan and a slight arching of her back. Hawkes seemed then to devour her lips, to taste their every surface with an avidity that sent a thrill of intense pleasure gliding the length of her spine.

Her heart crashed about in the cage of her ribs like a terrified bird. Pulling away as quickly as she had pressed herself to him, she breathed, "No! Stop."

When Hawkes spoke his voice was remote and cold. "I beg pardon, madam, for an unpardonable blunder. The beast in me does, on occasion, take possession of my better senses."

How could Sarah confess that the "beast" had taken possession of her as well—when she dared not admit it to herself?...

Th

The Silent Suitor

by

Elisabeth Fairchild

A SIGNET BOOK

SIGNET
Published by the Penguin Group
Penguin Books USA Inc., 375 Hudson Street,
New York, New York 10014, U.S.A.
Penguin Books Ltd, 27 Wrights Lane,
London W8 5TZ, England
Penguin Books Australia Ltd, Ringwood,
Victoria, Australia
Penguin Books Canada Ltd, 10 Alcorn Avenue,
Toronto, Ontario, Canada M4V 3B2
Penguin Books (N.Z.) Ltd, 182–190 Wairau Road,
Auckland 10, New Zealand

Penguin Books Ltd, Registered Offices:
Harmondsworth, Middlesex, England

First published by Signet, an imprint of Dutton Signet,
a division of Penguin Books USA Inc.

First Printing, April, 1994
10 9 8 7 6 5 4 3 2 1

To George,
my not so silent suitor.

Chapter 1

LIKE a shadow come to life, Ashley Hawkes Castleford, fourth Earl of Henley, detached himself from the deep, early morning shadows where he watched, with cynical interest, the house he leased in Heddon Street. His mood was as black as the shapeless garrick redingote that draped his shoulders, as black and bleak and starless as the sky had been all night while he grew stiff and cold with watching. Hope had faded with the night. The only thing warming Hawkes now, driving him toward the house, was a sense of injury that burned like a knife wound in the pit of his belly. It was time to bring the curtain down on the tawdry little drama that had played itself out before his very eyes; time, perhaps, to give up women, even the kind one paid for in coin.

Catlike and graceful, Hawkes swung down from his horse without a sound, his coat swirling about him like a thundercloud, his heart heavy with the knowledge the long night's waiting had brought to him. It was not Hawkes's way to deny truth or broken promises, no matter how difficult they might be to face, nor was it within him to slink off and lick his wounds. He must face those who injured him now, before the dawn ushered in a new day.

Fitting key to lock, he opened the door with the ease of familiarity. Catherine's calico cat scooted out to weave about his legs, her purr rasping loud in the morning quiet. He leaned down to scratch her ears, a grim sadness pulling down the corner of his lips. Then, like a larger, more dangerous feline, Hawkes stepped in the door and up the stairs, taking the risers two at a time without a creak. He hesitated outside a door at the top of the stairs, long enough to wonder if he expected too much of the people he allowed close to him. His muscles bunched with the coiled menace of the predator about to pounce.

There was no turning back, no undoing what had been done, no mending broken promises. He flung wide the door. It smashed back against the wall of the room with a bang that shattered the early morning still like pistol-shot.

The occupants of the room were not aware that the earl had intended to call. Both the man and the young woman bolted up in the bed with exclamations of surprise.

"Who is there?" cried she.

"Bloody hell!" said he, and in sudden haste to quit the bed leapt up, only to scramble back under the covers when his sleep-fogged mind awoke to the fact that he had not a single stitch of clothing on his person.

"But who else could it be, *chère amie?*" Hawkes purred from the darkness of the doorway.

"Do not kill him, Ashley!"

Hawkes ignored the "him" she referred to, lazily walked to one of the long windows beside the head of the bed, and threw back the heavy drapery. A smoky gray light illuminated the room.

"I've no intention of going to such trouble, pet," he drawled politely.

Had Catherine Stone been a woman of keener perception she might have recognized in the Earl of Henley a gentleman well skilled in hiding disappointment beneath a facade of nonchalance. Miss Stone was not such a woman. She was quite incapable of reading between any lines save those she quoted on stage and best understood theatrically overblown expressions of emotion that projected across a room. To her way of thinking, Hawkes seemed quite out of character as the cuckolded lover when, with a tight rein on the white-hot anger that sizzled just beneath his cool veneer, he sat in a chair by the window and offered a polite suggestion.

"Perhaps you should introduce us." He indicated the man-sized lump beneath the covers beside her. "I've no idea how to address this fellow in order to ask him to leave."

The gentleman under the duvet groaned, but Catherine, her pretty hazel eyes still wide with the shock of having been found out in her infidelity, answered without thinking.

"But, he said he was a friend of yours!"

"A friend? Really?" The earl sounded mildly interested. Lifting himself up out of the chair, he plucked back the covers to expose the man's face.

"No, not a friend," he said firmly after a searching examination, with carefully schooled features. "We are, however, acquainted. Mr. Preston, is it not?"

Hawkes had counted Preston among his closest friends until this very morning. Bret cast the sheets away from his chest and sat up with a sigh.

"You know full well who I am, Hawkes."

The earl allowed no trace of the painful sense of betrayed trust that cut him to the very quick to reveal itself in a visage that seemed carved out of granite. "Will you leave us, Mr. Preston?" His tone was distant but flawlessly polite. He refused to look at Bret.

Catherine began to whimper.

"Hawkes, let me explain . . . " Bret pleaded.

Hawkes cut him short. "Only my friends have leave to call me Hawkes, Mr. Preston. I require you to refrain from addressing me as such. In addition, I neither asked for, nor desire to hear your explanation. Will you leave us?"

With a sigh, and an apologetic shrug to the pretty young woman whose bed he warmed, Bret adopted the same cool formality with which he had been addressed.

"I should be happy to oblige, my lord, if you will be so good as to hand me the buckskin breeches you have trod upon."

Catherine's whimpering turned to sobs.

Hawkes, his manner careless though his fingers shook, plucked up the buff leather breeches and turning his back on the man he had once called friend, tossed them onto the bed. He contrived to appear indifferent to Catherine's cries. Women—especially fickle, unfaithful, calculating creatures such as this one—should not have been blessed with such skill when it came to the touching art of tears.

Bret, who retrieved his confidence as swiftly as he regained the scarlet uniform that marked him as an officer of the Royal Horse, endeavored to say something when he sat on the edge of the bed to pull on his thigh-high jackboots. Hawkes froze the words on his lips, saying with chilling finality, "You may see yourself out, Mr. Preston. It would appear you know the way."

The brusque finality of those words wrenched a contrite "Sorry, old man" from Bret's lips.

Mere words could not thaw Hawkes's icy self-control.

"Good day sir," was his only response.

Planting his cocked hat on his head, Bret saw himself out.

Catherine's heartrending sobs increased in volume. Not unmoved, Hawkes handed over his handkerchief.

"Blow your nose, Cathy."

The gentle suggestion brought her pretty hazel eyes, huge with surprise, darting up to regard him for a moment.

Hawkes felt foolish. Again the woman deceived him.

"You really must endeavor to produce some traces of moisture to make your moving performance complete, Cat," he purred.

She tossed the handkerchief back in his direction. It proved an ineffectual missile.

"A gentleman with any sort of sensibility would never insult a lady with such a nasty remark as that."

Her words were flung as ineffectually as the handkerchief.

"The point is moot," he said silkily. Laughter bubbled up in his throat. "I am the 'Beast,' pet, and as any female in town will tell you, the 'Beast' is no gentleman."

Petulantly she threw a pillow at him, with good aim, narrowly missing his left ear. "You are a beast. I was warned you could turn off all feeling in an instant. Go away, I'll not listen to your polite indifference anymore!"

He bowed.

"As you wish, madame. I shall not trouble you again."

She cried out against his leaving, for she was vain enough to believe he could not give her up so easily. Too late she remembered that it was by the earl's generosity that she kept herself well clothed and comfortable. She had much to lose in his leaving.

"Heartless creature!" she shouted after him.

The words neither halted nor hastened his exit. She tossed another pillow his way.

Hawkes dodged, unruffled, as the shot sailed past him. He watched, feeling a strange kinship with the abused cushion as it arced over the balustrade to explode upon the landing in a volley of feathers. His eyes dark and cold and unfathomable, he turned one last time to regard the young woman whose looks had captivated him from the moment he saw her treading the boards at King's Theater, eight months ago.

"You are welcome to take advantage of these rooms until the end of next month," he said, "but I do not intend to renew the lease. You may wish to make arrangements to vacate the premises."

"You've no regard for my wishes," she shouted after him as he made his way down the feather-strewn stairs.

Hawkes realized she was quite correct. He had no regard at all for her wishes, wiles, or explanations at this point. He was far more distraught over the confrontation with Bret than with the loss of Catherine's favors. He had expected passion, not constancy of her. That was too much to expect of a woman of Catherine's character and occupation—perhaps too much to expect of any woman other than his mother, who took constancy to the opposite extreme. She remained constant to the dead.

Bret was a different matter. Bret had betrayed his trust, wounding him to the core. Feeling strangely numb, he swung into the saddle, whirling the long black redingote out of his way before Catherine got the window open and leaned out in an intriguingly disheveled state of undress.

"Heartless creature!"

Doffing his hat to her, he set spur to the black horse, feeling as if indeed his heart were missing.

"Beast!" Her shriek sounded strangely defeated. He could not be sure whether she intended to insult or recall him with the title. Either way, it did not matter. He had, as Catherine accused, turned off all feeling for her.

The window slammed behind him.

Catherine Stone's wild shouting could not be heard above the rumble of wheels in nearby Piccadilly, where the road narrowed as it led into Leicester Fields. Carts and cabs, carriages and cattle rattled along with purpose until the abrupt turn and narrowed street slowed their passage, for by way of the Haymarket, one drove into Whitehall and the Strand.

It was therefore a trifle unusual that a gentleman of advancing years and balding pate, stood stock-still on the northwest corner of the intersection, engaged in earnest conversation with a striking young lady, for she was forced to tilt her head quite often in his direction in order to understand what he chose to say to her.

That she was a lady of means was quite clear, for while her white chip cottage-bonnet was not as high-crowned as the latest kick in fashion decreed, she wore a well-cut, high-necked walking dress of quality cambric, trimmed out professionally. It possessed a ruff of triple lace and full bishop's sleeves that tied in three places with ribbons of a muted sea green shade called Pomona, that had only recently begun to be seen in the shops. The silk-lined mantle that fell in soft folds from shoulder to knee was Pomona as well, and those who passed close enough to tell, could see that the color was well chosen, for it brought out the color of the young lady's eyes.

It was the first-glance, breath-stopping impression of a perfect female form, not the woman's impeccable taste in matching colors, that caught the attention of every pair of masculine eyes that strayed in her direction. But it was the unaffected expression of joy on the charming face that held their attention. Traffic, which normally slowed at this juncture, inched along as carters, cab drivers, and tradesmen reined in their teams to stare.

The drivers of a milk truck and a hansom cab that waited to pass, had agreed over their horses' rumps that they did not mind the delay so much. In fact, the cab driver, though he was a married man, turned to the milkman as their teams stood blowing a fog of warm breath, to wink and nod.

"Never thought as I'd be ogling a Venus at the crossroads this morning."

The milkman grinned. "Aye. A happy picture she be."

Miss Sarah Wilkes Lyndle, the Venus-at-the-crossroads, was as unaware of the heads that swiveled in her direction as she was of the beautiful colors that lit the eastern sky behind her. Sarah Lyndle was blind. The beautiful sea green eyes that so perfectly matched the sea green ribbons fluttering in the breeze, saw nothing.

The look of rapt attention that lit her face was due to sounds not sights. Wheels rumbled and hooves clattered on the cobblestones. Voices, babbling at a faster, harsher rate than what she was used to in the country, spoke in dialects she found difficult to decipher. The cacophony of sound pressed in on her ears as invasively as the confusion of smells filled her mouth and nose.

At home, Sarah knew where every step took her. Every sound, every scent was familiar. Lord Lyndle kept his daughter and her blindness, wrapped securely in the cotton wool that was Lyndle Hall. Every need was met, and Sarah's past, present, and future, meticulously arranged. There were no surprises, no obstacles to trip her up. All of her past and most of her future was predictable regularity—safe, secure, and cushioned from shock.

This new world she had stepped into was distracting and bewildering and all-enthralling in ways she had never anticipated. In London, each step was unfamiliar and fraught with obstacle. A simple stroll down the pavement was a hard, bruising, noisy adventure. Sarah was confused, dizzied, and exhilarated beyond all expectation.

Dr. Turvey had been nervously clearing his throat and mumbling under his breath from the moment they set out on this morning's errand. These slight noises, along with the slowing of his steps the closer they got to their destination, left Sarah with the uncomfortable conviction that the good doctor wished himself anywhere but here, on his way to the home of one of his best patients, Lady Amelia Castleford, the Dowager Countess of Henley.

It was her godmother Lydia Turvey's idea that they should be here, just as it was at Lydia's invitation that Sarah had come to London. Seven years in a row Lydia had written, pleading with Sarah's father to allow his daughter a taste of the ton. Seven years in a row Lord Lyndle had refused her generosity. This year the letter from Lydia had come again, fatter than before and bolder in entreaty.

"You cannot keep your daughter forever ignorant of the world of her peers, solely because of her blindness," Lydia's pen had scolded. "And I will not allow you to punish Sarah for her mother's folly."

Father read Lydia's crossed and recrossed lines and then read them again. Sarah held her breath and dared to hope that this year he might see fit to allow her to go. She had long ignored a faint, gnawing hunger centered in the area just beneath her heart, accepting her life, and her father's plans for it, without question or discontent, but there was an undeniable restlessness triggered by the letter. For years Sarah had felt its tug. In the past she had managed to squash the feeling when her father refused to let her visit Lydia. This year had been different. Sarah could not again deny how much the idea of a Season in London drew her. The hunger within her grew. Its ravenous gnawing seemed bent on devouring her peace of mind.

Sarah's mother had been drawn to London like a moth to flame, enticed away from her husband and young daughter, seduced by the lure of new clothes, courtly ways, and a whirl of entertainments. And, like the moth, Lady Lyndle's delicate wings had been singed. She had lost a vast sum of money in games of chance, spent a fortune on dresses and hats and shoes, and came close to scandal with flirtation gone awry. All of which Lord Lyndle might have forgiven, but his wife had come fluttering home again to Lyndle Hall, brought low by a feverish malaise, from which she never recovered. That he could neither forgive nor forget, for the same fever took from his daughter her sight.

Sarah had lived to mourn the loss of her mother. In mourning her, she determined to be different. She resolved to avoid London, card games, dancing, and any wildness of spirit she might have inherited. She convinced herself that London held no lure, and when to her dismay it did, with the yearly arrival of her godmother's invitation, she thought to satisfy the gnawing hunger within her by agreeing to her father's favorite plan for her future. She would, she promised, marry Geoffrey Garvey, the unwed eldest son of her father's best friend and neighbor, Sir Garth Garvey, when he returned from his two years of service overseas. She would, she resolved, be a good and faithful wife, unlike her mother in every way.

To her disappointment, her curiosity concerning London, was not diminished in the least by her promise. It seemed, to the contrary, to grow stronger.

Driven by the specter of her mother's sad end, which she felt she must exorcise before the commitment of marriage was fulfilled, Sarah had dared to add her own voice to Lydia's. Perhaps a Season in London would satisfy her growing discontent.

"I'm soon to be a married woman, Father," she had pointed out. "I know little enough of what that change in my life will mean, but I do know that I would be a good wife, content in her married state. It seems inappropriate to saddle Geoffrey, well traveled and wise in the ways of the world, with a wife as green as any schoolroom miss."

Her father had amazed her by agreeing, but it was not really her argument that won him over. It was, in the end, the fact that Lydia Turvey's husband George was a doctor that tipped the balance in Sarah's favor. Of all the people, a doctor might best keep her out of harm's way.

The fact that George Turvey was a doctor might ease her father's mind, but that same fact in no way eased Sarah's entrance into society. A doctor, even one descended from noble lineage, had the unfortunate taint of trade to contend with, in a society whose yardstick for the measure of a man was title, land, money, and the ability to survive without actually working. George and Lydia Turvey led a quiet, industrious life that touched upon the mere fringes of the whirl of activity and excess, that constituted the London haute ton.

"There's nothing for it but to approach one of the lady matrons who jealously guard the vouchers for Almack's," Lydia had informed her husband.

The doctor, who trusted his wife's judgment in all things related to social form, agreed to approach one of his patients, the Dowager Countess of Henley. Lady Castleford was one of the very dragons of respectability who had the power of the vouchers at her fingertips.

"We need not do this, Dr. Turvey," Sarah said with feeling, as she pivoted gleefully, her ivory cane as axis. Her ears were alive with the sounds of the city. "I need never go to Almack's. There is no end of other things to see and do; Astley's Ampitheatre, Mr. Towneley's statue collection, the Whispering Gallery in St. Paul's . . . "

The doctor, who was in the midst of rehearsing what he meant to say to the dowager, interrupted her.

"Lydia has the right of it, you know. Deuced vouchers will make all the difference in the world. Vouchers bring with them the proper connections—like people with theater boxes. Must have them."

"Must I?" Sarah reversed direction, smiling. She was enjoying herself enormously, with no more than the street to entertain her. This push to get passes to Almack's seemed ridiculous.

"Absolutely. Lydia knows best. Strong-minded woman your godmother, and very knowing when it comes to social niceties. She might have married any number of titled gentlemen, you know. Her family meant she should have a knight at the very least, but she told them, and in no uncertain terms, that she would have only me."

Sarah heard the swell of emotion thicken the doctor's words. He sounded moved, almost to tears. The metal arms of his spectacles clicked together in shaking hands as he gave his nose a resounding blow that spoke somehow, both of his determination, and of his great appreciation for the sacrifice Lydia had made in marrying him, the youngest son in a family whose wealth and power had been decimated by two generations of gamblers and rake-hells.

Had he not had his face swathed in the square of linen, and his thoughts elsewhere, the doctor might have noticed sooner what Sarah was completely blind to—trouble was headed their way, and it was moving fast.

No longer numb to the ache in his heart over the cruel betrayal of both friend and lover, Hawkes was pushing his horse to a pace faster than might be considered judicious, given the backup of vehicles. His grim concentration focused on navigating his mount between wagon spokes and slowly moving wheels in the face of the rising sun.

Light broke over the tops of the trees, low and blinding, and into that light stepped what appeared to Hawkes (as he scowled against the glare) to be not so much a woman as a perfectly formed goddess, set down on the curbstone in a blast of heavenly color. Despite having spent most of an uncomfortable night vowing never again to be swayed by a female, Hawkes's attention was riveted. Bathed in the nimbus of light, his goddess was not to be ignored. Her back was to the sun, smeared butter-soft as it angled through treetops laced with dew and fog. The light sought her out, concentrating itself like liquid gold in the thin muslin of her dress so that her shapely figure was gilded from the top of her hat to the hem of her skirt.

The face of this glowing vision was not revealed to him. A halo of fair, upswept curls peeped from beneath a bonnet brim tipped at such an angle as to reveal no more than a set of gently smiling lips and a softly rounded chin.

For an instant Hawkes forgot that he had spent a sleepless night uncovering the infidelity of his mistress, forgot the deceit of his friend, forgot indeed the press of traffic around him. He saw not where his horse was going, saw naught but the exquisite vision before him. He was wishing she might tip her head back so that he might see more of her face when Brutus reared.

It was Sarah's ivory walking stick and not her dazzling, sun-struck shapelineness that made an indelible impression on the horse. A veteran of Wellesley's Battle of Talvera, Brutus mistook the stick for a much deadlier weapon. With a toss of his head and a disgruntled rumbling in his throat, he reared up to avoid perceived danger in the stick Sarah waved back and forth at an odd angle in front of her, not unlike a drawn sword.

"Ho, Brutus!"

Hawkes wrenched his attention away from Sarah as swiftly as Brutus wrenched at the bit and came crashing down against the end of a two-wheeled haycart.

"Blast!" Hawkes thundered.

The cart, unbalanced, reversed direction with a loud cracking sound and dumped its contents in the road. The driver let loose a steam of heated cant and fought to steady his team.

Walleyed, Brutus danced back from the avalanche of straw with a twist that would have unseated many a fine rider, but Hawkes managed to cling to his back with remarkably good form, shouting forcefully, "Ho, Brutus. Ho! Be still, you devil!"

Brutus would not be still, backing instead beneath the noses of a team of dray horses, and then reversing direction with great suddenness and an unhappy snort, due to his distaste for a nip in the rump. He bolted forward, the bit between his teeth.

"Out of the way!" Hawkes shouted, leaning into Brutus's mane and grappling for the bit as the horse leapt onto the walkway and took to his heels.

The sun still hung like a corona about the head of the Venus-at-the-crossroads, who stood like a statue, directly in Brutus's path.

Hawkes dragged on the reins, roaring.

"Confound it, woman! Out of the way! Are you blind?"

Sarah had no doubt that the angry shout was directed her way, but she did not move, for in moving, she knew she might step directly into the horse's pathway, and this was no time for error. Pressing her arms to her sides, she made herself as small a target as possible, and bravely stood her ground, balanced on the balls of her feet, her ears alert. She was trusting in the acuity of her hearing to tell her, in the end, which way to leap. The brief moment of waiting seemed endless as the thunder of shod hooves bore down on her, but she stood her ground, like a toreador who stands waiting for the bull. In the last instant, she swung out of the way, as if trained to it, and the massive, leather-creaking, cloak-flapping bulk of man and beast rushed past her, so close, their wind whipped her skirts and flung curls of her hair across cheek and brow.

A rush of impressions, as unsettled as the air, assailed her senses: the smell of horse, the damp tang of fear, sweat, leather, and something else, a faint, clean, masculine odor, like the woods after a rain. There was, subtler still, a strange, charged quality to the air that washed over her in the wake of horse and man, like the atmospheric disturbance one experiences in the wake of a lightning storm, as if something larger than life, something elemental, and powerful, and life-changing, had just swept past.

"Damnation, woman! I might have killed you!"

The oath, flung back over the man's shoulder, buffeted Sarah as much as the wind of his passing. She was quite unused to being shouted at, to being roughly handled in any way. There was something grievous about having so much bloated anger focused on oneself. Surely the uncontrolled antics of a horse and her own innocent error of standing in the way, did not merit such an unseemly outburst.

"Dear God, Sarah! Are you all right?" Dr. Turvey was beside her in an instant. "You might have been killed!"

"Stupid fool! A man should not be permitted to take to the streets if he cannot control his horse," she insisted, her color high. She had no inkling that her walking stick was in good part responsible for the runaway horse.

"The man has too much horse under him," he said.

"And no rein on his tongue," Sarah replied tartly.

Faintly, they could hear the receding thunder of hooves and the horseman's shout, "Out of my way!"

Dr. Turvey led her around the cascade of straw littering the cobbles.

"Come, we've Lady Castleford to call on," he said, "and neither haycarts nor runaway horses shall stand in the way of vouchers to Almack's."

Chapter 2

THERE was something vaguely disquieting about the Countess of Henley's town house after the commotion of the streets. The servants were too obsequiously hushed and the rooms too still, with a sweet, closed-in mustiness that hung in the air, despite their grand size.

"Is the countess very ill?" Sarah whispered to the doctor, conscious of the resounding acoustics as they sat waiting in a vast, chilly drawing room for a summons to Amelia Castleford's bedside.

The doctor answered in a low murmur.

"You must never tell her I have said so, Sarah, but the countess has no physical complaint for me to mend. Her constitution is lowered by a constant state of melancholy, which magnifies every ache and pain and flutter she experiences. This melancholy has plagued her since the death of her eldest son, Aston, who was unfortunate enough to break his neck in a fall from a horse. That unhappy incident alone might not have so affected her, had not an apoplectic fit then struck down her husband George, close on the heels of which her sister and brother-in-law also fell, victims of smallpox. Convinced she must soon die of a broken heart, Amelia took to her bed and has not since stirred from the confines of her house."

"How dreadful!" The words echoed mournfully down the stuffy length of the room. Sarah's heart went out to the woman upstairs. She understood the depths of such loss. Her own mother had passed away when she was no more than seven. For months, in her newly darkened world, she had been completely inconsolable, convinced she was somehow responsible, and plagued by the dreadful fear that her father might just as swiftly be snatched away from her.

"Dreadful, dreadful." The word swam softly in her head.

"Dreadful indeed," the doctor agreed. "It is a dreadful waste for a perfectly healthy woman to pine for lost loved ones, when she has family still living and the soundness and vigor that so many of my patients are desperate to regain."

"What do you do for her then, if she has no real complaint?"

The doctor's laugh was a self-satisfied one. "I visit as often as I can, so that Lady Castleford is obliged to dress herself and see to her toilet and sit up in bed. I am determined that she shall get up out of it eventually."

When, at last, Sarah and Dr. Turvey were ushered by yet another hushed servant into the presence of the dowager countess, Sarah could neither see nor appreciate the black silk kimono that Amelia had taken pains to don in expectation of her visitors, but she had some clue to the painstakingly artistic arrangement of Amelia's freshly curled ringlets in the faint odor of singed hair that the curling iron had left behind. She gave the doctor's arm a squeeze.

"Come in, come in, Turvey. Do not stand in the doorway. Who is this lovely young woman you bring to see me?" Amelia beckoned with the imperious tone of a woman who is used to having her every command instantly obeyed.

Sarah dipped a curtsy. "I am Sarah Wilkes Lyndle, my lady. Of Lyndle Hall."

"Lyndle? Elisabeth Lyndle's daughter?" The countess leaned forward in her bed, with a rustle of silk, for a more probing look. Sarah felt the intensity of her perusal, indeed she heard the sharp intake of breath that signaled the widow's realization that she was blind. Sarah had heard just such stifled gasps many times before.

Close upon the heels of that gasp came inevitably the hint of sorrow, of genuine distress, in a voice stretched too high, as Amelia said, "You have your mother's looks, child, but you cannot see that, can you?"

"No, I cannot see, but I remember how my mother looked, and I am flattered if you feel there is some resemblance. I used to think her the most beautiful woman alive when I was a child. She had the loveliest dimples when she smiled."

Sarah was relieved that the first moment of shock had been met with regard to her sightless condition, for once it was past one might hope to carry on a fairly natural conversation. Lady Castleford's cheerfulness sounded forced, but Sarah did not mind. The questions directed her way were polite and typical and unlaced with meaningless expressions of pity or sorrow for her handicap. In fact, on discovering that Lyndle Hall was in Buckinghamshire, within a short day's ride of Brantley, her son's favorite property, even the preternatural cheeriness gave way to real curiosity.

Lady Castleford, who had by her own hand locked herself in seclusion for nigh upon five years, was, rather ironically, most dismayed to learn that Sarah had been confined to the country since childhood.

"Never been to London, you say? How tedious, my dear."

Dr. Turvey cleared his throat.

"You may recall that Miss Lyndle's mother succumbed to a fever contracted in London. That same fever, passed to Sarah, left her sightless. Understandably, Lord Lyndle has no desire to visit a location that brought him such misery."

Sarah nodded. "Father has been of the opinion that to allow me a Season was to risk losing me to some incurable malady borne on the city air."

Lady Castleford fanned the air before her.

"Oh my! Your father must have loved your dear mother very much."

Sarah knew not how to reply. There was no denying Father had doted on her mother. The problem lay in the opposite direction. Mother had not truly returned his affection. She wondered if Lady Castleford knew as much. Her mother had at one time been the subject of a great deal of speculative gossip.

The doctor was wise enough to redirect her thoughts. "Do you know, Sarah," he said, "Lady Castleford will not mount a horse for the selfsame reason that your father refuses to come to London?"

"Indeed, 'tis true." Amelia allowed herself to be distracted from thoughts of future catastrophe by the memory of past ills. "My eldest son, Aston, was tossed on his head by his favorite hunter while jumping fences. I find I cannot trust my person to any horse, on the basis of that tragic breach in equine etiquette."

Sarah leaned forward, her voice confidentially lowered. "Do you know I find myself quite in sympathy with your fear of horses, for while I enjoy posting about on the back of a steady cobb under the watchful eye of a groom, any creature with undue spirit leaves me quaking. Why just this morning we came close to being trampled by a runaway horse of ungovernable temper."

"Oh my! You never did." The dowager plied her fan a little more feverishly to stirring the air.

"It was quite an adventure," Sarah confided with an insouciant smile of such unruffled composure that Lady Castleford's fan stopped flapping. "But"—her voice took on the secretive hush of a conspirator—"we must never allow Father to hear of the incident, for he would most assuredly whisk me home into the country again, where one might just as easily encounter a runaway horse. Do you not agree? I should not like to confine myself to the country again, so soon. Lydia and the doctor have made all manner of entertaining plans."

Lady Castleford interrupted with the enthusiastic energy of a woman who ran other peoples' lives far better than her own.

"You must hear the Philharmonic Society perform. I have a private box begging to be used at the Argyle Rooms."

Sarah smiled. "How very kind of you to extend such a luxury, Lady Castleford, but we would not intrude. . . . "

"No, no, for nearly two years the box has been empty, my dear. My son, knowing full well that I am confined to bed, must needs tease me by continuing to rent it for me. 'In case I should have a sudden whim to go,' he says."

Amelia shook her head with a wistful little smile that Sarah had not the privilege to see.

"How very kind of your son, my lady," she said, misconstruing the sadly put-upon air with which the widow recounted the rental of the box, and before Amelia could draw breath to set her to rights, she leaned forward and changed the subject by observing, "I know my question may seem impertinent, but is that Chinese silk you are wearing?"

Amelia did not find such a question impertinent in the least. "How ever did you know that?" she inquired.

Amused that most people assumed her sense of hearing was as limited as her sight, Sarah chuckled, little knowing that of all things about her, Amelia found this sweet sound of mirth the most delightful.

"There is a marvelous and quite unmistakable rustle to fine Oriental silk," she explained.

Delighted, the countess moved just enough to bring forth the desired effect. "Quite right you are, my dear. I am pleased you noticed, for this is quite my favorite negligee. Silk is so kind to the touch, do you not agree?"

Sarah's fingers tested an imaginary length of silk in the air between them. "Like warm water running through one's fingertips," she murmured.

"Such a prettily turned phrase, my dear." Amelia thoughtfully pressed a soft fold of the fabric into Sarah's hand. "My nephew Stewart won it for me."

"Won it, madam?" Sarah said.

"Oh yes, Stewart is forever winning things. He is well known for his luck."

Dr. Turvey cleared his throat. "One must be lucky, or have bottomless pockets, in order to continue indulging oneself with games of chance."

"Yes, that is so," Amelia agreed. "Now and again, such a way of life cannot but land my nevie under hatches." She laughed dismissively. "But, 'tis not often. He has not borrowed significant sums off me above a half dozen times." Fondness dismissed all hint of reproach. "Stewart has, I'm happy to say, other talents to recommend him. He is quite handsome, with a keen eye for fashion and fast horses. I dare say, in matters of elegance and refinement, the boy has no equal."

"He is called Beauty, is he not?" Turvey asked politely.

Sarah did not mistake the stiffness that took sudden possession of Amelia's tongue. "Yes. In some circles. Just as, most regrettably, my own dear Ashley is called Beast."

"Beast, my lady!" Sarah's expressive mouth gave evidence of her genuine distress. "What a cruel title."

"Indeed," sighed Amelia, and it was a long-suffering sigh, the sort that only a mother, who has done all that may be expected of her, and still her child does not conform to her expectations, can sigh. "Ashley cares naught what society thinks or says of him. He is sadly lacking in sensibility for such things. Indeed, he seems amused by the term, but it is a matter of no little consequence in the eyes of a mother, I am sure you understand."

Sarah did understand. Her mother had cared not a fig for proprieties, no matter the distress it brought her family. She responded with a very satisfying degree of sensibility, by reaching out to pat Amelia's hand.

"Perhaps it is best that your son can laugh, for were he pained by the name, surely 'twould serve only to vex you the more."

"Having never considered the matter in that light, I find strange comfort in your words," the countess leaned forward to whisper in a voice so moved it trembled. "You see things, my dear, that most of us with eyesight would do well to observe."

"You are very kind, Lady Castleford. Would that I might see you more clearly."

"If I could but make it so." The countess sounded genuinely distressed that she could not.

Dr. Turvey took up Sarah's hands. "Sarah can see, my lady, after a fashion. With these."

"Can you really, child? I have heard that King George saw the face of Lady Sarah Lennox by passing his hands over her face when she was presented at court. They say he wished to see if she bore any resemblance to her namesake and great-aunt, Lady Sarah Lennox, and declared her 'very like.'"

"Lady Lennox was most kind to allow the king such a courtesy. Most people do not care to have their faces handled."

The doctor agreed. "There was some fear that such an exchange might excite the king unduly. He was prone to bouts of dementia even then."

Gently, Amelia lifted Sarah's hands to her soft, powdered cheeks.

"You may look at my face if you like."

Sarah was pleased. Light as butterflies, her fingertips began to trace the outline of Amelia's profile.

The countess started and pulled away. Sarah paused and might have stopped had not the dowager whispered, "Go on." She sat very still, a smile rounding her cheeks, until Sarah had done with the contours of her face.

"It is no wonder they were concerned for the king," Amelia said. "There is something most intimate in having one's face passed over in such a manner."

Sarah was moved that a countess should care to understand the limitations of her visionless world. "Thank you, madam, for permitting me such an intimacy," she said. "I have a lovely picture in my head now to accompany your kind voice."

"My lady . . ." Dr. Turvey hesitated delicately, and Sarah knew that he meant to take advantage of the moment to make good his promise to ask for vouchers. "I would be most indebted to you if you could consider granting me a favor."

A sudden stillness was Amelia's immediate response.

"Indeed. A favor?"

Sarah cringed, wishing fervently she had insisted they forget the stupid vouchers.

"I do hesitate to ask . . ."

"Dear God, Turvey. You have me in a quake. I shall need my smelling salts if you keep this up. Out with it. What is this favor?"

"Could you find it in your power to sponsor Sarah's entry to Almack's?"

Amelia sank back into her pillows with a genteel little huff of relief.

"Vouchers? Is that all? Such ado about nothing," she scolded. Without a trace of condescension, she said, "I'd be enchanted. How old are you, my girl?"

Sarah lifted her chin. Her reply was bound to provoke a response. "I am four-and-twenty."

She heard Amelia's sharp intake of breath and let loose a throaty chuckle. "Almost in my dotage."

"Nonsense!" The countess protested forcefully. "You're not on the shelf yet. But what, pray tell, have you found to keep yourself occupied these four-and-twenty years, locked away in the solitude of Lyndle Hall?"

"You shall not pity me, my lady," Sarah insisted. "I have been under the tutelage of not one, but two exceptionally talented ladies of reduced circumstances. Due entirely to their patient efforts, I speak both German and French, have learned the steps with which to accompany a variety of dances, am accomplished at both the pianoforte and the harpsichord, and knit passably well. I do not think my husband will find me too sorely lacking in social graces."

Lady Castleford's voice lifted with interest. "You are engaged then?"

Sarah blushed. "Not officially, but there is an understanding that I am to marry my neighbor's son, when he returns from his service to Wellington in Spain."

"And do you care for this young man?" Amelia leaned forward, intent upon the answer. "Will he make you happy?"

Sarah's hands moved nervously around the gold filigree top of her ivory cane, echoing the uncertain dance of her feelings. Of course she cared for Geoffrey. He had been her playmate, her closest friend before and after the fever. He had helped her to grow fearless in the strange dark world into which she had been thrust. But they had grown apart and now she had no idea at all as to what kind of young man Geoffrey made. How did one answer such questions? She sighed.

"We were inseparable as children, but I am sad to say our relationship suffered when Geoffrey reached an age to go away to school. A Grand Tour extended his absence and immediately upon his return, before we could begin to

renew our acquaintance, he persuaded his father to purchase his colors so that he might advance a career in the
military. I have not been in his company above a dozen
times since we climbed trees together." She laughed, heard
her own uneasiness in the sound, and forced both her hands
and tongue to be still. "Our fathers think we are a perfect
match."

"And do you?"

"I've no idea," she said in all honesty, "but I should not
like to be a burden to my father forever."

An unfathomable silence fell, during which Sarah felt
she must surely have lowered herself in the widow's eyes
with such a remark.

"And now you are come to London." The dowager's
voice offered no clue as to her thoughts.

"Yes, is it not wonderful! There is so much to hear, and
smell and taste and do!" Enthusiasm warmed Sarah's voice.
Her very features were touched by its glow.

"There was this inexplicable yearning within me . . . ,"
she tried to explain, with no idea how ethereal her expression became, nor how impassioned her voice. "I wonder if
you will understand when I describe it as an insatiable need
to explore a little of the world beyond the tiny sphere in
which I have for so long quite happily passed my time."

The words that sprang from her mouth seemed suddenly
too wild and unconventional, too much like something her
mother might have said, to be bantered about in polite conversation. A sense of decorum and duty quenched the light
that had momentarily illuminated her features.

"I should not like to be an antidote among my husband's
connections, so of course I had to come to London."

Amelia, who was fast becoming an antidote among her
own connections, firmly grasped her hand and gave it an
encouraging squeeze.

"Do you know, I have myself been troubled by just such
a yearning of late."

"Shall we explore together?" Sarah's enthusiasm bubbled up like a spring. "An adventure such as I have under-
taken is most invigorating."

"Perhaps." Amelia's voice shook with uncertainty. "The

next function at the Assembly Rooms will be Wednesday next. I shall contact Lady Tipton and Cornelia Candish to inform them of my patronage, and if I can prevail upon my nephew to accompany us, I just might rouse myself from this bed and go with you."

Chapter 3

A S the countess spoke, a man entered the room. Sarah knew him at once for a gentleman. She caught a whiff of an expensive sandlewood scent and heard the brush of leather tassles dangling from Hessian boots. She had no way of knowing they belonged to Stewart Castleford, who looked a fashion plate of sartorial perfection in a chin-grazing, double-breasted, swallow-tail coat of sky blue, over a figured, white waistcoat and skin-snug pantaloons. The Beauty, who was for the moment ignorant of this sad fact, struck a pose, and lifted a gold beribboned monocle to one discerning china blue eye.

"To what purpose would you prevail upon the good nature of your favorite nevie, Auntie dear? You know that you have but to ask, and I am yours."

Sarah knew Lady Castleford's relative examined her. She could feel his gaze in its searching perusal of her person, and she felt at an immediate disadvantage, as if he knew more of her than she of him, for she had no means of reciprocating such an examination. She listened carefully for some change in the pattern of this newcomer's speech that would indicate to her that he realized she was blind. Sarah suffered some concern as to how well society would accept her physical failing. This was but the second of many such excruciating introductions she must endure over the weeks to come.

"Stewart!" Amelia said. "You come most opportunely. I would introduce you to Miss Lyndle. I have just been promising to seek her endorsement at Almack's."

"Yes"—the gentleman paused, both in his speech, and in his progression across the room—" 'tis where I came in."

There, Sarah heard it, the pause, the faint surprise in the words that followed. That was the only evidence Stewart Castleford gave of having taken in her unfortunate condition. Sarah was pleased by this mannerly reaction to her blindness. Introductions were made all around, and the purpose of Mr. Castleford's presence as escort to Almack's repeated.

"Nothing would please me more," the young man said. Bowing graciously over Sarah's hand, he lifted it to lightly brush his lips with the smooth, self-assured elegance of long practice. The gesture, Sarah decided, as performed by him, was social perfection, an exquisitely unruffling pleasure. The light, unencroaching support of his hand, the brief salute of his lips, was neither too firm, too rough, too hot, too damp, nor too cold. Such a gesture spoke to Sarah of all that she had imagined London would prove to be. There was something in such an exchange that made her better understand her mother's having been enchanted by London, and reminded her of all that she must expect her betrothed to be accustomed to. She wondered if Geoffrey had perfected such a faultless salute to a lady's hand.

"Will you grant me the undeniable honor, Miss Lyndle"—Stewart Castleford's words and tone were as smooth, as practiced, as undemanding as his hand—"of accompanying my dear aunt and myself to Almack's? It should be among the first places one appears when embarking on a Season in London. You will, I dare say, cast every beauty there quite into the shade."

Sarah could not be startled by such unabashed flirtatiousness, for this too was what she had been led to expect in the City. Stewart's flattery was offered with controlled finesse and in the company of so many witnesses that it posed no threat of seduction. Sarah could not help but be pleased. It was rather nice to have pretty things said to one. She found herself inclined to like Lady Castleford's nephew.

Brave enough in this friendly company to jest, she retorted, "I am told you are called Beauty. Do you find yourself overshadowed in my company, sir?"

A momentary speechlessness communicated his surprise.

She wondered if he, like everyone else, expected a blind girl to be of a more retiring nature.

"It was a blackened eye that did earn me the title, fair lady. Not the beauty of this poor face of mine."

She playfully wagged her finger at him. "I do not believe such nonsense. Your aunt tells me you are quite the pink of the ton."

"If I am pink then you are vermillion, Miss Lyndle," he teased her without malice.

Sarah was pleased when Stewart offered to walk with her to the top of the street. She could not know that his purpose in visiting with his aunt had not been met, nor that Stewart was quite sensitive to timing when approaching a lady, especially a relative, on the subject of a pressing need for a loan.

All she knew, was that he seemed to find her fascinating, and that there was something likeable in his interest. Sarah was not accustomed, either to attention or flattery, and to have both delivered in such a polished package lifted her spirits immensely, and made her more inclined than ever to understand her mother.

With a steady hand, Hawkes guided a lathered, but now tired and obedient Brutus, among the press of curricles and phaetons that thronged about the east entrance to Hyde Park.

The earl was in the midst of a most trying morning. He wished for nothing so much as a bite of breakfast and an hour's uninterrupted sleep, but neither would be his until he had dealt with a matter of far more pressing importance: Stewart.

Rather like a cart horse wearing blinders, Hawkes was not to be diverted from his course. He had every intention of catching up to his cousin, and none at all of being given the slip. The Beast had it in mind to give the Beauty a severe, and possibly prolonged, tongue lashing.

Before Hawkes could reach him. Stewart's party separated; Dr. Turvey and his companion moving down the path toward him—while Stewart, upon whom his baleful gaze remained locked, headed in a leisurely manner up Tyburn

Lane, of all places, where public hangings had been held in London for years.

When Dr. Turvey called out a pleasant good morning, Hawkes never so much as took his eyes off Stewart. With a weary touch of his hat brim, he said, rather ironically, "Nice to see you, Turvey."

It would have surprised Hawkes to have heard the brief, damning dialogue regarding his identity that passed between the doctor and his companion after he had passed.

Sarah clutched at Dr. Turvey's sleeve, her voice shaking with pent-up emotion, "That was the gentleman who came close to riding us down earlier!"

"Are you quite sure, Sarah? I must admit that while the horse is black and of a similar size, I cannot say with any surety that the man is the same. I saw nothing but the backside of him this morning."

Sarah felt a familiar impatience rise up in her breast. So many people assumed that because she saw naught, her recognition of something or someone was justifiably questionable.

"I was very nearly killed this morning, Doctor. I am not likely to forget my impression of who was responsible. Every aspect of this horse and man, other than the visual, is printed upon my senses with permanent ink. There is no mistaking his voice. I could never forget it! It is so indelibly written in my mind, that even now, when I am perfectly safe, my hand trembles with the reminder. Who is he? I should like to ring a peal over his head."

"That . . . ," the doctor said, "is the 'Beast.'"

"The 'Beast'? Lady Castleford's 'Beast'?"

"The very same."

"Oh! How vexing. I shall be obliged to politely hold my tongue, as a courtesy to his mother."

The 'Beast,' despite his brusque attitude and a long-standing reputation for ignoring the niceties of polite society to a point bordering on rudeness, had no more intention of cutting Dr. Turvey than he had of allowing Brutus to trample Sarah, but he was very much in a mood to wring his cousin's neck.

Brutus needed little urging to catch up with the high-heeled dandy he pursued. Coming abreast of the Beauty, the Beast spoke no word of greeting, only swung down gracefully from his saddle, riding crop in hand.

Stewart, to his credit, turned and stood his ground, raising his beribboned quizzing glass with a dainty hand to examine the great height of his clearly agitated cousin.

"If I didn't know you better, Hawkes," he said, peering with arrogant dismay at the riding crop in his hand, "I'd wager a monkey that you intend to use that whip on me. Right here, in plain view of all London."

Hawkes smiled ruefully at the notion and tapped the short whip against the side of one of his mud-splattered boots. "You tempt me sorely, Stew, indeed you do."

Stewart waved his glass at the far end of Tyburn Lane with an irrepressible sense of whimsey. "Hang me, cousin. You should have brought a rope."

Hawkes laughed wearily and ceased his impatient tapping. "A moneylender would seem to be more in order."

Stewart shrugged. "Meaning that you have just come from your ward, who I daresay was unable to hold his tongue about what I now acknowledge to have been a most absurd request I made of him."

"How deep are you?" Hawkes inquired, in no mood to prevaricate.

Stewart extracted a dainty ormolu box from the small pocket in his tight jacket, shot his cuff so he might pull forth the handkerchief he had tucked therein, and with a practiced twist of the wrist, took a pinch of snuff. "Oh you know me, Hawkes"—he sneezed delicately into his handkerchief—"my pockets are always to let."

Hawkes knew Stewart too well to be fooled.

"Coming it too strong, cousin. Why badger my nephew, if things are no worse than usual?"

Stewart shrugged. "Truth to tell, the paltry sum I am in need of is all on account of a waistcoat."

"A waistcoat?" Hawkes's wide mouth began to twitch.

Stewart bristled. "You, dear cousin, dressing as you do"—he sniffed, lifting his quizzing glass to gaze with raised eyebrows at Lord Castleford's riding attire—"have absolutely no appreciation for the perfection Monsieur LaFette can achieve with embroidered silk. You cannot begin to understand. Such a pity too being blessed as you are with those shoulders." He placed unmistakable emphasis on the last two words. "The ladies about town would undoubtedly compete for the honor of undressing those shoulders, if you did but offer a little more attention to what you shrugged onto them."

The shoulders in question lifted slightly.

"I do not dress so that women may take joy in undressing me, and thus it is quite possible that the finesse of your tailor is beyond my understanding, Stew. I much prefer the simplicity and comfort Stultz gives me, to the skin-tight elegance of a coat such as you now wear. I have no doubt that you call upon the aid of a stout valet armed with shoehorns and smelling salts in order to coax such a confection onto your back. Do you not live in fear that you will enfold yourself in a coat so tight that any lady bent on unpeeling you will faint away with the exertion required, or in the very least, fight fabric so long that the heat of her ardor will cool and reason return?"

Ignoring all else, Stewart latched on to the name of Hawkes's tailor. "Stultz?" he demanded. The quizzing glass came into play once more. "No wonder it hangs well."

Hawkes was beginning to enjoy himself. His cousin could not be in too dire a strait to carry on so comically without the least hint of remorse for begging money off a lad half his age. "I gather," he said with a hint of purring sarcasm, "that you cannot pay for this waistcoat. Is the tailor camped out on your doorstep?"

Stewart closed his mouth with a snap. "Don't be daft. Things are never as bad as that. The silly man simply won't give it to me."

"How very peculiar." One dark eyebrow lifted.

"Precisely! He has never refused me in the past."

"You are a customer of long standing?"

"I should say so. Fully a dozen waistcoats have I commissioned from his very hand."

Hawkes's voice was too honeyed to be sincere. "The

ladies about town must be delirious with joy. Your tailor is not so impressed. Have you paid him faithfully in the past?"

"Why, of course I have paid him in the past."

"How far into the past?"

"Whatever do you mean?"

"Of the twelve waistcoats, how many have you paid for?"

"What an impertinent question."

"Ah!" The earl's voice was smoother than velvet. "We come at last to the heart of the matter. My guess is that you paid for the first, perhaps the second, but most certainly not the third. Thereafter, whenever presented with a bill, you thought to keep the poor tailor happy by commissioning still another article of clothing."

Stewart was glaring at him. "However did you know that?"

Hawkes's voice hardened. "I have heard that is how debts are dealt with in certain circles. I have yet to hear, however, of any of the beau monde extracting pocket change from young relatives barely out of leading strings."

Stewart languidly tucked away his snuffbox. "Have no fear. I shall not pester Nate again."

"Of that, I am quite certain." There was an implacable firmness that underlined the seriousness with which Hawkes regarded the subject, but before Stewart could give further voice to his wounded sensibilities, his cousin halted all complaints with the words, "Shall I pay off your creditors, Stew?"

The china blue eyes fairly started from their sockets.

"Certainly not," Stewart blustered. His face was for a moment a picture of offended pride, but he tempered the rejection of assistance when he went on to say with a good show of unconcern, "You may pay Monsieur LaFette for my waistcoat if you so desire, cousin, but by no means clear the reckoning. Word would soon be out to everyone. Just think if my tailor, hatter, and bootmaker all refused me service in order to be paid."

"Are you as deep as all that then?"

"Deeper," Stewart said with the nonchalance of one accustomed to owing a great number of people money. He went on in a rallying tone. "But have no fear, cousin, I shall not depend on you to foot my bills. Luck is bound to turn in my favor. She always does."

"Devil's to pay, Stew. You cannot continue indefinitely in this fashion."

"I have no intention of doing so. Too tiresome by far."

Hawkes made no attempt to disguise his contempt. "You could do quite well with the monthly stipend my uncle left you, if you did not insist on playing hazard and deep basset as well as possessing fully a dozen women-pleasing waist-coats."

Stewart waved a pale, beringed hand about his head. "You would have me practice economies, I know, cousin, but you really must not preach, for I have it on good authority that you have dropped a pretty penny on your flaxen-haired high-flyer."

"No more," Hawkes drawled, and then wished the words unspoken, for Stewart's bored vagueness vanished.

"What? Do you intend to mend your wicked ways?"

It was Hawkes's turn to sound unconcerned. "I refuse to support a mistress who embarrasses me with her generosity."

"Generosity?" Stewart looked confused.

Hawkes bit the words off. They left a foul taste in his mouth. "She shares her sheets with one man too many."

"No? Who would dare?"

"This morning it was a Mr. Preston hiding under the covers." The earl's sarcasm was vitriolic.

A flash of pity touched Stewart's countenance. Hawkes saw it and flinched.

"Bret's a fool. Whatever did you do?"

Hawkes shrugged. "Not much really. Just handed him his unmentionables and required him to leave."

Stewart slapped his thigh. "You never did."

"He was all over gooseflesh. What else could I do?"

Stewart managed for a moment to sound both wise and condescending. "You could find yourself a wife."

Hawkes found humor in the suggestion. He wagged his

eyebrows up and down suggestively. "Who's to say I shouldn't still be handing men their breeches?"

Stewart grinned. "There's the rub," he admitted. "One must endeavor to find a faithful creature."

Hawkes sighed, smile fading. "I am not convinced that such a female exists. Do you know, I saw a woman this morning, who looked like a Boticelli Venus; a goddess, a vision, an angel of light . . . " He paused, remembering. "Looks can be deceiving. This goddess frightened Brutus into the back of a haycart by waving her bloody walking stick right under his nose."

Stewart chuckled. "A haycart, by Jove! I should have liked to have witnessed that. What happened to your Venus?"

"The featherhead! She stood frozen in Brutus's path when he took the bit and headed straight at her."

"Don't tell me you killed her?"

Hawkes pursed his lips. "I came as close as I should ever care to. She—" He stopped, picturing the scene in his mind. There was no disguising the admiration in his voice,— "somehow, she managed to step back out of the way at the very last moment. The sun was in my eyes. My heart was in my mouth. I'm still amazed she wasn't knocked flat."

Stewart grinned. "Who was she?"

"Don't know. She was gone by the time I settled Brutus." Hawkes's brow furrowed. "Where does Venus go, when she has changed some poor mortal's life?"

"Mount Olympus. Has she changed your life?"

"Yes. I have decided her appearance was a portend."

"Ah, and her celestial message?"

"I must give up women. They're dangerous creatures."

Stewart laughed at his cynicism. "It follows that it would take divine intervention to encourage such restraint in you, Hawkes, but it will not do. You have far too many responsibilities as earl to give up the idea of providing your line with an heir. As for myself, marriage sounds far more appealing than standing forever in debt to some tight-fisted tradesman. I intend to visit Almack's come Wednesday. Shall I have an eye out for a young lady of excellent breeding and faithful nature among the latest offerings?"

Hawkes snorted derisively. "An angel, a vision, a god-dess of light?" he suggested dryly. "No, thank you. I should think you would have your hands full searching out your own Venus."

His cousin grinned. "I have, just this morning, met a young woman who is blind to all my failings, and rich enough to settle with any tradesmen no matter how steep the reckoning. I have offered to escort her to Almack's."

Hawkes cynically clucked his tongue. "If that is all you require of a wife, you shall doubtless be handing some chap his breeches before you're wed a year."

Stewart took a defensive stance. "How so?"

"You've neglected to so much as mention whether or not you care for this well-endowed paragon, or she for you. Do you not require a modicum of affection in this marriage you propose?"

"Of course not!" Stewart laughed bitterly. "Love is too painful a business. Do not tell me you require so much in a partner, for if that is the case you must indeed abandon the idea of happiness."

Chapter 4

HAWKES did not take the proposed solution to his cousin's financial woes too seriously. Stewart was constantly betting on some harebrained scheme to build himself a fortune. This latest, to marry a wealthy heiress, seemed equally unlikely to succeed. Hawkes conducted a mental search among the monied widows and eligible daughters currently residing in London, but could think of none who would be foolish enough to fall in with Stewart's scheme. It crossed his mind that his cousin might be referring to the recently widowed Baroness DeValle, but dismissed the notion as ridiculous. Sylvia had not so much as spoken to Stewart in all of five years. She was, Hawkes was certain, the very reason Stew had given up on the notion of love.

So it was, that when Hawkes next saw his cousin seated in the crimson box that he kept reserved for his mother in the Argyle Rooms, it never occurred to him that the woman seated beside Stewart, half hidden behind Dr. and Mrs. Turvey, could be the heiress his cousin reckoned on winning.

Hawkes assumed that the doctor and his cousin had accomplished a task he found himself unequal to, in coaxing his mother out of her fondly fostered illnesses, and the excess of her mourning, long enough to enjoy the pleasure of her rented box. It also occurred to Hawkes that Stewart, with pockets to let, was not above asking his mother for a loan as brazenly as he had asked his ward.

Thus, the occupants of Lady Castleford's box heard a rap upon the door when the gong sounded for intermission.

"Cousin"—Stewart allowed no more surprise to enter into his voice than was polite—"come in, come in."

"No, no, I will not interrupt. I was but pleased to note that this box was at last engaged."

"Join us," begged Mrs. Turvey. "Your dear mother has been good enough to offer us this lovely treat, and made us aware that we do so at your expense." She drew him into the box.

"She came not with you then?"

Hawkes discovered that there was an attractive young woman seated in the spot where he thought to discover his parent. She did not look up at his entrance, apparently too interested in staring down into the crowd below, but he found it difficult to drag his own gaze away from her perfect profile. There was a warm radiance in the high plane of her cheek, a sheen to the curls that clustered at her brow, and a luminous glow along the smooth line of bared neck and shoulder. There was too a strange feeling of déjà vu, as if perhaps he had met her before. He drank in her beauty like an elixir and concluded, from the absence of blushes and a remote coolness of expression, that this vision was quite accustomed to being stared at.

"Do not condemn your mother too harshly, Lord Castleford," she said. "She would be here but for a mild fit of sneezing."

She spoke, without turning, addressing him with her voice, but not her eyes. The fact that she dared to do so intrigued the earl. Conversation between a proper young lady and a gentleman she had not yet been introduced to was a bold practice usually accompanied by bold looks.

Her voice was low and throaty and as soft as the velvet that molded tightly to her bosom. Having once heard it, Hawkes wished nothing more than to hear its tone again, despite, in fact perhaps because, there seemed to be some hint of derision in its depths, as if she found reason to disapprove of him.

"Sneezing?" Intrigued as much by the news that his parent intended to step free from her self-imposed cocoon, as by she who brought it, Hawkes would have said more, had not in that instant Dr. Turvey entered the box behind him, laden with refreshments.

"Ah, Castleford. I see you have met our Miss Lyndle."

"On the contrary," Hawkes purred. "I have not yet had the pleasure."

Blandly, Stewart introduced the young woman as Sarah Lyndle, of Lyndle Hall, and then picked up the subject of sneezing where it had left off.

"Ten to one it's my fault, Hawkes, that your mum took to her hankie. Most regrettably, I had forgot that she is allergic to primrose and allowed several to be included in the nosegay I presented to her. She had no more thanked me than she began to sneeze, and despite Nanny Hatcher's conviction that it was the 'dashed nosegay,' Aunt Amelia would have it that she had contracted a fever and must not expose us to contagion."

Hawkes murmured in sarcastic agreement that it was indeed most regrettable about the primroses and politely declined Dr. and Mrs. Turvey's request that he stay and listen to the rest of the concert in their company.

"I've come with a group of cronies," he begged off. "And while they are a craven lot of ruffians, they would nonetheless feel slighted were I to abandon them."

Taking cordial leave of the ladies, Hawkes had again an impression of a remoteness—he would have gone so far as to say a cool animosity—from Sarah Lyndle as he bent over her hand—until their fingertips met. Then, despite the fact that both wore gloves, he felt, from the heat that small contact generated, and the flush of color that started at the base of her neckline and swept up to the roots of her wheat-colored curls, as if they had connected in a more intimate manner.

Yet, like some shy schoolgirl, the beauty refused to meet his look. Hawkes held on to her hand a moment longer than was strictly proper, in the hope that her lashes would lift. To no avail.

He would have left her then, relinquishing the delicious warmth of her hand and soon forgetting he had ever wondered at the color of her eyes, had she not spoken in the velvet voice that so completely enchanted his ear.

"I am pleased to meet you in person at last, Lord Castleford." Her downcast lashes and heightened color were the picture of a demure innocent, but the sensual quality of that voice pulled him irresistibly closer.

His brows lifted in amusement. "You have met me in some other guise, Miss Lyndle?"

Even now she refused to meet his look, but he detected an indefinable edge to her words when she said, "Yes, my lord, I suppose one might say so. Your opinion and your reputation have both been made known to me."

Brows drawing together in a disconcerted frown, Hawkes released her hand and drew back, as though bitten. Of all things, he abhorred gossip the most, for through its machinations he had been made to suffer more than once. She would not look up at him, even while insulting him, choosing to regard her shoes rather than allow him to read in the depths of her eyes the meaning of the riddle of her words.

A defensiveness took possession of Hawkes's features.

"Reputations, like shadows, rarely fit the man, Miss Lyndle." His tone was politely chilling.

Without another thought as to the color of the young lady's eyes, Hawkes turned on his heel and quit her company.

So intent was he in that goal that he neither recognized in Sarah the woman whose walking stick had so frightened Brutus, nor so much as noted the marked attention he received from the occupants of a box to his right.

The gentleman and the lady therein sat at the back, as if to avoid prying eyes. Both wore full mourning. The tall, narrow, slightly stooped gentleman was clad in funereal hue from the velvet evening cape thrown loosely about his rounded shoulders to the boots that encased his skinny shanks. Even the artistically arranged neckcloth that completely hid the regrettably prominent Adam's apple that wobbled when he spoke was black. But, for all his sober coloring and the retiring arrangement of their seats, he yet managed to draw attention to himself because of the way he craned his neck in watching Hawkes through black-rimmed pince-nez that slid down off his nose when he bent to scribble something into the black, calf-bound book laid out across his knees.

"Is that not the Baroness DeValle?" Sarah heard her godmother whisper to her husband. "The recent change in status from wife to widow does not seem to trouble her overmuch, for her to appear in public so soon."

"Can't blame her. God rest her profligate husband's soul," the doctor replied with a hint of distaste.

"Why do you say that? Was he not a good husband, worthy of a proper period of mourning?"

Sarah strained to listen. The name DeValle was well known to her, though she had never heard it spoken in anything above a whisper. Her mother's name was usually mentioned in the same hushed breath.

Beside her, Stewart had gone unnaturally still.

"No, the baron was not a good and decent husband." The doctor was not so difficult to hear as his wife. "A rogering rake and a rapscallion, though you would never know it to look at him. I have heard he loved none so much as himself, nor so little as his wife. Died of the pox. David Billings physicked him. Said he was riddled with the stuff. Said the baron was so intent on ridding himself of it that he tried any number of wholly unorthodox treatments." He whispered something unintelligible in her ear.

"Oh, no!" Mrs. Turvey started. "As if despoiling virgins could cure a man. How awful."

"Indeed. It's a wonder his wife is not cursed with the stuff as well, but the word among his servants was that he frequented the petticoat merchants more often than his own bedchamber."

Stewart swallowed hard, as if it pained him to do so.

Sarah's godmother whispered again. "Do you know, I had heard that the marriage was in name only. I could scarce credit the tale that he would have nothing to do with her once it came out that she was one of the Beast's conquests. There was some talk that the marriage was to be annulled. Such a story makes more sense to me now. Poor girl! Black becomes her. Do you not agree?" Lydia's voice was soft with sympathy.

The doctor nodded. "I should think she's very happy to be wearing black."

The Beast, quite contrary to what might have seemed more fitting behavior of one who had been dubbed with such an unflattering monicker, paid a call on his mother the very next day. It was his purpose, both to encourage his only living parent to accompany Stewart or the doctor when next they visited the Argyle Rooms, and to judge with his own eyes the severity of her sneezing fit.

He found to his dismay that his mother, far from continuing to dwell on this sign of potential demise, had all but forgotten her allergic reaction. She sat upon her bed in the midst of a welter of cambric, satin, and dimity, as her dresser, Anne Dunnock, obligingly turned her lady's wardrobe inside out, searching for just the right frock to wear to Almack's.

"Almack's?" he repeated, his lip curling with distaste. "Of all places, Mother, why should you wish to go there?"

Amelia shook her head crossly. "But of course it must be Almack's Ashley. I know how you despise the place, but the girl must be introduced, and I am well versed in the accepted way to go about it, even if you are not. No, no the dimity will not do, Anne. I look positively bilious in that shade of gray. I cannot think what ever possessed me to purchase the thing. Do you prefer the striped tobine or the watered silk, Ashley?"

Hawkes paid no attention to the dresses, making instead a valiant attempt to comprehend her conversation. "Is Cornelia come out of the schoolroom then?"

"Cornelia? Whatever brought her to mind?" Amelia pulled her attention entirely away from her wardrobe, a hopeful light in her green eyes. "Do you care for Cornelia, Ashley?"

"Care for her?" Understanding dawned. Hawkes's eyelids drooped lazily down to conceal his distaste for yet another reference from his parent to his unmarried state.

"No more than the ordinary, Mother."

The light in Amelia's eyes was replaced by a flash of impatience. "Whyever did you bother to ask about her then?"

"You mentioned an introduction at Almack's," Hawkes repeated with infinite patience.

"But of course I did. Why else would I be choosing a frock to wear there?"

"I've no idea, Mother. I have, as you well know, no inkling why anyone should ever choose to go to Almack's."

Amelia blinked a moment. "Oh! 'Tis Sarah Lyndle."

"Sarah Lyndle?" Hawkes frowned, remembering the name. It belonged to the angel-faced chit who had insulted him.

"Yes. A dear, sweet girl."

Hawkes found the remark amusing. He wondered once more what color eyes the insulting young dazzler had. Would they have mocked him had they lifted to gaze into his own? What tattered vestiges of his reputation could Miss Lyndle have encountered to make her fingers burn so hotly in his palm?

His mother announced as though it were no more than a commonplace, "I have committed myself to sponsoring her entrance to Almack's, for while she is past the age of coming out, she must be introduced. I am sure the effort will quite do me in, but she is a dear, naive thing and I have quite taken her to heart."

Lord Castleford refrained from comment. No matter how little he esteemed Miss Lyndle, he could not but be pleased she had somehow induced his parent to cast off her blacks and appear in public.

Amelia studied the two frocks Anne Dunnock stood patiently holding with a heavy sigh. "If only Stewart were here. He is most helpful when it comes to choosing the correct attire for an occasion of moment."

Hawkes dismissed the intrusive vision of Miss Lyndle from his mind. "Stew is, by the way, in the suds. I would appreciate it, should he come to you begging a loan, if you will send him my way."

"Poor Stewart, the boy is always in debt, but he does no more than ask on occasion for pin money, which I am happy to give him. After all he is a most attentive nephew. Did you know he brought me an exquisite little nosegay yesterday, all tied up in silver ribbon?"

"So I am told. I was also informed that you were feeling not at all the thing yesterday."

"Nonsense. Nothing but an allergic reaction to some primroses. Stewart was quite put out that he had forgotten my disinclination for them. Indeed, Ashley, I am feeling quite well this week. Dr. Turvey complimented me on my condition upon his latest visit, although I am sure I feel a headache coming on this morning." She fluttered a dismissive hand at Anne, whose arms had begun to tremble under the weight of the tobine and the silk.

Hawkes took up his mother's plump hand and lightly kissed her fingertips. "I take my leave of you then. I should think the stripe would be just the thing for Almack's. I have always felt that frock did lend you a most distinguished air." And with the slightest of nods to acknowledge Anne Dunnock's grateful smile, Hawkes set his beaver upon his head and strode from the room. He wondered as he did so, how the haute ton would choose to regard Miss Sarah Lyndle; as innocence personified, or as an outspoken temptress with the face of an angel.

Chapter 5

SARAH was not at all bored by Almack's. Her appearance, in the company of the reclusive Lady Castleford and her nephew Stewart, sent a ripple of commentary through the main Assembly Room the moment they stepped through the door. Society's worthy matrons and their suitor-seeking daughters approached the trio in avid curiosity, and word was soon spread through the card rooms that an oddity was to be witnessed in the main salon.

The crowd grew. The countess was complimented on her looks, and Sarah was pronounced the image of her mother, whose name evoked crows of recognition, hints of stories better left untold, and a bit of scandalized whispering. The rumors were old ones and apparently not substantive enough to halt a breathtaking number of invitations. Teas, soirees, drums, and nuncheons were mentioned, and the promises of printed invitations detailing times and places for each entertainment did at one point overwhelm Sarah with the feeling that this was exactly the tide that had engulfed her mother.

The attention was exhilarating, and for the most part pleasant. There were, however, a few introductions Sarah suffered through. It was not that there was any open insult or censure, but Sarah was an excellent judge of character and could read between the lines of conversation what people meant, in contrast to what they said. A broad range of emotion was exhibited among the host of women who sought her out. There was some dismay that it was on her account that Amelia Castleford should at last come out of mourning. There was a hint of jealousy, too, among those whose social connections the countess did not intimately number. What surprised Sarah the most was an encounter with a gentleman by the name of Sylvester Naughtley, an oily, wheedling individual whose clammy hand reminded her of a fish and who seemed bent on reiterating to her the fact that he had known her mother, and known her well.

Lady Castleford rescued her from his attentions and introduced her to her friend, the Lady Beale, a woman of great girth and creaking stays, who told her she too had known her lovely mother, and that it was vital that she avoid empty rattles like Naughtley. When she discovered that Sarah had only just met the Castlefords, she was quick to inform her stoutly that the Beauty, Stewart Castleford, of all men in London, was a welcome guest at any function, and that she could not have chosen more wisely her escort. Her fan wafted rhythmically to a litany of Stewart's attributes.

"He is fashionable, gracious, punctual, and obliging enough to ask the most awkward young wallflowers and the feeblest of matrons to whirl about the floor should the occasion involve dancing. He is blessed with wit and humor, speaks with fascinating detail of the interesting places he has been, and is usually well versed in the latest gossip. Above and beyond all of these traits to recommend him, there is"—Lady Beal lowered her voice, and snapped her fan shut with emphatic vigor—"hope to be cherished that where the Beauty goes, perhaps the Beast will follow. Have you met him?" She lightly rapped Sarah's knuckles with her fan and chuckled throatily. "Now, there's a desirable catch, despite his dark, brooding ways, my dear. I have often said so to my own daughter, Anne."

While Sarah was digesting this information, Amelia dragged her off to meet yet another distinguished matron. Before long, Sarah's head whirled with names and titles and bits of gossip.

"Stewart promised me a chair," Amelia said at last, pausing in what had seemed to Sarah an endless circuit of the Assembly Rooms. "I wonder where he can have gotten off with it. . . . "

As Lady Castleford breezily flapped her fan, Sarah found

herself plying her own little painted ivory confection and asking what might be considered an impertinent question.

"Why is your son called Beast? How came he by that unhappy name?"

Amelia stifled a gasp of indignation, dropped her fan, and fumbled about the contents of her reticule with some explanation of searching for smelling salts.

Wishing she could bite back the hasty words, Sarah blushed as pink as the embroidered roses on her gown.

"I beg your pardon, Lady Castleford. It is not my intention to pry. If you would rather not speak of the matter, please forgive my unseemly curiosity."

Fortified by a stout whiff of smelling salts, Amelia patted Sarah's arm with the open bottle to still the flow of apology.

"Tut, tut, my dear girl. Of course you find the name a curiosity. It is quite refreshing that you have the courage to ask me to my face, instead of discussing the subject in whispers behind my back."

Sarah wished that both her tongue and her curiosity might be governed with greater strictness, but at the same time she could not regret her question. She was far too fascinated by the Beast, not to try to understand him better. Lady Castleford's son was unlike any gentleman of her acquaintance. Never, in Sarah's experience, had she found herself both drawn to and repelled by anyone, as she was to him. That she had unintentionally succeeded in putting his back up, with both action and word, was undeniable, but what she found even more intriguing, was that he seemed bent on repaying her in kind. This Beast had not once, in the brief moments they had shared, shown any inclination to be careful of her feelings. To Sarah, who was used to everyone around her being careful—not to mention her blindness, not to let her run into things, not to offend her in any way—such carelessness was a novelty. No doubt the Beast dealt with everyone around him with equally caustic sarcasm. In that perhaps lay his perverse attraction. He treated Sarah just as he did anyone else, as if she were not special, or different, or set apart—not even in her blindness. It had been refreshing somehow to be released from that distinction, if only for a moment. Sarah wondered if this was the kind of man who had seduced her mother away from home and family.

Lady Castleford sighed. "I do not pretend to fully understand how Ashley came to be called Beast," she said. "People assume it is because he is rough and rude, the antithesis of Stewart's polite polish. As different as night and day though they may seem, the two were not always so diametrically opposed. In their younger days, the two spent almost every waking moment together. Both of them mad about horses."

Sarah thought of the wild first impression she had had of the Earl of Henley on a runaway horse in the back of a hay-wagon in Piccadilly. Her image of this woman's son was inextricably linked with that of the horse he had been mounted upon.

"It was not until they went away to school that they began to drift apart." Lady Castleford went on. "Their interests and intellectual pursuits proved quite different, as did the friends they cultivated. The two did not agree on much of anything, until they met Sylvia."

"Sylvia?"

"Sylvia Hupton, now the widowed Baroness DeValle."

"DeValle?" Sarah could not believe her ears. For the second time since coming to London, the name DeValle was raised. Did Lydia know it was DeValle who had seduced her mother?

"Poor girl, she is not seen much in public these days. Still in mourning, you understand. Beautiful, Sylvia is. Titian hair. She took all London by storm in her first Season. Dozens of young men, and a few not so young, made great cakes out of themselves over her."

"Your son numbered among them?" Sarah was astonished. She could not imagine the caustically sarcastic Lord Castleford making a cake out of himself over any female.

Amelia laughed fondly. "Oh yes. Ashley and Stewart. Both of them head over heels. Sylvia is credited with christening the boys, Beauty . . . "

"And Beast!" It was Stewart who finished the statement. He had arrived with the awaited chair in time to overhear the last of their conversation. His voice sounded strange. "Sylvia caused a stir at the Philharmonic the other night, Auntie. Made an appearance with Sylvester."

"She is seen with that awful toad?" Amelia sniffed. "He is here today, scribbling down whatever gossip anyone is foolish enough to let slip. He was annoying Sarah with his neverending questions only a moment ago, wasn't he, love?"

Sarah nodded. She understood now why Naughtley had made such a point of mentioning his connection with her mother. He was somehow connected to the late Baron De-Valle.

Stewart laughed. "Sylvester lives for gossip. He has become a chronicler of wagging tongues. I am told he makes a living out of blackmailing anyone foolish enough to get themselves talked of. You and Auntie offer him fresh material, Miss Lyndle."

"Perhaps so, Stewart, but I find it excessively ill-mannered in you to point it out to Sarah. Now, if you will be so good as to excuse me, I see Lady Beale beckoning." With a purposeful rustle of striped tobine, Amelia sailed away.

"Your pardon, Miss Lyndle"—Stewart courteously took Sarah's elbow into his possession—"I have been, as my aunt was so quick to point out to me, excessively ill-mannered. Would you care to take advantage of the chair I have appropriated?"

Having settled her comfortably in the chair, Stewart leaned upon the back of it and bent closer to her ear. "I'll wager, Miss Lyndle, that you shall find yourself both misinformed and bored if you depend on my aunt to supply you with the family history."

Sarah felt the blood rush to her cheeks. She was quite unused to the sensation of a gentleman conversing in such proximity to her ear that she might feel the very warmth of his breath. She wished that she had held her tongue between her teeth rather than to have been caught prying into the affairs of this gentleman's extended family. "I must apologize, sir . . . "

"For gossip!" He interrupted her with a condescending chuckle. "But I find nothing to condemn in gossiping—

only in misrepresenting the facts, or in abusing the innocent with its power."

"Your aunt—" Sarah began. He cut her short.

"My aunt did but begin to tell you the entertaining story behind the names Beauty and Beast. You see, Hawkes—"

"Hawkes?"

"My cousin, Ashley. He is Hawkes to everyone in London given the privilege of addressing him so, save his mother."

"Oh, do pardon my interruption and go on."

"Hawkes and I, both young and foolish, easily fell under Sylvia Hupton's spell. We had no real hopes of success, mind you, but at the time we were both of us fresh out of school, and chose not to believe the harsh realities of fortune and title. Miss Hupton, you see, came from the Devonshire branch of Huptons, a top-lofty bunch if ever there was one. They took pride in their pride, if not in the managing of their money. High in the instep, but with pockets to let, Sylvia Hupton was given a lavish coming out so that she might go to the highest bidder."

Sarah gasped.

"My aunt neglected to tell you as much, did she? I'm not surprised. Well, Hawkes and I had nothing but our undying love and good names to offer at the time and that was not enough by a long shot. Miss Hupton and her family had no way of knowing my cousin was within three months of coming into his inheritance through the death of not only his older brother, but his father as well. As for myself, I would have given Sylvia anything her heart desired . . . would have plucked the moon down out of the sky, were such a thing possible, but"—his voice flattened—"as the youngest of a long line of brothers, I had not even the expectation of wealth to offer, unless, heaven forbid, a plague swept through the ranks of my siblings. No plague came."

He paused and Sarah began to suspect, by his silence, as much as by the bitterness at the edge of all he had said thus far, that Stewart still nursed a great deal of pain over the events leading to his being called Beauty. She wondered if the intriguing Sylvia Hupton had left an equally indelible impression on Stewart's cousin, the Beast.

Stewart sighed dramatically.

"When we discovered that our hearts sought the same prize in earnest, my cousin and I, ignoring the daunting economical disadvantages which rendered us both quite ineligible as suitors, resolved to fight for the lady."

"A duel, sir?"

"Never that. Merely a rousing bout of fisticuffs. I was, of course, soundly beaten. Hawkes has always been my superior in boxing. But I managed to get one good swing in. His nose has never been quite straight since."

"Oh my, and then what happened?"

"Why, when I drew his claret we stopped milling to assess damages, and Hawkes started to laugh. His nose was all-over red, and puffing up like a bun on the rise, and the black eye he'd given me was already beginning to color. I had the devil of a time seeing out of it for the swelling. We knew the odds were against either one of us ending up in Sylvia Hupton's arms. It struck us both funny that of all things we should be ripping up at each other over an unattainable woman. Hawkes was wheezing through his mashed nose like an organ grinder's monkey. I was squinting through my swollen eye trying to make out what he was on about, and we ended up in whoops, rolling about on the grass, two grown men, or so we thought at the time, laughing fit to burst. We rose, exhausted, but best of chums again."

Sarah tried to suppress the amusement that swelled up into her throat at the vividness of his description, failed miserably, and dissolved into soft peals of laughter.

Stewart laughed as well, stopping himself manfully to say, "We determined, over breakfast, which I could not see to eat, and Hawkes could not smell to taste, that neither of us should have her."

He had her laughing again. Stewart pinched his nose between two fingers and flattened his voice cynically. "'Stew,' Hawkes says to me, 'let us never again dishonor our friendship, or our faces, by fighting over females.'"

"But, how came you to be called Beauty?"

Stewart sat back with a sigh. "The incomparable Sylvia, having suddenly lost not one, but two fawning cavaliers

from the audience that groveled at her feet, set out to discover why. It didn't take her long. Neither sympathetic nor
amused by our wounds, Sylvia was incensed by the thought
that boyhood bonds proved stronger than her own lovely
lure. She determined to give us a setdown, to mock us pub-
licly, while we still bore the awful traces of our scuffle."

"She named you Beauty and Beast?"

"Yes, to the profound approval and amusement of all
who heard. She remarked that I had a beauty of an eye, and
Hawkes a beastly nose. Unfortunately, the names stuck."

"Not so unfortunate for you perhaps," Sarah chided gently.

"You have the right of it, I fear. My title has done nothing to discredit me. My cousin was not so fortunate. The
gossip mill would have it that Hawkes had seduced Sylvia.
Hence the name Beast. Once begun, the rumor could not be
squashed. Most decent young women began to regard him
with trepidation, while those who were not so decent, either
scorned him, or flung themselves in his way, curious as to
what kind of a seduction might be termed beastly."

"And did they find out?" Sarah wondered.

"A few," Stewart muttered. "Hawkes was suffering
mightily at the time over the death of his brother, Aston.
When his father snuffed it as well, he was thrust suddenly
into his inheritance, and . . . suffice it to say he sowed a few
wild oats until the death of his aunt and uncle knocked the
wind out of his sails. He was left with the guardianship of
young Nathanial. Of course, by that time, Hawkes's beastly
reputation was set in stone."

"And reputations, like shadows, rarely fit the man,"
Sarah murmured under her breath. Sadly, she did not know
exactly where reality ended and reputation began, even in
her own mother's gossip riddled history. Sarah felt a
strange empathy for Lord Ashley Hawkes Castleford, the
Beast, and wondered if she would ever have occasion to
discover just what kind of creature he really was.

Safely ensconced in Amelia Castleford's elegant, if out-
dated barouche, Stewart Castleford posting alongside on a
rented hack, Sarah settled comfortably back against the

squabs, drank in the moist, cooling air of nightfall, and wondered if either of the Castleford cousins still bore a *tendre* for the recently widowed Baroness DeValle. There had been a trace of raw emotion in Stewart's voice when he had admitted himself ready to give her anything her heart desired.

The dowager interrupted her thoughts.

"Well, dear, I am not feeling at all pulled, as I was quite sure I would. One can only hope not to have contracted something contagious in that awful squeeze. Did you enjoy yourself?"

Sarah smiled. "Above all things. I have never met so many people who wished to make my acquaintance. Thank you."

"You are more than welcome, my dear girl. You took splendidly. I could but wish that Ashley might have seen fit to accompany us today."

Sarah fought back a wave of amusement. She could not imagine the Beast at Almack's.

"From what your nephew tells me, ma'am, such a gathering could not but try the earl's patience. Do you think your son would find such a function at all to his taste?"

"No, and it is enough to give one palpitations. Do you know I begin to despair of his ever presenting me with a grandchild? He has virtually no opportunity to meet with respectable young ladies in his current style of life. For all he may think Almack's a very insipid entertainment, he could not but meet a perfectly suitable young lady there."

"Dozens!" Sarah agreed, and she fell for a moment into a silent study. What type of woman would the Beast consider suitable? Not she. They were like oil and water together. Her face grew hot as she recalled the warmth of his hand on hers.

The countess sighed from her side of the barouche.

Sarah felt a bit like sighing as well, but then a thought struck her so forcibly she felt she must share it with Amelia.

"Surely, madam, Lord Castleford comes to the entertainments you, yourself, present. He might meet any number of perfectly amiable females in that manner."

The widow sat up. "He always did so in the past," she mused, "but, I have not been in the habit of entertaining these past five years, due to my uncertain constitution."

"No need to despair then, my lady. He is not an old man, yet. Eventually you must be able to put him in the way of some pleasant damsel and perhaps when that time does come, he will have become more receptive to the notion of a wife and family."

Amelia seemed quite struck by the idea. "You are quite right, Sarah. It is high time I thought of entertaining again, despite the frailty of my constitution."

Chapter 6

HAWKES would have raised his dark eyebrows to their most mocking heights had he but known how stimulating certain conversation had become with regard to his name, reputation, and marital status. Instead, blithely unaware, yet with the question of the color of Miss Lyndle's eyes like an itch he must scratch, he returned to his mother's house, with the express purpose of discovering how the ladies had fared in their outing to Almack's.

He was startled to find one of the housemaids on her knees at his mother's doorstep, scrubbing down the bricks with soapy water. The woman greeted him with unusual good humor considering the task she had been assigned.

"Good day to you, Master Ashley. My lady will be happy to see you've returned, sir."

"Is something afoot, Maisey?" he drawled, leaping from the ground to the top of the step with feline agility, thus avoiding the ruination of her work.

"Yes, sir. Your mother's planning a do, for that lovely Miss Lyndle who is always coming round with the doctor."

"For Miss Lyndle, you say?" Hawkes found the news both irritating and interesting. What spell had Miss Lyndle cast to convince the intractable invalid to abandon her bed?

Maisey smiled warmly. "It does my heart good, sir, to see your mum and the old place begin to come right again. We've gone mad with cleaning, don't you know."

Gone mad with cleaning they had. Timmons, his mother's normally staid butler, answered the door wearing a great linen apron that covered the majority of his attire. He stepped back to allow the earl entry, revealing with wounded dignity that he held in his grasp a silver candelabra and a polishing rag.

"I can see that I have arrived with poor timing, Timmons. You were about to inform me that my mother is not home to visitors?" Hawkes suggested with understated irony.

"Quite so, sir." Timmons inclined his head.

His mother, her hair encased in a dusting turban, called down to him from the landing. "Is that you, Ashley? I have no time for you today, dear. The whole house is upside down."

"It has not escaped my notice," Hawkes agreed with a lazy smile. "You look well, Mother, despite that awful Persian headpiece you are wearing."

Amelia tugged at her turban. "One makes sacrifices when one intends to entertain, even to one's appearance. For your part, you must solemnly promise that you will sacrifice the whole of an evening in attending the little soiree I am planning."

"But of course. Have I not always made an appearance at your entertainments, Mother?"

"This time I insist that you arrive early to help me greet our guests." Lady Castleford's tone was severe.

Hawkes frowned. His aversion to entertainments, was rooted in the prospect of warding off a long line of round-eyed young ladies, who, having been warned of his evil reputation, were still thrust upon his attention by pushing mamas who hoped their darling offspring might snare an earl. It occurred to him that his own mama might have joined in the lineup, and that the young lady she was pushing was the much-praised Miss Lyndle. With a cynical lift to his lip, he bowed to her command with the remark that he would be happy to oblige her on this auspicious occasion. After five years of waiting, Hawkes was immensely pleased to see that his parent had begun to take interest in anything, other than disease and death—even Sarah Lyndle.

"How did you and your protégé fare at Almack's?"

His mother blinked at him, as if surprised he should ask. "Splendidly, barring the presence of that obnoxious gossip-

monger, Sylvester Naughtley, who is always prying and
scribbling and biting the end of his pencil as if struck by
profound thought. He cannot have had anything but nice
things to say about Sarah though. Everyone took to her, just
as I knew they must. She is an exceptional young woman,
not at all like her mother, who while nice enough, was a trifle . . . frivolous.''

Hawkes could think of several words that better described Sarah's mother, if rumor was to be believed. But he
knew better than to rely solely on rumor. He judged Sarah's
character far more by her own forwardness than by any
transgression her mother might have committed. It occurred
to him, as his mother sang the girl's praises, that he had
only to ask her what color the young woman's eyes might
be to still the question that had been niggling his curiosity
for days, but he dismissed the thought and asked instead if
he could in any other way be of assistance.

When refused, he took up his hat and cane, made his way
past Timmons, and leapt down from the step over the
laughing head of Maisey. He did not make good his escape
however, for just as he set foot in the stirrup, Timmons
called out to him to wait, for milady had just come in mind
of something she would have him do.

Once more he avoided the wet steps, endearing himself
forever to the maid, who later told the cook, "I cannot think
how anyone can call him Beast, for one could not ask for a
more considerate gentleman.''

Hawkes found his mother quite out of breath from having run down the stairs after him. With a mocking smile
that masked his concern, he led her to a bench and insisted
that she sit and say nothing until she had regained her composure.

"Do have a care, Mother," he said. "You will bust your
stays if you insist on galloping after me in this manner.''

"Ashley!" She found it difficult to scold him, so out of
breath had the exertion left her, but she directed a speaking
look at Timmons, exuberantly polishing silver within
earshot, and croaked, "How can you speak so?''

"Have I not always done so, Mother?" He removed his
hat and shot the butler a roguish wink. "I have never seen

the sense in stays. You must agree they make it most difficult for a lady to move about with any comfort, and in my
opinion whalebone does little to improve on nature's
curves."

"Ashley!" Lady Abigail wheezed.

"It has on more than one occasion occurred to me, having smelled as many burnt feathers as I should ever care to,
that society could well do away with the contraption."

"Ashley Hawkes Castleford!" Lady Castleford had good
control of her breath. "I forbid you to say another word in
my presence on this subject."

Hawkes was unperturbed by her ire. "You sound quite
yourself again. Now, what sent you all in a pelter after me?
It must have been important."

He was amused to find that she was willing to put aside
her irritation with his manner long enough to ask a favor.

"Be so good, Ashley, as to send for Button. I would have
her brought up from the country."

Hawkes's eyebrows zoomed upward. "Button, Mother? I
must make a point to compliment Dr. Turvey on the
strength of his tonics if you are inclined to go riding."

"Of course I shall not ride, dear boy. You know I have
not set foot to stirrup since Aston died."

"If not to ride, then what need have you of your mare?"

With a defensive toss of her head, Amelia said, "Miss
Lyndle has confided in me that she does, on occasion, take
great pleasure in riding, given a gentle cob."

Miss Lyndle again! Hawkes suppressed a snide laugh.
Button was more than gentle, she was positively languid.
Sarah Lyndle must be a desultory horsewoman indeed, if
Button was as much as she could handle.

"Of course, Button came to mind," his mother said.

"Of course," Hawkes said dryly. The girl would appear
to have both his mother and her household, wrapped firmly
around her little finger. What was she after, he wondered?
Most women were after something.

"It will make me very happy to loan the girl the use of
my mare."

"You are most thoughtful in attending to Miss Lyndle's
needs," Hawkes could not resist observing.

"Nonsense!" she retorted with surprising firmness. "Sarah Lyndle is an extraordinary girl. She has been denied many things. I would bring her what small pleasure I might when it lies within my power to do so." The turbaned head shook emphatically. "I cannot imagine what her father can have been about, to neglect her introduction to London for so long." She smiled. " 'Twill make me very happy if Sarah chooses to trot around a bit on my mare."

And, with that admirably selfless remark, Amelia straightened her headpiece and sailed back up the stairway, leaving Hawkes to wonder if Button could be goaded out of her customary lethargy long enough to "trot around."

In due course, Button arrived from the country, reviving Hawkes's curiosity regarding the riding skill of the audacious young enchantress who had so completely won over his mother. He renewed his resolve to discover the color of the downcast eyes that had refused to meet his. He could not but wonder if Miss Lyndle's look, on meeting his at last, would burn with the same warmth that had radiated from her fingers.

An effusive note of thanks, in his mother's sprawling hand, found its way to the earl's desk. It was followed to his surprise, two days later, by a second note of thanks, this one in a fair, feminine hand he did not recognize.

The second note was unusual in two respects. First, it was written on a piece of paper remarkable for its expensive tooth and weight, decorated by both an exquisite French watermark and a lovely if somewhat ostentatious deckled edge. Second, it was addressed to him in Mrs. Lydia Turvey's neat hand. She wrote that this was at Miss Sarah Wilkes Lyndle's express request.

The note was decidedly informal in tone, saying simply that Miss Lyndle was thrilled to take advantage of Button's presence and that she and the bay mare were fast becoming close friends.

It made no sense to Hawkes, who maintained ignorance regarding Sarah's blindness, that a young woman of station should: first, reside with a medic, second, not know when it was proper and improper to address a gentleman to whom she had never been introduced, third, ride no better than the likes of Button, and fourth, require Lydia Turvey, the granddaughter of a duke, to serve as her secretary. The only reason Hawkes could fathom for such bizarre behavior was to disguise the lack of a proper background and education.

Along this train of thought it was not such a far leap to assume that what his mother had described as the "much denied" Miss Lyndle might in fact mean that the young woman was penniless. With Stewart's own vow to marry into money fresh in his memory, it occurred to Hawkes that the intriguing Miss Lyndle might be attempting to worm her way into his notice, and thus the Henley inheritance, by way of his relations.

He resolved to pay very close attention to the much-denied Miss Lyndle and her encroaching relationship with his mother. Dipping quill to ink he dashed off a reply.

There was no endearment to begin the epistle, just:

> Please lavish all kind thanks on my mother's deserving brow. The mare is by far too docile for my taste, but she is steady, pretty, and has pluck. I am most humbly pleased you approve.

And then, without flourish, or closing sentiment, simply A. Hawkes.

When it had been received, Sarah found nothing to object to in the note, for its content was the most civil exchange she had as yet enjoyed with the Earl of Henley, and she was far too happy with the unexpected riding privileges to find reason to complain.

There was no disguising the disapproval in Lydia's clucking tongue however, when, having read it once aloud, she turned Lord Castleford's note over in her hand, saying, "How very odd. That's all he wrote. Such brevity cannot but be offensive."

"He knows the horse far better than I would have guessed," Sarah observed.

"Three lines! No more." Lydia complained.

Sarah was used to the casual manners of the country and refused to be offended.

"I expected no more and certainly"—here she did laugh—"no less."

She was soon to be seen riding Button in Hyde Park at an hour of the morning when most of the ton were still snug in their beds. No one fashionable frequented the park until five in the afternoon, when, she had been told, a virtual parade of horseflesh and smart carriages jammed the riding circuit. Sarah took no joy in crowds. She preferred the park when it was empty, for it was then she could most easily hear the hoofbeats of the groom who went before her, leading the way.

She heard Mr. Naughtley's approach before she knew who it was and judged him a poor horseman before ever he spoke, by the rhythmic slap of his buttocks in the saddle.

"Hallo! You ride, Miss Lyndle?"

She recognized his voice with sinking dread. There was something snide and denigrating in Naughtley's manner that she could not like.

"I ride, Mr. Naughtley," she acknowledged.

Sylvester pulled his horse in beside Button. "Recognized me by my voice, did you? Well, I recognize the mare you are mounted on. I was at Tatt's the day Ashley Castleford purchased her."

"Lord Castleford purchased her?" Sarah could not stop her inquiry, any more than she could the smile such an image engendered. "That must have proven amusing. I have it on good authority the earl prefers the sort of animal that might leap into a haywagon if provoked."

"Exactly so. Any horse considered fit enough to merit a stall in the Castleford stable is scrutinized with great attention. You can imagine the surprise"—Sylvester's laughter was heavy with sarcasm—"nay, the consternation with which quizzing glasses were raised when this fat, mild plug stepped up to the block and a Castleford began to bid on her. The mare's gentle mien in and of itself would have been funny enough, but even more laughable, a number of us got the addlepated notion the Beast wanted the mare for breeding and began to bid as well." He laughed maliciously. "Drove the price up considerably. I devoted several paragraphs to the incident in my journal."

Sarah wished herself rid of Sylvester Naughtley. She should never have encouraged his tale-telling. "I would prefer you did not refer to my friends by those awful nicknames," she said.

"Of course, I would not offend you, Miss Lyndle," he agreed smoothly, although something in his tone suggested otherwise. "It is, you know, out of a desire not to offend, that I sought you out today."

Sarah frowned. "Whatever do you mean?"

"You may recall my mentioning that I knew your mother?"

"Yes?" Sarah said with wary distrust of his suggestive tone. "You have the advantage of me. I knew her but little. She spent the great majority of her time here in London."

"Yes. She adored the city, and the city adored her in return. She was most popular." Unpleasant innuendo oozed like oil from his words. "A particular favorite of the Baron DeValle's. She is often mentioned in my journals. I could read them to you sometime."

The hair at the nape of Sarah's neck stiffened.

"I do not think so, Mr. Naughtley. Memories of my mother only serve to upset me."

He clucked his tongue like a parent disappointed with his child. "As you wish, but it is most interesting I assure you."

She thought he surrendered too easily.

She was right. He had not given up.

"I have given some thought to publication, you see, and it did occur to me you might wish to hear anything that concerns your family so intimately before it goes public." His hint that he held information that might prove embarrassing was too broad to mistake.

Sarah's first reaction was contempt and anger. How dare he threaten her with a past about which she knew next to nothing? How dare he attempt to defame her mother to her? What could he possibly have written about her?

Her head came up and her back went ramrod stiff.

"I shall let you know if I change my mind," she said, sugaring her words, when she would much rather have spat them at him. "For now, I must bid you good day."

Directing the groom to lead her back to the Castleford mews, where Button was stabled, she rode away from Sylvester Naughtley with the shaken feeling she had just crossed paths with a man who was not so much annoying as he was dangerous.

Chapter 7

O
N the evening of his mother's soiree for Sarah Lyndle,
Hawkes arrived early, as promised. Two weeks of
waxing, dusting, and polishing had proven a worthwhile
endeavor. From the glittering crystal chandelier to the honeyed hue of the parquet floor, the Castleford town house
shone. Tapers glowed warm yellow in all the wall sconces,
and polished candelabra added their flickering brilliance to
the hallway that invited one into the ballroom, from whence
came the faint sound of violins being tuned. The scent of
roses and lilies and burning wax suffused the air, stirring
thoughts of the last ball Hawkes had attended here.

Sylvia Hupton had been one of the guests then. In fact,
the last time Hawkes had spoken to the beautiful girl who
would become Baron Otto DeValle's wife, had been in this
very hallway. The candlelight that long-ago evening had
thrown a soft warmth on her proud features, and strangely,
it was always that dreadful moment that came to mind
when Hawkes allowed himself to remember his feelings for
Sylvia.

She had been pulling on her gloves, preparatory to leaving and had looked up smiling when Timmons opened the
door. He and Stewart, as they came in together, still bearing
the evidence of their fight for her, had been chuckling over
their debonair appearance in patches and plaster.

Smoldering brown eyes locked on the two of them.
Sylvia's smile was brittle, her chin high. Two red spots col-
ored her cheekbones.

Stewart, as surprised as she and still smarting from the
ego-bruising blow she had dealt him by mocking his black

eye, now rakishly covered by a black satin patch, had been the first to remember his manners.

"Miss Hupton," he said politely, "I did not expect to see you here."

Hawkes could see Sylvia would have liked to cut them both cold, as she had chosen to do every time they had chanced to encounter one another in public for several days, but Stewart stood waiting for some response, and she had already acknowledged their presence with a direct look, so after an awkward moment of silence in which she looked right through them, she said with the same forced smile, "Ah, but, Beauty, I had great expectation of encountering you here."

Feeling forgotten in the background, Hawkes darted jealous looks from Sylvia to Stewart. Her simple words had fired a light in his cousin's one unpatched eye.

The light did not warm her.

"I have the pleasure of informing you that I am to be wed," she said, dashing her words like cold water on the fire of Stewart's open desire for her.

Hawkes had been stunned by her statement, but in looking at Stewart he realized with sudden, crystalline clarity that his cousin's feelings for this woman ran far deeper than his own. Stewart had been staggered, literally knocked unsteady on his feet by her announcement. His mouth had fallen slightly agape, and though he tried to speak, no words came.

Sylvia, her mouth tight, her dark eyes huge with what looked like angry concern, had darted a look at Hawkes as though she required some assistance.

"Felicitations!" he had said in his most mocking manner. "Your news devastates us, eh, Stew?" His arm had risen, like a brace about his cousin's shoulder.

Stewart swayed a bit, but strength returned to his backbone. "Who is the lucky chap?"

Sylvia went white about the lips. Her brown eyes centered on Stewart's pale face a moment before she set her jaw and said fiercely, "The Baron DeValle."

"DeValle?" They had echoed her in harmonious disbelief. DeValle was a confirmed bachelor. Never had he shown the slightest inclination to end that state. It had even been suggested that he was somewhat deviant in his sexual preferences. He was known to frequent a coffee house in Covent Garden that catered to the meaner inclinations of the flesh if one had the money to purchase such favors. That he should wish to marry, and marry the lovely girl before them, sickened the very heart of the Castleford cousins.

The baron, who stood taking leave of his host, heard mention of his name. Slender and fastidiously elegant, though well past his fiftieth year, he broke away.

"Hallo! Who calls?"

Lifting a gold-rimmed pince-nez to the bridge of his narrow nose, the gentleman examined the Castleford cousins.

"Beauty and the Beast, is it not?" He snorted, amused by his own cleverness. Leaning in close to Stewart's face, his cloying sweet cologne washed over them like aspic.

"I say, dear boy, that's quite an eye you're wearing. Nasty shade of eggplant. Clashes awfully with your outfit." He rocked back on his heels, bringing his eyepiece to bear on Hawkes. "Still, I must say it is preferable to trotting about with a nose the size of a boot."

Hawkes sketched a bow and drawled acidly, "Far rather a boot for a nose, than a tongue that requires a leash."

The baron's eyes narrowed behind the pince-nez, and a lazy, knowing smile curled his fine upper lip as he deliberately misinterpreted the remark. "Ah, my intended has been telling you of our approaching nuptials?"

Stewart managed a nod.

Hawkes merely glared at the man, astounded by his gall.

"Can you credit it? All of London had determined I should never be brought to heel, but even an old dog must learn new tricks when it behooves him. Instead of seducing other men's wives, I must see to the winning of my own." He chucked Sylvia under the chin. The look she threw at him was not a loving one.

The baron was unperturbed. "The banns are to be published in the morning's *Gazette*."

Grasping Sylvia's elbow, he drew her to his side, his cool gaze flitting from one Castleford to the other. "We shall honeymoon in the Alps, you know. Stunning country. Absolutely stunning."

Stewart stiffly offered Sylvia his congratulations.

Hawkes could not bring himself to wish her happiness. She would not find it with this dreadful man.

Sylvia had looked up at them for a moment, the corners of her mouth pinched tight, her great, dark, terror-touched eyes swimming with unshed tears. Blinking energetically, she had accepted the baron's arm and left them.

"Our guests are arriving, Ashley. Is aught amiss?"

Hawkes raised his head, a trifle dazed. His mother was descending the stairs.

"After all my work," she fretted, "are you not pleased?"

He blinked and turned his dark, brooding eyes in a searching perusal of the entryway. He then turned his gaze in an equally searching manner upon her person, and smiled.

"You have outdone yourself, Mother. I am happy to see both you and the house in such good looks."

"Yes, your father would have been proud," she whispered, the words catching in her throat. She caught up his right hand and kissed the heavy gold signet on his ring finger. "He would be pleased you have decided at last to wear his ring."

Hawkes fingered the ring. It felt strange to be wearing the signet. He had always thought of it as Aston's inheritance, not his. He did not play the part as gracefully as Aston would have, but he had the look of an earl about him tonight, in the understated elegance of an austerely cut jacket of Devonshire brown, an eggshell white waistcoat, and matching smallclothes that clung to his legs like a second skin. Even more remarkable than his careful grooming, his mother, it would appear, was no longer bent on wasting what was left of her life. His father would have heartily approved.

The instant Dr. and Mrs. Turvey crossed the threshold, bearing the lovely Sarah Lyndle between them, Hawkes raised his head, as though scenting prey. He stood a moment thus, head up, blinking in dismay. The encroaching Miss Lyndle was, in person, not at all the picture of the conniving fortune huntress his imagination had painted in her absence. Her attire and deportment was all that was to be expected in a lady of taste and quality. Her dress was an understated vision of cream vandyked crepe and white satin. A choker of pearls bound her slender throat. No other jewelry adorned her person, only creamy, rose-tipped camellias nestled in the gold thread of her curls, their perfume drifting about her like a sweet cloud.

Hawkes stepped forward with every intention of furthering their acquaintance, but Dr. Turvey stood in his way. "Glad to see you, Turvey," Hawkes said, though in contradiction to his greeting his gaze swept irresistibly past the physician to the young woman who followed in his wake.

Hawkes could not deny her lure. A faint blush rosied the creamy bosom and crept up the gently curving column of her neck. His gaze followed the sweep of color past the pearls, past the pulse beating in the hollow of her throat. It was time he discovered the answer to the question that had been in his mind since the moment they last spoke. What color were her eyes?

She was looking right at him, in fact; past and through him, as Sylvia had on that long ago evening, as if he were not worthy of her focus. He frowned. Miss Lyndle's were strange eyes, their color, an indeterminate shade somewhere between blue and green and gray. Cold and flat and fathomless, like the ocean on a still winter's day, her strange, doll-like gaze held rigidly aloof from him, spared him not a glance. He found such disregard challenging. He would like to plumb the icy depths of that stare.

Dr. Turvey's voice lay claim to his attention. "I am pleased your mother has chosen to entertain again."

"Yes," Hawkes agreed. He was thrilled that his mother had come out of her self-imposed seclusion, but he would much rather be discovering what part Miss Lyndle played in the recovery. Did the young woman's strangely distant gaze avoid his out of embarrassment, contempt, or guilt? He must do his best to melt the ice of her disdain and find out, for he took no pleasure in the idea that his mother had come out of seclusion only to fall prey to a beautiful and clever fortune huntress.

Stewart arrived, resplendent in a fitted cutaway coat of Spanish blue superfine and a shot-silk waistcoat worked subtly in gold thread. Immaculate chalk white smallclothes complemented the pure white folds of the stock at his throat, tied for the occasion in the elaborate Orientale, so stiff and high that Stewart was unable to turn his head to either side. Despite his limited peripheral movement, the Beauty lost no time in taking Sarah Lyndle's arm. He led her away, before Hawkes could so much as say hello to either of them.

Dutifully remaining by the door to greet the flood of guests, Hawkes did not so much as catch a glimpse of the intriguing Miss Lyndle for upward of a quarter of an hour, but his thoughts returned to her far more than he would care to admit. Before stepping into his customary safe harbor, the card room, he stopped to scan the ballroom and found his gaze drawn to Sarah like a compass point. She sat, a pale rose among thorns, in the midst of the dowager set that found comfort and a cozy gossip in the grouping of chairs against the far wall of the ballroom.

What detained Hawkes from joining in the hand of piquet that was forming was the unguarded look of longing that had stolen over Miss Lyndle's exquisite features. The rhythmic tapping of one cream-tinted slipper peeking from beneath the elegant fall of vandyked crepe drew him irresistibly to her.

It did not occur to Hawkes that it was somewhat strange to find so lovely a young woman as Miss Lyndle not already endowed with a waiting line of dance partners. It was not his habit to worry about such things. He was determined to set fire to an iceberg—no more, no less. He stalked across the room, bowed before Sarah, and ignored the startled inhalation that whistled from the combined throats of fully a half dozen of those who sat within hearing range, when he purred, "Do you care to dance, Miss Lyndle?"

Without so much as the good grace to tear her gaze from the very activity she disavowed interest in, she said, "I do not, my lord. A young man has gone off to fetch me a glass of lemonade. I should not like him to suffer the misapprehension that I care not for his company, should he find me missing upon his return."

Cruelly rebuffed, for he knew by her tapping foot that she yearned for the floor, Hawkes declined to press his suit. He bowed with civility, but without so much as a glance toward any of the other women who would have gladly taken him to partner, made his way back to the card room.

An hour later, he stood up from the smoke-ringed gaming table and stepped into the cool garden through the low window that was built with just such escape in mind. His brows flew together in a frown, and what sounded remarkably like a growl rumbled in his throat, for there on the moonlit terrace Hawkes discovered none other than Sarah Lyndle.

She was dancing!

To dance in this dark, lonely spot to muted music, with any man, was decidedly indecorous, but that she chose to dance with his ward, the earl found personally offensive. Had he not recognized the tall, awkward young man, Hawkes doubtless would have left Miss Lyndle to her own scandalous devices, but he had no intention of allowing this woman of confoundingly contradictory moral certitude, to lead Nathanial astray.

He stepped from the shadows of the lawn, into the half-light thrown through the doors that opened onto the terrace, his voice silky with sarcasm.

"Does my nephew teach you the waltz, Miss Lyndle?"

The couple fell apart with a guilty start. Nate recovered first to answer him. "No, no, Hawkes, you have it in reverse. Miss Lyndle is helping me to master the steps."

"Nathanial," Hawkes said formally as he made a rigid little bow to Sarah, "I have it on very good authority that Miss Lyndle does not care to dance."

Nate squared his narrow shoulders. "Of course she cares to dance, sir. You have just seen her."

"Mr. Trent," Sarah spoke in the low, throaty tones that so captivated Hawkes's ear, "do not fly to my defense. The earl does but throw my own words back in my face."

"But that's rude. . . . " Nate spluttered, shoving his spectacles to the bridge of his nose.

Hawkes laid a calming hand on his ward's shoulder. "You are quite right, Nate. It would appear that Miss Lyndle does care to dance—with you."

"I must apologize, sir." The young woman's throaty voice was almost believably contrite.

"Must you?" He purred dangerously, irritated that he should care to hear what next the voice chose to say.

Miss Lyndle cut Nate's indignant protestation short, asking sweetly, "Will you be so good as to fetch me my walking stick, please, Mr. Trent?"

With an irate look directed at Hawkes, Nate agreed through clenched teeth and strode away.

"I admire the dispatch with which you manage to place yourself quite improperly alone with not one, but two different gentlemen on a poorly lit terrace, Miss Lyndle."

Hawkes glided closer.

Too close it would seem. She backed away. The odor of camellias hung sweet and heavy in the air between them. The light from the moon surrounded her flower-strewn hair. Her face was hidden in shadow.

She laughed softly. The sound, thick and honey-sweet, touched his spine in such a way that like a bee hovering over a blossom, he felt compelled to close once more the space that separated them. She stood her ground, and Hawkes, grimly satisfied, edged closer still, his desires fueled by what he mistook for a sign of surrender in the blind intimacy of the darkness.

Half hidden as she was, in shadow, he could not see if a hard frost still glazed the windows of her sea green eyes, but her voice was velvet soft, as sensually provocative as the heady odor of camellias.

"Oh dear." She sighed. "It was never my intention to become fodder for gossip mongers, but it seems that I have stepped once again on the toes of propriety."

She retreated deeper into the shadows, and Hawkes, convinced by her words that this would not be the first time the cool Miss Lyndle flew in the face of convention, pursued her, as if he were no more than a marionette, and her voice pulled the strings. She gasped when he reached out to stop her from backing out of reach, his hands enjoying the silken flesh of her upper arms. She turned away with a smothered cry when he bent to kiss her, so that his eager mouth, meant for her lips, met the cool softness of her cheek.

"Stop!" she said breathlessly, shrinking out of reach.

Hawkes had no intention of stopping. As though he were indeed a hawk, and she the hare, he swooped, and this time his lips did not miss their mark. She froze, her lips hard and unyielding beneath his, her back and arms like rigid blocks of wood in his embrace. This was not the response of a willing and wanton young woman.

"Stop!" she said again when he withdrew his lips from hers, puzzled. He had been certain this was what she wanted, the reason she had ensured they would be alone together on the terrace, the reason she had led him into the shadows.

Nate chose that inopportune moment to return.

"Here you are!" Cheerily he interrupted them, even as Miss Lyndle's breath caught in her throat in a little sob and she broke away from the hold he had taken on her wrist.

Hawkes whirled on his ward, frowning, but Nate, momentarily blinded by the brilliance of the light from the ballroom, did not seem to realize what it was he interrupted. He advanced on them, blinking and squinting, an ivory and gold walking stick clutched in his fist.

An oath passed Hawkes's lips as he took in the pale filigreed object. His hand shot out to stop Nate short, even as he turned to demand of Sarah, "This is yours?"

"Of course it's hers," his ward said defensively. "You don't think I would pick up the wrong one. . . . "

Hawkes wasn't listening. This ivory stick was unmistakably the same one that had been used to frighten Brutus into the back of a haycart. He took it from Nate with grim distaste.

"Is it your custom, Miss Lyndle, to step under the nose of every man's horse waving this stick about, like a bayonet, or have I had that singular pleasure?" His voice was deceptively mild.

"Hawkes, really!" Nate protested weakly.

With sinister grace, Hawkes clasped Sarah's hand to the shaft of the walking stick with the pressure of his own, and as if he meant to dance with her, he whirled her out of the shadows and into the light of the doorway, using the pressure of the walking stick, and the whip of his sarcasm to maneuver her. His face too close to hers for comfort, his voice mercilessly teasing her ear, he deliberately, languidly, made her dance away from his words.

"Did it amuse you, Miss Lyndle, to see Brutus mounting a haycart?" he breathed.

Sarah's mouth fell open in an O of shock. Speechlessly she retreated from his verbal attack.

As if this were a strange waltz, he pursued her, physically and verbally. In a rush, words coursed through his lips, soft—so only she could hear—but relentless. His cheek pressed into the camellia-scented hair. His breath burned hot and fast in her ear. He defiled her with the smooth, purring insinuation of his voice.

"Did you laugh to see him take the bit and run away? Or would you rather he had tossed me in the street? Is this, Miss Lyndle, how you step on the toes of propriety?"

She wrenched away from his cruel dance with a little moan, waving her stick on the terrace in front of her, much in the manner she had on Piccadilly Street, in a strange, clumsy rush to get away from him. The light from the doorway fell full upon her face; on the mute agony of her trembling mouth. It illuminated the unfocused quality that never left the strange sea green eyes. Her outstretched hands desperately groped the air for direction.

"Miss Lyndle," Trent called out, bolting after her, "have a care!"

Hawkes's mouth, which had begun to curl into a grim smile, fell open.

"Blast my eyes!" The words hissed through his teeth even as he leapt forward to stop her headlong rush.

"No!" she cried, struggling to get away from his embrace, even as she tripped and his hold kept her from crashing into the flagstones.

"Stop! No more," she cried, her understandable anguish

like a physical blow to Hawkes's heart as he pinned her to his chest.

"I did not know you were blind," he said hoarsely, the words torn from his throat as she continued to twist away from him. "I did not know. I thought your act a malicious one."

Her struggles ceased, leaving her limp and somehow defeated in his arms.

"Are you all right?" Trent's distress pushed his voice an octave higher in the middle of the last word. "Whatever possessed you to run?"

"I'm sorry," she said wretchedly. "My stick . . . what have I done with it?"

"It's rolled off into the grass," Trent reassured her. "I'll find it for you."

He jumped down off the flagstones into the shrubbery, anxious to calm her in any way he could.

Miss Lyndle released a shuddering sigh.

Hawkes was having some trouble working his jaw.

"Can you stand?" He was surprised that his wretched tongue could manage to sound tender.

"Yes."

He winced when she flung herself away from his touch.

"Was all of the shouting and hay in the street on my account?" she asked tragically, sounding wounded and remote.

Heat blistered Hawkes's cheeks, but he knew not how to lie to her. "Yes." The word caught in his throat and broke apart.

One shaking hand flew up to twist the pearls at her throat. "I'd no idea," she said.

"Nor I, that you could not see. I am a fool."

Hawkes wanted nothing more than to still the tremor in her hand. He reached out to take it in his own, but stopped short. He had no reason to believe his touch would comfort her.

She straightened and took a deep, calming breath.

"About frightening your horse, my lord . . . I must apologize. . . ."

"No!" he blurted. The word seemed too loud. Frowning

at his own clumsiness, he said again gently, "No, you must not, Miss Lyndle. I deserve no apology. I have behaved abominably. My tongue is like a viper. . . . "

"I've found it!" Flushed with victory, Nathanial bounded back to them.

Sarah turned her back on Hawkes. "Good," her voice quavered. "Will you take me in now, Nathanial?"

Hawkes's jaw worked. He could not let her walk away like that, not while her voice still shook, not while she thought him beast in both name and deed.

"Miss Lyndle . . . " he said, his voice gruff.

She clung fiercely to Nate's arm, chin trembling.

He cleared his throat uncertainly. "Would you care to dance, Miss Lyndle?"

Nate blinked in dismay.

Sarah's mouth worked an instant, but no words came. She sighed and allowed an uncertain but very brave smile to lift the corners of her lips, as if she understood that with his request he offered both an apology and an opportunity for atonement.

Her voice was low. "It would be ill-mannered of me to reject the generous sacrifice of your toes for crushing a second time this evening," she allowed.

Hawkes, whose brows had settled into a single, troubled black line, closed his eyes briefly, so profound was his relief. When he opened them, it was to see that she held out a small, gloved hand to him.

As if that hand were fine crystal, he gently took it up and tucked it into the crook of his arm.

Shame, contrition, and a growing admiration ruled Hawkes's thoughts as he led Sarah firmly off the terrace and into the center of the ballroom.

The dancers made room for the pair, a good many of them startled, not only to see that it was the Beast who had at last coaxed the lovely Miss Lyndle to join them, but by the ferocious looks he threw at anyone unwary enough to threaten the swirling path down which he led his partner.

Sarah knew naught of the war of emotions that disturbed him, nor of the ferocious tilt of his brows. She found in the

Beast an unexpectedly gentle guide. All her fears of both his cruel temper and the perils of the noisy, moving dance floor were dispelled as he led her with adroit skill among the swaying couples. The release of clutching fear that she had so recently experienced at the hands of this unusual man, who now seemed to mirror her every thought and move, was a strangely exhilarating experience. The music, the firm heat of his hand at her waist, the joy of a partner who would certainly not let her fall, surrounded Sarah with the sensation that she floated in sound.

She began to relax, to recover from the defensive posture that had stiffened her movements. A grace and confidence she had never experienced in the schoolroom, with Miss Washburn leading her through the steps, gradually took over her limbs. Sarah had never perceived herself as capable of fluidity of motion. She was far more used to crashing into things than to floating on air. She felt she had just been released from an incredibly powerful spell.

Like the porcelain figures from a music box come to life, the two whirled around the polished floor, their feet sure, while several unsuccessful attempts at conversation stumbled into silence. It was the heat and pressure of his hand on her back and the parallel sway of their bodies that spoke more articulately than any language of tongues. The balm of this silent conversation, began to heal the wounds inflicted by his sharply biting sarcasm on the terrace. Sarah reeled in a soothing bath of sound and motion.

When the set was over, and far too quickly in Sarah's opinion, an army of young men descended on them, all wishing to fill her dance card.

The earl, as meek as a lamb, all sarcasm in abeyance, took his leave.

He lifted her hand to lightly brush his lips, and Sarah, grown accustomed to the unruffling social perfection that was the Beauty's salute to these same fingers, could not pinpoint just what the vital difference was that made her hand tremble every time the Beast bent to press his lips there. She wondered, illogically, if some of the acid sarcasm yet laced the earl's mouth, burning through the protective covering of her glove, for a prickling heat rushed through her hand, on its way to meet a similar vibrating heat that hummed in the small of her back, where the pressure of his palm had so recently guided her around the dance floor.

"Compliments, my dear. You do not lack for partners."

He released her with the words, and Sarah acknowledged to herself that this was the third time that the earl had addressed her as 'his dear,' and while it was most improper of him to do so, she could not find it in herself to be offended while her fingers still hummed from their singeing contact with the very same lips that dared to address her with such cavalier familiarity.

Chapter 8

HAWKES could not dismiss his thoughts from Sarah Lyndle as easily as he had his person. He found himself unable to concentrate on the headlines of the paper propped before him on the breakfast table the following morning. Vacillating between berating himself for the unconscionable ass he had been on the terrace, and congratulating himself for having managed to convince her to dance, he obsessed over her. Their dancing had been an enlightening experience, nay, a revelation. Sarah had blindly followed his lead as if the two of them saw with the same set of eyes, as if they functioned from the same mind. It had seemed for the length of a song that they careened along, body and soul, as a single entity. This uncanny affinity she demonstrated for echoing his movements, as if she were his own distorted shadow, or a mirror image turned female, rattled him far more than he would have cared to admit. He had seen no more of her after their intoxicating whirl, he had in fact distanced himself from her in the card room, but his mind, objecting to the arrangement, had occupied itself with thoughts of nothing else, and he had played miserably.

Last night she had invaded his dreams. This morning he made no effort to dismiss her from his thoughts. He was, in fact, plotting the circumstances under which they next might meet, and so deep were his imaginings that he did not look up when the door to the morning room swung open.

"Well, what think you, Hawkes?" Stewart demanded, arms akimbo.

Hawkes did not often have the pleasure of his cousin's company before the hour of eleven, Stewart being not at all the early morning riser he himself made custom. Caught off guard by the untoward appearance of his kinsman, he could make neither head nor tail of Stewart's question.

"Morning, Stew. Forgive my fog, but I've no idea what you've just asked me."

"Your thoughts, cuz . . . " Stewart repeated, lifting his quizzing glass to examine the contents of the sideboard.

"Yes, yes, that much I gathered," Hawkes said vaguely. "My thoughts on what subject, pray tell."

"Thoughts on my heiress, of course." Stewart waved a fork at him. " 'Twas green with envy I found myself when you of all people did coax her into taking the floor, after I had spent the better part of the evening to absolutely no avail, pleading with her to accompany me in that very pursuit."

Hawkes put aside the *Times.*

"I'd no idea Miss Lyndle was your heiress!"

"I beg you will not next tell me that you have fallen slave to her charms, for 'twould be dreadfully tiresome if we should come to blows over yet another woman. I might feel compelled to cut you off, as completely as you have cut off Bret Preston." Stewart smiled archly as he poured a cup of tea. "With so many females in London, you would think the three of us could settle our sights on different ones, eh?"

Had this been an ordinary sort of morning, Stewart's thoughtlessness would have met with a catlike smile and some wickedly biting remark. But this was no ordinary morning. Hawkes had spent a great part of it wishing beastly words unsaid and beastly deeds undone. He had been thinking that he would like to begin again with Sarah Lyndle, so that her impression of him might be other than a beastly one.

Hawkes stood and paced to the far end of the room. The expression he bent on Stewart when he turned revealed no more than passing interest in the topic they discussed. He spread his arms deprecatingly, convinced he was being faced with just punishment for trusting too much in rumors.

"We have agreed to never again dishonor our friendship by fighting over a female. I do not pledge my word lightly." A weight seemed to settle in his chest, and the

words came slowly to his tongue, as though dredged up
against the resistance of his soul. An image of Sarah as he
had first seen her filled his head, stirring within his heart a
wistful yearning that had nothing to do with distant
promises to Stewart.

"You have no designs on her then?" Stewart pressed.

"I am quite certain that Miss Lyndle is not the sort of female that would have me," Hawkes dodged the question.

"Capital! In that case, I shall avoid calling you out, and
have some of your cutlets and gravy instead."

With an odd little smile for Stewart's enthusiastic in-
roads on the sideboard, Hawkes stared without seeing at
headlines that did not interest him in the least, and tried
without success to banish the perfumed memory of camellias from his mind.

Sarah breathed in the faded essence of one of the crushed
and browning flowers that had adorned her hair the night
before. She had a strange feeling of hunger this morning
but no appetite for the food set before her. The sensation
within her was very like the feeling she had experienced
her first day in London, as if her perspective had somehow
changed, as if she were caught up in something new and
disturbing and completely exhilarating.

The diverse impressions she had of Lord Castleford
plagued her like a question that knew no answer.

"What manner of man is the Beast?" Sarah asked herself
as much as Lydia.

"What manner of man?" Lydia repeated vaguely as she
buttered her toast. "Such a question, child. Whatever do
you mean? He is just a man, like all other men."

Sarah toyed with her spoon, considering what little she
knew of the Earl of Henley. There was something shadowy,
something oddly shapeless and mercurial about her concep-
tion of him. He did not easily conform to the mold of any
other man of her acquaintance.

No other man could so stir her emotions with the heat of
his breath on her neck and ear, or the heat of the words he
threw at her. No other man in her memory had ever moved
her with his unguarded anguish in admitting ignorance of

her blindness, or struck such a chord in her heart with an unvoiced plea for forgiveness. Never before or since had she so trusted the gentle, guiding force of any man's hand at her waist as he led her into the blissful, heady whirl of the dance.

Sarah felt as if she struggled with the frustration of trying to define an element of nature; a wayward gust of wind, perhaps, or the charged quality of the air before a lightning storm. She was used to reading people rather well, despite her sightlessness, but she had neither the words to express the rather fanciful notion of having met the incomprehensible, nor the intention of sharing her raw thoughts and newborn feelings with her hostess.

"He is not like other men, Lydia. That I know. And while I will admit that his manner is not at all the polished smoothness his cousin is master of, had he not succeeded in coaxing me onto the dance floor I might have passed a rather uneventful evening."

"I cannot regret that he encouraged you to participate, Sarah, but it was most inappropriate of the earl not to stand up with even one other female. Such singular attention from a gentleman with Lord Castleford's history cannot be considered a feather in any decent young woman's cap. It will not do for people to suffer the misapprehension that you are fast, love."

"Like your mother," Sarah almost expected Lydia to go on. Lydia did no such thing, but the thought hung between them as if she had. Sarah found it remarkable that she had been the only recipient of Lord Castleford's attention. To be singled out in such a manner might not please the notions of society, but she found herself quite warm with pleasure at the distinction. She wondered if this sort of giddy elation was what had compelled her mother to stray so far from home and family. She shook away the thought and let her head sway instead to the memory of last night's music.

"I'd no idea the pleasure dancing could bring. I am confident that I am not so clumsy as I would have supposed."

"Clumsy, my dear. Not at all. You were a picture of grace. Why, both Mrs. Loden and the Widow Rodenberry

complimented you quite prettily when you took the floor
with . . . Stewart Castleford. You do make a most striking
couple, being of a height, and equally fair."

Sarah was surprised that it was her dance with Stewart
that should draw compliments, for there had been something so appropriate, so perfect and lyrical about her movements with the strange gentleman known as the Beast that
she had been certain it must be noticed. It did not occur to
her that Lydia might lie to her, or that Lydia might have noticed the unusual rapport and feared now for the safety of
her heart.

"How very kind of Mrs. Loden and the Widow Rodenberry," she mused, plucking a petal from the camellia. It
was strange, she thought, how sometimes those gifted with
sight could look and still not see what she would have described as nothing less than an earth-shattering experience.

Hawkes had promised to keep his hands off Sarah Lyndle, and meant to hold fast to that promise, but his thoughts
were entirely too wayward to obey. As if another mouth
must voice his thoughts, so powerfully did they intrude on
his consciousness, the first words uttered by his ward as
Nate breezed into the morning room in an ebullience of
high spirits were, without so much as a good morning,
"Sarah Lyndle is a marvelous young woman, think you
not?"

Blithely loading his plate with a growing young man's
ration of kippers and eggs, he joined his kinsmen at the
table in the silence with which this pronouncement was
met.

"She is, despite her blindness, as beautiful in mind as she
is in her person. I find there is a tragic poignancy in flawed
beauty," he said. "As if the fragile quality of perfection
were somehow intensified in the reminder of how easily it
is marred."

Stewart blinked and raised his quizzing glass.

Hawkes closed his eyes and thought of Sarah. He agreed
wholeheartedly with Nate's assessment.

His ward was not through. "Do you know, Miss Lyndle
is the first female I have ever encountered who under-

stands, and can in fact hold intelligent discourse regarding the works of Plato, Homer, and Aristotle? Her father is, of course, an expert on the subjects, which would account . . . "

"Good morning Nathanial." Hawkes's interruption was quellingly polite.

Nate blushed. " 'Tis a good morning, isn't it?"

Is it? Hawkes wondered, for while he did not in any way disagree with Nate's opinion of Miss Lyndle, he was in no mood to hear anyone else sing the praises of a treasure he had just vowed to leave exclusively to Stewart's plundering.

Stewart was not so averse.

"I am happy you approve," he said, patting napkin to lips. "I have it in mind to marry the girl."

"You?" Nate exclaimed, shooting a disbelieving look at Hawkes, who merely nodded in acquiescence, his eyelids at half-mast.

"Yes," Stewart went on, voice and chest swelling with pride as he shoved back from the table to rise. "I mean to press my suit this morning with the delivery of a posy. Lilacs perhaps, to prove I am suffering the first pangs of love, and red carnations, for my poor heart."

Nate rolled his eyes expressively, a smile in possession of his lips that brought to Hawkes's mind the image of a cat who has gotten into the cream.

"Good luck," he said with the flippancy of one who believes such luck highly improbable.

Stewart raised his monocle as he donned his cloak, the closer to examine Nate's cheeky grin.

"Thank you," he said, polite but dubious as he took himself out the door.

Hawkes, who saw nothing to smile about in the image of Sarah Lyndle accepting flowers from his cousin's hand, wondered what inner thought so affected his ward's demeanor.

"How do you intend to entertain yourself today, Nate?" he queried, more with the purpose of taking his mind off the scent of camellias and the image of moonlight on golden tresses, than out of any real curiosity.

Nate cleared his throat and blushed fiery red. "I'm off to the bookstalls," he said with such a guilty look that Hawkes wondered what mischief he might be bent on.

"Do you mind if I accompany you? There is an unusual French book I have seen mentioned in the *Times* this morning that would be a lovely gift for a friend of mine, should we come across it."

Hawkes's interest rose when Nate choked on his coffee in response to this request.

"Shall I search out the book for you?" his ward offered with such desperate goodwill that Hawkes's determination to accompany him was doubled. Nate was hiding something from him about this morning's business. He had best forget Sarah Lyndle and see to his duties as guardian.

He rose from the table, curiosity roused. "I am in need of a diversion," he said pleasantly. "Shall we go?"

Chapter 9

SARAH wound her way through the stacks of books that made Hatchard's an unequaled reader's paradise, reminded of how woefully uneducated she must be, locked by her blindness forever from the riches that so many pages represented here. She was reminded too of the book that Sylvester Naughtley had mentioned, a book that would appear to detail her mother's activities, of which she herself was ignorant, for all who should care to read it. She did not falter from her purpose however, and with the assistance of a clerk, she and her godmother made their way to the floor that Nathanial Trent had promised would offer up a book for her father.

He met them, as promised, at the top of the stairs. "Good morning, ladies. I have secured a copy of *Prolegomena ad Homerum* for you. Shall we browse?"

Sarah agreed, her mind swinging between thoughts of what Sylvester had written about her mother's foolishness and her own foolishness in dancing with this young man's guardian. Nate did not notice her preoccupation. Happily, he led Sarah through the intricacies of Hatchard's, Lydia trailing in their wake.

So powerful were Sarah's memories of the night before that when she caught whiff of a faint, woodsy fragrance, she did at first wonder if her imagination played a trick on her senses, until Nate said, "Hallo, Hawkes, only look who has come book hunting today."

Hawkes did look and in looking he realized that Miss Lyndle was the reason for his ward's blushing discomfort. There was no disguising the ardent light in Nate's eye. It would seem that all the men in his extended family worshipped at the feet of this particular goddess.

Small wonder. Sarah Lyndle was an exquisite piece of work—his memory but a pale shadow of reality. There was a goodness to her face, a calm, intelligent, self-certainty that he found both surprising and admirable. A young woman with Sarah's handicap had many reasons not to look so self-assured—had reason too not to look so pleased they encountered one another so close on the heels of last night's uncomfortable misunderstanding on the terrace. Was it possible she had forgiven him?

It struck Hawkes afresh that there was much to regret in the promise he had so recently made to Stewart. He would like to know Miss Lyndle better. He would like to erase all traces of vicious words he had so carelessly thrown at her.

He pulled his gaze away from her, mindful of his claim to Stewart that he had no designs on the lady, mindful too of the surprising dryness that assailed his mouth from the moment he said, "Good morning, my dear."

He made a point to address all further conversation not to Sarah Lyndle, but to the doctor's wife. Had he but known it, his time was well spent, for Lydia did begin to wonder afterward if perhaps she had too harshly judged him.

"I hope you found pleasure in my mother's soiree, Mrs. Turvey," he said pleasantly as the four of them fell into step outside the bookstore. "I am no judge of such things, but it did seem to come off rather well." He allowed himself a glance at Sarah's reflection in the mullioned windows of the shops they passed.

His intense looks at first baffled Mrs. Turvey, for she could not fathom what in a milliner's shop could so fascinate a peer of the realm. But, as his searching perusal continued, at the cobbler's next door and then at the bakery on the corner, she at last determined it was Sarah's reflection that drew his eye, and not the goods.

"She is a rare girl, isn't she?" she suggested softly.

"Yes," he agreed. Wistfully, he stopped darting looks at the windows and was surprised to see Lydia Turvey's expression change in response to his self-control, as if she saw something unexpected and likable in him.

"Mrs. Turvey, I would beg a favor of you, of a most delicate nature. Would you be so good as to slow your step, so that we might be out of earshot of our companions?"

Mystified, but too curious to refuse him, Mrs. Turvey drifted a pace or two to the rear as he requested. Hawkes drew from beneath his arm the paper-wrapped purchase he had just made at Hatchard's.

"Please give this to your husband."

Mrs. Turvey took the bundle from him, clearly puzzled. "Of course," she said. "What is it?"

Hawkes allowed his eyes to follow Sarah's passage away from him for a moment before he answered. "It is a rare and wonderful book that I saw mentioned in this morning's *Times*. I would prefer Miss Lyndle knew not whence it came."

Sarah knew nothing whatsoever about the mysterious book until late that evening. Dr. Turvey returned home from surgery then and having satisfied his hunger with a modest repast, he excused himself from the ladies on the pretext of stepping into his study for a smoke. She did notice that Lydia was unusually impatient with the crochet she was working and that she sighed with relief when the doctor returned to the parlor.

"I've something for you, Sarah," he said, the lilt of excitement in his breathless delivery.

Sarah put aside her knitting. "You should not ply me with presents, Doctor. I shall go home terribly spoiled."

The doctor laughed. "This gift comes not from me."

"Who then?"

Lydia noisily cleared her throat. "A friend, who wishes to remain unidentified," she said.

Sarah tried not to panic. The book that immediately came to mind was the journal that Sylvester Naughtley threatened to publish. Surely this could not be it.

" 'Tis an altogether new sort of book by a Frenchman named Valentin Hauy. Fascinating, I'm sure you'll agree, for it is a book designed to be read by the blind."

Sarah sat as though frozen in her chair, hope mingling

with disbelief. A book she could read? "I do not understand."

The doctor sat down at the card table that occupied one
corner of the cozy room. "Come here, and you will. These
pages have been embossed. The letters are in relief. You
have only to run your fingers along the words, which are
regrettably in French, but in this fashion you will be able to
read."

Sarah let loose a shaky laugh, as she rose, her eyes
swimming in tears. What a ninny she was to worry about
Sylvester Naughtley and his journals.

"My dear Sarah, whatever is the matter?" Lydia begged,
starting up from her chair.

Sarah pulled out her handkerchief.

"N-nothing. I'm terribly sorry for this fuss."

"Sarah, love"—Lydia's concern only served to make the
tears flow faster—"if 'tis nothing, whyever do you cry?"

Sarah sniffed. She could not unburden her heart concerning her fears with regard to Sylvester to these good people,
for she had no clear idea what it was that her mother had
done that might be used against her. She did not like to de-
ceive them, however, so she settled for half of the truth.

"This morning, as you led me through room after room,
each filled to the ceiling with all manner of reading material, Lydia, I was absolutely wretched with self-pity for my
blindness. It occurred to me, you see, that while I have
learned my letters and know how to spell in both French
and English from blocks with raised letters, that I should
never have the good fortune to delve into the wonders of
any book, least someone be so kind as to read it aloud to
me."

Lydia gasped. "Oh dear, I'd no idea."

Collecting herself, Sarah wiped away the tears and with a
very slight quaver, said brightly, "This book sounds quite
amazing. You will be sure to thank the thoughtful person
who so kindly thought of me, will you not?"

"Of course."

Her godmother sounded as if she, too, had been brought
to tears.

* * *

Before Lydia Turvey's thank-you note had time to reach him, Hawkes was pleased to glimpse firsthand the success of his gift.

Drawn from the stuffy confines of his mother's study by the promise of sunshine and the heady lure of honeysuckle and jasmine, he walked the narrow, grassy path that led to a vine-covered arbor which was an especially favorite haunt of his. He was surprised to find that he was not alone in seeking its peace.

Sarah, her upswept tumble of curls framed against the dark green of massed ivy climbing the wall at her back, occupied one of the wrought-iron benches in the arbor. A bulky book lay open on her lap, and slowly, laboriously, her fingers passed and repassed over the surface of each page.

Miss Lyndle's strange sea green eyes were open, but they found nothing to hold their interest in the book. They stared blankly in his direction, and Hawkes closed his own eyes a moment, wondering what it must be like to go through life in perpetual twilight, unable to see light or color or form. There was something chilling in the prospect, something so out of keeping with the visual pleasure that the creature he opened his eyes to gaze upon brought him that Hawkes felt suddenly very fortunate, in an elemental way that might never have entered his head had it not been for Sarah Lyndle.

Reluctant to interrupt her concentration, he was as loath to turn away, for he found pleasure and inspiration in observing the interest with which this young lady regarded his anonymous gift. It was, at last, the memory of his words to Stewart that spurred him to turn upon his heel and go.

The sound he made as he turned startled her from her reverie. Her hand fell still upon the page and she called out in the pleasantly throaty voice that always pulled him closer. "Who is there?"

The earl answered the lure of that voice.

"Ashley Castleford, my dear. Pardon my intrusion."

"Intrusion?" The ripple of her laughter shook him. "How can one intrude in one's own garden?"

"I make it yours to enjoy, Miss Lyndle," he said with a little bow, and would have left her had she not stopped him.

"Do not go on my account, Lord Castleford."

He laughed, gently mocking her invitation. "Fear you not to fare too long alone again in the company of the Beast, my dear?"

"Should I, sir? Are we not within plain view of your own mother's windows? As I am quite certain you would never wish to offend her sense of propriety, I can live in no fear for my own."

"Brave puss," he purred. "Your logic is irresistible."

Sarah wondered as he reversed direction to approach her if he addressed all the women of his acquaintance so freely. "Brave puss" and "my dear" were not at all the proper references for an unattached female. Suffering from the confusing sensation of being both repelled and incredibly drawn to this man, Sarah wondered for an instant if he meant to abuse his power over her as Sylvester Naughtley meant to do. She could not forget the heated embrace into which Hawkes had swept her, nor the strange, provocative taste of his lips on hers. He had tried to take advantage of her once. Would he do so again? She had been terrified of him in that moment of unleashed passion, terrified that he might rouse within her some vestige of her mother's wanton nature. She was wise to fear as much, for even knowing what he was capable of, she was too stimulated by his presence to send him away with proper dispatch.

"As to whether I should fear this Beast you mention," she said, with the fervent hope that she was not a naive fool, "I have found, sir, all too often, that names do not fully encompass the nature of the person or thing they are meant to designate. Someone was once good enough to point out that 'reputations, like shadows, rarely fit the man.'" She wondered if he recognized his own words. "I must admit, it had been so long since I had the pleasure of seeing a shadow, that I asked various acquaintances if they would be good enough to describe mine to me. No two people offered up the same description, of course."

"No?"

"No. It would seem an elusive creature, my shadow. She

shrinks and exaggerates and distorts, and yet, in some small way at all times is representative of who I am."

"Very like a reputation," he sounded mildly sarcastic.

"Very like," she agreed, feeling a little flustered that he chose to stay and test her wit with his own. "When you ask me if I fear the company of the Beast, that, sir, is to ask if I fear the company of a shadow."

"And do you?"

She shifted nervously, aware of his scrutiny, and yet unwilling to equivocate. "I have reason to fear only one thing in you, my lord."

"Said thing being?" he drawled.

"I have reason to fear your tongue, sir, for it is dagger sharp."

An unusual note of sadness supplanted the bite of sarcasm in his tone. "I would not have you fear me in any way, my dear. Perhaps my tongue may make amends. Will you hear its description of your shadow?"

"If she is to be seen," she agreed, wondering if she had imagined the fleeting hint of sadness.

He laughed. She liked the sound. It banished sadness, without mockery. This man was no Naughtley.

"You have right to wonder, for, seated as we are beneath a canopy of leaves, the retiring shadow does seem to play hide-and-seek."

She closed up the book in her lap, her lips parted in anticipation. There was something changed in his tone, as if he were a storyteller with a tale of moment to unfold.

"She is here, your shadow," he said softly. "And seated as we are, the elusive creature has become one with all of nature. She is bound, however loosely, to the shadows around her, the shadows of leaves and tree branches and, indeed"—his voice fell so low she felt compelled to lean into the space that separated them, so as not to miss a word—"your shadow and my own have become attached, entwined in such a way that we resemble nothing earthly, but instead have become one marvelous, mythic creature that cannot survive the full strength of the sun."

Sarah was stunned. His imagery was highly evocative. It lifted the hairs at the nape of her neck. The book she had been studying, her precious new book, slid, unheeded, from her lap.

She did not realize that they had both bent to retrieve it, reaching out simultaneously, until her fingers found the heat of his for the breadth of an instant.

She pulled back as though scalded; touched and shaken, both by his flesh and by the erotic poetry of his description. There were good reasons why sitting alone in a private garden, with a gentleman one barely knew, was behavior discouraged for an unattached young woman. Something strangely akin to fear lit up like a flame in Sarah's breast. This Castleford, the Beast, roused in her person an unusual heat, a heat she had never experienced before. His very nearness muddled her thoughts, stilled her tongue, and possessed her with the ridiculous notion that she might like to lean her head against his shoulder to drink in more of the woodsy aroma of the vertivert root the earl's valet must keep hanging in his clothespress. Alarmed by her own inappropriate desires, she abruptly took up her ivory walking stick and stood.

Biting sarcasm almost hid what she thought must be real concern as he too, rose. "My tongue offends you?"

She laughed and immediately regretted having done so, for the sound of it was forced, even to her own ear. "Your tongue? Not at all, my lord. He behaves quite prettily, but he would turn my head with such prose."

He did not deny the claim.

"Then I shall banish the cheeky fellow and mutely offer my arm instead, so that he might lead your lovely shadow wherever she should wish to go."

His hand took up hers, very lightly, to settle it, quite appropriately, on the smooth fabric of his sleeve. Sarah was amazed to discover that her fingers were alive with feeling, as if his touch charged her extremities with an awareness of everything they came into contact with. Such an awareness had been, until that moment, beyond her scope, and that surprised her, for she had always thought her hands incredibly astute. They saw so much her eyes could not. This heightened sensitivity was most unusual. She had felt its power only once before, on the evening they had danced together. That he, and he alone, could conjure up such hidden resources within her very senses, both stimulated and unsettled her. She was not quite sure she liked the sensation, for these newly unleashed powers of observation and awareness seemed beyond her control.

"Will you be so good as to return my shadow to the harsh reality of the sun, and myself to Dr. Turvey?" She wondered as she made the request how it was that what she desired, and what she said, could be so diametrically opposed.

"I am yours to command, my dear."

She imagined she heard a trace of disappointment in his gracious reply and felt compelled to explain.

"I would say good day to your mother if she is not feeling overly pulled as a result of her entertaining, and thank her for the precious book I just now so carelessly let slip. I believe it must be she who has seen that I should have it."

Lord Castleford, who assured her he had tucked the volume safely in the crook of his arm, suggested, "Perhaps, as we proceed, you will tell me what makes this book so wonderful."

Sarah did just that, with considerable relish, and to both their satisfaction.

Chapter 10

WHEN a short time after the following morning's post had been delivered, Hawkes's study was intruded upon by his ward, he refused for a moment to look up from a missive that he read with more than passing interest. The smile softening his hard-edged features as he perused the single sheet from Mrs. Lydia Turvey, thanking him profusely for Sarah's special book did not fade when at length he put down the letter.

"Good news?" Nate ventured.

"Mmm? Yes, in fact it is good news." Hawkes allowed his eyes to skim the page again. "Need something?"

"It had occurred to me, my lord," Nate said, warily, as though expecting to be refused, "that I have within my power the means to bring some pleasure and enlightenment to the dark world of our new acquaintance, Miss Sarah Lyndle."

Hawkes looked up sharply. "How so?"

Nathanial had practiced this speech. It came out as if by rote. "It has crossed my mind, sir, having heard Miss Lyndle explain her own superior mind with anecdotes of a father who spends a great many hours engaged in reading aloud to her, that I might serve in some small capacity the same role while she visits London."

Hawkes's inclination to chuckle at Nate's verbiage, was stifled. Fear of denial spoke too plainly from the boy's eyes.

"You wish to read to Miss Lyndle?"

Nate nodded, mutely expectant.

"I've no objection to such a kindness." Hawkes said.

"Borrow whatever you think might strike Miss Lyndle's fancy from the library."

"Thank you, sir." Nate voiced his gratitude with a gusty sigh of relief, but he made no move to go.

Hawkes raised an eyebrow. "There is something else?"

Looking rather like a cat that has swallowed a canary, Nate blurted with youthful enthusiasm, "I would, in addition, sir, greatly appreciate being included in the sight-seeing tour to St. Paul's Cathedral."

"St. Paul's?" Hawkes stared at him blankly.

Nate's face fell. "Aunt Amelia did not think you would mind."

Hawkes tilted his head, a puzzled frown knitting his ferocious eyebrows. "What else did my mother say?" he drawled.

Nate blinked at him quizzically. "She said, sir, that Miss Lyndle had expressed a great desire to experience the mysteries of the Whispering Gallery, and I thought . . . ," Nate trailed off. "Is this a private excursion, sir? I've no wish to intrude."

Hawkes smiled ruefully, his understanding now clear. His mother meant to throw him together with Miss Lyndle in such a manner that he could not refuse. "You are welcome to come with us, Nate," he said briskly. "In fact, you will do me a great favor in inquiring of the Turveys and your cousin Stewart if they should care to accompany us."

While quick to join the growing party of sightseers to St. Paul's, Stewart took unexpected umbrage to the book-reading scheme.

"I'm quite put out," he told Hawkes.

"Indeed?"

"Yes, I'm finding it very difficult to pursue my suit with the Lyndle, you see."

Hawkes tried to look bored. He was in no mood to hear his cousin detail the way in which he wooed Sarah Lyndle.

"That pup Trent must always be underfoot. He and Mrs. Turvey are all the time shushing me during the afternoon readings. Your ward especially takes unmitigated offense if

I try, even in the smallest way, to interrupt with conversation, no matter how diverting."

"You find it unusual that the others want to read at these readings?" Hawkes made a sarcastic attempt to squash the topic. To no avail.

Stewart plunged on with his complaint.

"I have sat through the entirety of a perfectly nonsensical story about a man who is shipwrecked in a land peopled by tiny humans. I am not at all fond of the author. He does us the greatest disservice by creating a situation where any lasting relationship between his hero and any female is absolutely out of the question."

Hawkes took pains to control the twitching of his lip. "Miss Lyndle shares your aversion to Swift's satire?"

Stewart shook himself like a cock with ruffled feathers and took out his ormolu snuffbox. "No, Hawkes, I do not think she does. In fact, I have noticed that she follows Mr. Gulliver's arduous progress with rapt attention, even to the dropping of her knitting on occasion."

He was silent a moment, his mouth pursed in a rather pained expression, which was relieved but for an instant by the delicate sneeze that followed his inhaling a pinch of the blend of snuff he took such pride in.

"Reminds me of that dashed spaniel I had when we were boys. Do you remember? Always under foot."

"Corky? I do not quite see the connection between your cocker spaniel and Gulliver."

"Not Gulliver, cousin, 'twas your young Trent I was referring to."

"Nate?" Hawkes's bored look vanished. He did not like to hear his ward ridiculed. "But again I find myself at a loss." His sarcasm was pronounced. "Corky adored you. That was the reason he followed you about. I dare swear that if Nate follows you it is not out of adoration, Stew."

"Dash it all, Hawkes, forget the stupid spaniel. I am well aware the lad does not adore me. He makes no secret of the fact that he is not obliged to answer to my wishes, and has come to the point of rudeness on more than one occasion. It is not me, but Sarah Lyndle that he hounds. Do you know he has had the gall, not only to offer to escort her around

St. Paul's, but to invite me along, like so much extra baggage? Be so kind as to call the boy to heel. He would not dare disregard your wishes."

Hawkes studied his cousin's expression. "You are correct in assuming the boy does not disregard my wishes. This jaunt to St. Paul's is my mother's idea, a clever one too. I am handling the arrangements. Shall we count you among our number, or do you mean to cry off? We've no desire to drag you along unwillingly. As to calling Nate to heel, as you put it, 'twould be an unkindness to do so. You have yourself just pointed out that the boy's readings are met with rapt attention. I am surprised that you would deny your heiress such innocent diversion."

"Innocent? You have not seen the calf's-eyes young Nate wears these days, if you would so call his motives."

Hawkes gave Stewart a rather more piercing look. "Be that as it may, I leave you to your own devices in diverting Miss Lyndle's rapt attention away from—what mixed metaphor is it with which you identify my ward?—a calf-eyed pup."

Chapter 11

SARAH was both dreading and looking forward to the St. Paul's excursion. It was odd that she felt drawn, not only to the adventure of exploring the cathedral, but also to the opportunity to again meet a man who had at first seemed bent on insulting her, and now would seem to be avoiding her. Sarah could not deny her fascination with the man called Beast, but Hawkes had shaken her confidence in their curiosity being mutual. His absence and his extended silence spoke of rejection. Was it possible that the kiss he had pressed on her was no more than a mistake, his talk of shadows nothing more than talk, and his offering to be her tour guide to St. Paul's merely a courtesy to his mother? Sarah had to know. Geoffrey Garvey, whom she meant to marry, had not the power to invade her dreams and thoughts as this Beast did, and it seemed there was something wrong in such a contradiction of sensibilities.

Three weeks dragged by with Hawkes's participation in none of the afternoon readings that Nate and Stewart unfailingly attended. It occurred to Sarah that perhaps it was her blindness that made Hawkes hesitate to further their acquaintance. The thought was lowering. Once it took hold she could not shake it.

On the day of the St. Paul's excursion, Nate met her with the disappointing news that Hawkes had arranged to meet them at the cathedral rather than ride with them. It was Stewart who helped the ladies into the carriage, and Nate who regaled them with trivia about Sir Christopher Wren's building of the dome in which they should soon be traipsing about. Stewart helped the ladies down again when they had arrived at their destination, and he took possession of

Sarah's arm in order to assist her in mounting the steps that took them up to the entrance. It was not until they were inside, in the cool, vast, echoing stillness of the cathedral, that Sarah, anticipation heightened, met up again with Lord Castleford.

At a time when most men of fashion favored tasseled Hessians that announced their presence with the faint slap of leather on leather, she had noticed that Hawkes preferred soft, heelless jockey boots. Their hushed tread was part of a patchwork of sounds and scents that came together in Sarah's mind as the shadowy image she carried of him, and she recognized their measured tread approaching her as clearly as if she could see.

The sense of Hawkes's presence was heightened by the woodsy fragrance she so closely associated with him. She could put some sculptural boundaries to the mass of him; his height and weight, and even the shape of his hands, but the rest of his physiognomy was a mysteriously shapeless mass. She wished she knew more, but could not imagine any occasion on which she might satisfy her curiosity, without the ruination of her reputation.

A thrill of apprehension ran along her spine at the idea of exploring the contours of any man in an intimate manner. As she wondered what she would find in a husband and her duties to him, a second shiver rocked her. She wondered what it would be like to be "seen" through the touch of the man who would take her to wife. Oddly enough, it was not Geoffrey Garvey's hands she imagined tracing her contours, but the Beast's instead.

The earl must have seen her shiver for the first thing he said, in the lowered tone one always adopted within hallowed walls, was, "Here. You'll be needing this. We shall be stepping down into the crypt to start our tour, and it is even chillier belowstairs than above."

The weight of his cloak, and briefly his hands, settled disconcertingly on her shoulders, so that she shuddered with a chill so violent her teeth chattered. The garment warmed her. The cloak that draped her from shoulder to heel had absorbed the Beast's body heat and was imbued with the pleasant smell of him. Warmth surrounded her,

soaked into her. Sarah felt the earl engulfing her in something far bigger than a mere bit of woolen. Standing very
still, she allowed him to do up the clasp beneath her chin as
though she were no more than a child, feeling all the while
that the guilty pleasure she took in the warmth of both the
fine wool and its owner's manner was somehow illicit and
improper, for she was promised to another, whose memory
stirred no such sensations within her.

"How very kind you are," she said softly, her voice
hushed by a reverence that had little to do with the nature
of the building in which they stood.

"Not at all," he said softly.

He pulled away as his cousin joined them, saying with a
hint of pique, "I should have been happy to loan you my
cloak, Miss Lyndle, had I known you were feeling the
cold."

"Good," her benefactor said briskly, "I shall require you
to give yours up to your aunt, Stew, and perhaps Trent's
will do for Mrs. Turvey. I had forgotten we should be going
underground today, or I would have reminded the ladies to
wear something warmer than muslin and shawls. Perhaps,
in order that this hitch may not delay our tour, you will lead
the way. A clergyman has been commissioned to show us
where Mr. Christopher Wren himself was laid to rest. I
would not care to keep him waiting."

Glowing with warmth and satisfaction within the encir-
cling cloak, Sarah allowed Stewart to lead her down some
steps that led beneath the body of the cathedral. In front of
them went a soft-spoken guide to direct their progress, and
behind, quickly, cloaks exchanged, came Nate and Mrs.
Turvey, followed by Hawkes and his mother.

Basking in the warm folds of the cloak and happy that its
owner followed close behind her, Sarah listened to their
guide's trivia with only half an ear. Not even the cold and
eternally finite stillness of the tombs they viewed could mar
the hope-filled awareness of life and its possibilities that
brought a contented lift to her lips. However, everyone else
seemed quite relieved when their sobering tour ended with
a demonstration of the workings of the pipe organ, and the
crypt was left behind them.

Traipsing cheerfully back up the stairs into the great Latin cross of the cathedral, the clergyman suggested they examine the famous carved-limewood choirstalls by Grinling Gibbons, as well as the carved-oak bishop's throne, before endeavoring to climb into the dome.

"Lord Castleford has made special provisions for your enjoyment," he said.

The special provisions turned out to be permission granted to use a portable stair, normally accessible only to those whose job it was to dust and polish the heights of the choirstalls.

"What's this?" Stewart exclaimed.

"A closer view, for those who care to clamber up," Hawkes said.

Nate rushed to take advantage of the stairs, his shoes ringing on the metal steps.

Sarah tilted her head to listen as he climbed what sounded like a great many of them. Hawkes, whose presence she seemed preternaturally aware of, stood beside the portable stair, guiding his ward's ascent. Behind her, both Mrs. Turvey and Lady Castleford insisted they had no desire to try the stair, but she could hear them breathing awed, murmuring exclamations of praise as they drifted away from the group to examine the beauty of the woodwork. When Nate came clattering down again, she heard him gleefully directing the ladies to "Come see the other side, for there is more."

Stewart, who had been standing at her elbow all the while, released her arm that he might "have a peek." His going left Sarah feeling isolated in an unfamiliar and echoing darkness, afraid to take a step in either direction for fear she might trip over something. She heard Stewart somewhere above her, words of appreciative wonder on his lips, and with a lonely sense of her own inadequacies, tried to imagine the grandeur that everyone else could see.

Lord Castleford gave up his post beside the stairs. She could feel his approach even from a distance, as if he reached out to touch her with his purpose.

"Your turn, my dear," he said softly.

She was relieved to be remembered, and pleased that he

should even consider including her, but the feeling that she was somehow judged wanting in her blindness had not been completely dispelled. Her voice faltered with uncertainty and disappointment.

"I, I do not think . . . I mean . . . I shall not be able to see even if I do manage to scale the stairs, my lord."

"Whyever not?" Hawkes said quietly, cutting her protest short, and before Sarah knew what he was about, the warm grasp of his hands had engulfed her own kid-wrapped digits as he guided her to the base of the portable stair.

"We shall have to do away with this, I think." His hands dropped hers to tug at the clasp that held his cloak about her shoulders still.

" 'Twill only get in our way," he explained.

The cloak was swept away, leaving her with the uncomfortable sensation that she had lost both warmth and security.

"But, my lord . . . ," she began.

"You cannot mean to send her up this stairway, Hawkes. 'Tisn't safe." Stewart condemned the idea, even before it could be enacted. Having reached the base of the steps, he sounded as if he stood on top of them.

Hawkes deferred to her judgment. "It is entirely up to you, Miss Lyndle. Would you care to see the carvings?"

" 'See' them?"

"Yes." He leaned in close to her. "The stair brings you close enough to touch the carvings, and as they are in deep relief, I think you may, in truth, be able to see them."

Sarah could not stop herself from smiling. Such an arrangement seemed tailored specifically to her needs, and it was rare that anyone so swiftly understood those needs.

"I would like to see them, if you do not think I should fall," she admitted.

"Not a chance of that!" His certainty calmed her fears and erased the doubts she had been suffering with regard to his possible contempt for her blindness.

"Take four steps forward . . . ," he directed with steady assurance. "Out of our way, Stew!"

Stewart stepped out of her way.

Hawkes lifted her right hand until it rested on the cold hardness of an iron railing.

"Now, step up," he urged without any trace of hesitancy, "just as you would on any stairway, with your skirt lifted a little, that it might not get in your way."

She shivered, her uncertainty returning. She was a little shocked at his mention of raised skirts, but did as he said, wondering all the while if she was improperly displaying her ankles in the process.

"Splendid!" he encouraged. "Now, up again . . . and again, slowly." His voice vibrated with bracing enthusiasm from the steps below her. It would seem he meant to follow her progress all the way up the stairs—with his person.

She felt the floor fall away beneath her. A draft of cold air swooped most disconcertingly beneath her lifted skirt. Hawkes, two steps behind her, sounded reassuringly solid. "That's it, my dear."

"Oh my!" Lydia Turvey's worried voice came floating up from what sounded like a great distance below. "Are you all right up there, Sarah? I'd no idea . . . "

"I'm sure she's fine with Ashley watching her every step," Lady Castleford said, but her voice, which trembled slightly, was far less reassuring than her words.

Sarah hesitated, concerned herself by the concern she heard in both the women's voices. Careless of her footing, her shin banged up against the next step.

Hawkes must have heard the sudden hissing intake of her breath. "Steady!" he advised, and he mounted another step, so that the bulk of him, closer than before, was palpable. "We're almost there, and you've nowhere to fall but into my arms." His voice held amusement, and a purring resonance that reminded her of nothing so much as a contented cat. "Unless that idea appeals . . . " he paused suggestively.

Sarah felt the blood rush into her face. With a nervous laugh, she carefully began to climb again, clutching tightly to both the iron railing and her raised skirt.

"There now," he said softly when she had reached the top. "That was not so difficult."

He was right behind her, two steps separating them, as had been his habit during the climb, but while she could go no further, he did not stop until he had closed the space between them, and stood on the riser just beneath. She could feel the muslin of her skirt brushing against the unexpected resistance of his leg. Unbidden, her body swayed a little in his direction, increasing the wickedly heady sensation of fabric brushing fabric. From her waistline to the spot where the hem of her skirt weighed heavy on the arch of her instep, Sarah had the tantalizing sensation of being caressed. It was for the briefest moment as if Lord Castleford had touched her in a most intimate manner without ever using his hands.

Sarah jerked stiffly back from the feeling, but in so doing, she succeeded only in banging her ankle.

"Relax, my dear," he murmured, amused. "I do not bite."

His head was on a level with her own. She could feel the warm wind of his breath on her cheek when he spoke. Her face burned, and her breath came too fast. "I am unused to standing in such close proximity to a gentleman anywhere other than the dance floor."

"Imagine we do but dance then, Miss Lyndle." Lightly, his gloved hand settled around the ball of her shoulder. Lightly, it applied pressure, until she was standing in a less exaggerated posture. She trembled and wondered as her skirt brushed up against the length of him once more if she was being unnaturally missish to allow such contact to disturb her equilibrium so. She could not stop thinking of the time he had dragged her into his arms and kissed her.

Her voice was a trifle unsteady. "What steps now, my lord?"

Like a dance instructor he directed her. "Lift your right hand, and reach out until you touch something."

She did. Her kid glove found only air. Dizzied, she was relieved to find herself suddenly, and quite literally in his hands; one steadying the elbow of her upraised arm, the other slipped around her waist.

"It would seem this were a waltz, my dear." His cool remark, if not the heat of his hands, had a calming effect, for indeed it did seem they were poised to dance, and she had never felt so graceful as when they had last stood in just such a position.

"Here! My hand will show yours the way."

The weight of the gloved warmth at her elbow slid lightly along her sleeve, raising gooseflesh as it went to take possession of her hand. Burning from such contact, her fingers found wood this time, hard and smooth and steadying. His guiding hand fell away and like a bird uncaged, her own flew swift and sure over the carved surface.

"Can you feel it?" Stewart's anxious voice drifted up from below.

"Can she tell what they are?" It was Mrs. Turvey, muted, addressing Stewart.

But Sarah was focused completely on what Hawkes might next say, or do, or touch.

"What do you see?" His warm breath in her hair sent a chilling spasm down her spine.

Her gloved fingers felt abnormally sensitive as they passed over the ridges and curves. "It is a face," she whispered with an air of discovery, and then, impatiently, she drew back a little from the carving in order that she might wrench the confining kid covering from her fingers with the aid of her teeth.

"That's better," she said as her bared fingertips played over the carving, unfettered. "It is a child's face. There is a garland of flowers in her hair."

"What else?" he insisted. As he leaned forward, the lapel of his coat raked lightly against her back. She was startled by the sensation. Her loose glove, which she had clutched against the railing, fell, unheeded, like a pale leaf, from the height of the stairs to the darkness of the floor below.

Sarah swallowed hard, concentrating on the wood beneath her bare fingers, and not the tingling ripples of sensitivity that spread out from the spot his coat had touched, like the little waves in a disturbed pond.

"The child is naked!" Even as she let slip the ill-advised word, her guilty, gloveless hand darted back from the carved torso of the wooden child as though it were caught in an improper act. Heat raced from the vulnerable nakedness of her exposed fingers to the base of her spine. Heat burned in her cheeks and in the tips of her ears.

"Yes," he agreed, unperturbed, and taking up her hot,

shaking, gloveless hand once more in dancing fashion, he placed it in contact with another section of the carving.

"Can you tell me what this is?"

"Feathers. Wings." She said, less guilty, on firmer ground.

"Exactly." His voice was soothing. "You will find that they are attached to the naked child that so needlessly disturbs you."

"Attached? Is she then, an angel?"

"Without doubt," he said softly. "There is, my dear, a long row of angels, stretching out on either side of you, wingtip to wingtip."

Her fingers flew out to confirm. With great excitement she leaned out over the iron railing of the stairs, to call down to the others, her voice falling as lightly as the glove, "I see angels! Beautiful angels."

Her words bounced about in the great vastness of the cathedral in a thousand, soft, rushing little echoes. Those who stood beneath them looked up and smiled, for there was no hint of sacrilege in such an outburst.

Hawkes was struck by her euphoria, as if it possessed mass and density. In a society of sycophants and mincing fops, who made boredom and cynicism an art, such unadulterated joy was a novelty. A smile so beautiful it rivaled the artistry of Gibbon's angels, sweetened Sarah Lyndle's parted lips. He could not stare at her hard enough, could not drink in the pure expressiveness of her delight deeply enough. She took his breath away.

Justifiably pleased with himself for inspiring such happiness, Hawkes did not like to see it fade, nor did he wish to consider the prospect of descending too quickly from such exalted heights. Witnessing the glory of St. Paul's through freshly opened eyes, he looked about, with the conviction that he must share more of the wonder of this place with Sarah.

"Clinging to those angels you will find fat cherubs," he said tentatively.

It was the right thing to say. She turned her attention back to the carving. He wondered what it would be like to have those fingers trace the lines and contours of his surfaces. The thought stirred him.

"They hold between them garlands of flowers"—his voice began to gain speed—"and below us, are more blossoms, each one so perfectly rendered that any gardener might easily identify them. Nearer still to the ground there are panels beneath pierced-iron grillwork, that abound in still more flowers, these wound through horns and ribbon and swirls of carved feathers."

She seemed transfixed by his description. Her head tilted, the better to hear his every word. Her mouth slanted at an attractive angle, lips slightly parted. He would like to transfix those lips with his own.

"Tell me more." Her words were breathless with desire.

He hesitated, eyes darting, overwhelmed for a moment by the hunger in her expression, his desire to kiss her, and the difficulty of describing such complex grandeur to one who saw none of it. And then, with a sense of commitment, he dove into a rich description of the carved stone pillars and the ornately painted and gilded arches that stretched above the choirstalls. He told her about what he could see of the dome from this vantage point and of the oil paintings by Thornhill depicting the life of St. Paul in a great wash of brilliant color. He went on to describe the lace of wrought iron that flanked the altar, and told her of colorful mosaics and marble reredos and stained glass, until he was breathless and she, laughing as he gathered wind to begin again, begged him to stop, for her mind could absorb no more.

Impulsively, she turned to clasp his hands in her own.

"Thank you for letting me see," she said, the fervor of her sincerity flowing for a moment like a river, from her hands to his. It was only with a great deal of self-control that Hawkes resisted the urge to lift her deliciously bared right hand to the warmth of his lips. He would like, he thought, to taste the intensity of her joy, to show her the arts of lovemaking, just as he had shown her the wonders of St. Paul's.

"I feel," she went on lightly, still trusting him with the gift of her touch, "like a tiny figurine, suspended in the midst of a lavishly iced and marzipanned cake."

"An apt analogy," he acknowledged, although he did himself regard the beauty of her aspect as if she might be one of Grinling's marvelous limewood angels, come to life. He could not claim to be relieved of his sudden burning desire to taste the lips of an angel when she released her hold on his hands.

"Shall we be off in search of the mysterious Whispering Gallery?" he suggested, for he could not wholly rely on his better instincts should they stand in such close proximity much longer.

"Yes, please." Her smile, like a benediction, filled him with an unusual contentment. Ashley Hawkes, Lord Castleford, in that moment did not feel in the least beastly.

He led Sarah down the steps, and while descending should have proved more difficult than ascending, there had grown a bond of trust between them that made the task effortless.

Hawkes's fragile bubble of contentment seemed ready to burst when it was discovered that not all members of the party were equally enthusiastic about climbing the requisite steps that it took to attain the height of the Whispering Gallery in the dome above their heads.

The ladies were the first to abandon the plan.

"I've climbed up and down as many steps as I would care to mount today, Ashley," his mother said. "Those of younger and stouter limb must undertake such, not I."

Mrs. Turvey followed suit.

"I shall stay and keep Lady Castleford company," she offered. "I've seen the Whispering Gallery many times."

"Nothing could deter me from going up," Stewart said stoutly as he sank down in the front row of a section of pews and discreetly pulled off one of his pumps, "had I been wise enough to wear some footgear other than these detestable, blister-raising contraptions." He rubbed his stockinged heel and winced. "As it is, I believe I would slow things down considerably."

"Well, I'm for setting off immediately."

Nate's enthusiasm was not to be denied, and Sarah, who had begun to look quite downcast, brightened.

"Oh yes," she said. "Let's be off."

Hawkes had gone straight to the spot where her glove had met the floor. He bent to retrieve it, his regard swinging from those in the party who would stay behind, to the duo of intrepid climbers who were off already in pursuit of the stairs.

"You cannot expect the boy to oversee such a climb alone, Hawkes," Stewart admonished.

His mother agreed. "Oh my, yes, only think if she should stumble. Perhaps I should go . . . "

"No need," Hawkes assured her as he gave his cousin a searching look. He found it rather unsettling, to be bade go where he would have thought Stewart would least like to see him wander.

"You cannot let the pup take her all that way alone." Stewart shot a meaningful look at him.

Hawkes's eyebrows rose. It would seem Stewart feared Nate's competition for the lady's favor more than his own. With a sigh of resignation, for nothing could have reminded him more pointedly of his assurances to Stewart that he had no designs on Sarah than this open show of trust, Hawkes nodded.

"As you wish, Stew." He set off in languid pursuit, and by the time he reached the stairs, Sarah and Nate were already out of sight. Above him, their voices echoed gleefully off the walls of Portland stone like errant children's. Smiling, he followed in their wake, delighting in their high spirits but feeling he had been placed in the untenably tempting position of an unnecessary third wheel.

Hawkes caught up to them in the gallery beneath the windows of the drum that topped the dome. Seated on the circling wooden bench that hugged the wall, the two faced one another from opposite sides of the dome, the great railed-off circle of space that fell down into the cathedral below like a dark well between them.

Sarah leaned into the wall, one of her ears almost pressed to the stone. Nate, lips moving, whispered from his side of the gallery until she nodded and whispered back.

Hawkes sank down upon the bench not far from his ward, hoping to catch what was being said. What he heard was Sarah Lyndle's voice, as clearly as if she sat beside him, whispering lines of poetry.

"Piping down the valley's wild, piping songs of pleasant glee. On a cloud I saw a child, and he laughing said to me, 'Pipe a song about a lamb . . .'" She paused.

Nate's voice came next. "Too easy. That's William Blake's 'Songs of Innocence' . . . " He wagged his hand, beckoning Hawkes to the spot where he sat, his exuberant appreciation of the place irrepressible. He patted the bench enthusiastically, saying, "Sit here, directly opposite Miss Lyndle, and whisper into the wall. She will hear you as clearly as if you were to speak directly into her ear. If you've no objection, I've every desire to press on to the Stone Gallery. I understand you can see all of London from up there, but it's a bit of a trot, and I've no desire to fatigue Miss Lyndle if the breeze is too brisk."

"Press on, by all means." Hawkes kept his tone deceptively mild as he sat down, though his heart leapt with anticipation at the prospect of a moment completely alone with Sarah. "We shall likely follow on in a bit, once we've both had a moment's more rest to catch our breath."

Satisfied, his ward left them.

The small, round, domed gallery fell silent. The stone walls seemed suddenly chill. Hawkes regarded the beautiful young woman seated directly opposite him. His hand, which had sunk out of habit into the pocket of his coat, came up again on encountering the soft resistance of her glove. He wondered if the hand it belonged to was unduly chilled.

Her voice swam in his ear. "This is a curious place."

"Indeed, my dear. But ought not one take advantage of the remarkable acoustics and whisper all conversation?" His voice dropped as he leaned into the wall so that he did in fact whisper the last few words. There was something deliciously sensual about speaking to her in such a fashion. He was delighted when her lowered voice came back to him with an appropriate quotation.

"Let me not to the marriage of true minds admit . . ."

Pleasure lifting one corner of his wide mouth, Hawkes picked up the prose where she had left off, rather than rush to name its source, for in so doing, his whispered words could speak a little of what lay hidden in his heart.

"Impediments. Love is not love which alters . . . " He paused, hoping she would continue the quote.

She did not disappoint him. The words were like a healing balm to his ear. " . . . when it alteration finds. Or bends with the remover to remove. Oh no, it is . . . "

" . . . an ever fixed mark, that looks on tempests and is never shaken!" he finished. A contented silence fell between them, but then, as though the hollow echo of empty silence somehow threatened them, they both rushed to fill it.

"Today has been wonderful. . . . " she began.

"I have your glove." He drew it forth and began to play with the soft kid fingers. "It fell."

"How silly of me to let it go."

He lifted the diminutive glove to his face, cradled in the bowl of his hand. Closing his eyes, he inhaled the faint odor of her perfume. Heliotrope. He opened his eyes to stare across the vast space that separated them. He was strangely touched to see her clasping and unclasping her one kid-gloved hand over the one missing its mate.

"Shall I bring it to you?" His voice, he thought, sounded too wistful, too hungry, too needy. He wished to be near her for more than reason of a glove.

She took a moment to respond.

Forced to wait, watching her, wanting her, he wondered if his voice revealed too much in its passage around the stone wall.

Her answer, when at last it came, was no more than a sigh. "Yes, please."

Swiftly, anxious on the heels of the intimacy of their whisperings, he trod the circumference of the dome.

There was an expectancy in her manner that reminded him of what he had seen in her expression when she had begged him to tell her more about St. Paul's, as though she waited, with slightly parted lips, for something of far more consequence than a glove. Her look slowed him.

Her posture was formal, her expression unremarkable, her hands clasped tight. Her eyes revealed nothing, and

Hawkes realized how much he relied on those windows of thought and feeling to determine what most people were thinking. He stood before her, unable to pinpoint in what way she communicated to him the undeniable sense of anticipation and hunger, but aware that it stopped him from giving in to the temptation of sinking down on the bench beside her, for his own hunger, his own needs, threatened to breech his self-control. He wanted nothing so much as to sweep her into his arms, his lips pressed to hers, and yet, there was a deep-rooted fear within him that such conduct would destroy the understanding, the sense of accord that was theirs today.

"Your glove." His voice was gruff with desire.

She reached out, uncertain of finding it. He pressed it to her palm.

Her fingers closed for an instant on his. "Thank you."

Hawkes could not resist all temptation. Encouraged by the slight pressure of her hand, swiftly he raised the bare bridge of her knuckles to his lips that he might plant a kiss there. Then, in a decidedly improper fashion, he turned the delicate wonder of her slender hand and planted another kiss in the cup of her palm.

Gasping, she pulled away from him.

"Forgive me," he said without any real regret, as he pressed the glove into her hand a second time. "I have been wishing to do just that for the last half hour and more."

Blushing, she clumsily busied herself with fitting her fingers into the snug confines of kid. "Do you always give in to your impulses, no matter the consequences?" Her voice shook.

"Usually," he said mildly. "Quite beastly, I'm told."

She gave his comment a moment's consideration, all the while clasping the hand he had kissed quite tightly with the one he had not, as if it might choose to run away from her.

"Perhaps it would serve us both best if we chose to forget this particular impulse."

Her voice no longer shook.

His, was thick with the desire he so closely guarded. "Well, my dear, if you take no pleasure in kisses, as I do, perhaps it would be best if you forgot. I must be content to carry the memory for both of us."

She did not look completely comfortable with his answer, but letting go of the clenched grasp on her now safely covered hand, she tilted her head toward the stairway as if indeed his kisses disturbed her thoughts no more. "Nate returns," she said.

He heard footsteps, faintly, a moment after she spoke. As he marveled at the acuity of her hearing, he realized with a feeling of guilt that made him think of Bret Preston's expression when he had stood up out of Catherine Stone's bed in the middle of the night, how close they had come to Nate's walking in on something quite inappropriate to his role as guardian, and quite out of keeping with his promise to Stewart.

His ward bounded through the stairway door. "Come on, you two. The view's spectacular, and the noise—I never knew the city raised such a din." Trent's voice raised its own unintelligible din in the drum of the curved ceiling.

Miss Lyndle stood. "Shall we go?"

Hawkes took possession of her safely gloved hand and settled it on his sleeve. "I am yours to command, my dear," he said in all seriousness, wishing her commands might involve a return to kisses, for the heat of passion blazed within him, in a conflagration that threatened to burn away both self-control and good intentions.

Chapter 12

A N entire week passed before Sarah again came in contact with the Earl of Henley. It was a miserable week,
seven days of fog and a drizzling rain that shrouded the
city, and everyone's spirits, with gloom. Sarah's only diversion in that time—the doctor and his wife being far too
busy fighting an outbreak of fever that seemed to accompany the weather, and the dowager and her nephew Stewart
laid low with sniffles—was the daily coming of Nate with
the books that he read to her. Even then, it was fond memories of the trip to St. Paul's that primarily occupied her
thoughts. Every moment was relived, every word reexam-
ined. The palm of her hand still warmed whenever thoughts
of the kiss that had been placed there resurfaced. Sarah had
to admit that she had thought Hawkes meant to take her in
his arms, and deep within herself she came to terms with
her disappointment he had not done so. She wondered what
it would be like to be kissed by this man, and kiss back
with equal passion. The kiss thrust upon her unwilling
mouth the night of the ball was no measure to go by. Then
she had neither expectation nor desire for kisses. Now her
wayward thoughts brought her to the blush. She would end
up like Mama if she did not push such dangerous inclinations completely from her mind.

The weather cleared, and Sarah, who thought that her
clouded mind might clear as well in the rain-washed air, accompanied Dr. Turvey on his rounds. While the doctor was
privately closeted with the widow, she would practice her
music on Amelia's fine pianoforte and concentrate on
thoughts of a happy marriage.

Sarah loved to express her feelings with music. There

was a power that seemed to flow from her fingertips in the expression of sound. Her father called it a gift, her governess insisted it was nothing less than a miracle, and the music teacher who had come in to give her lessons pronounced her in possession of an "ear." Whatever it was, Sarah had only to listen to a piece of music and after a few halting tries she was able to reproduce it chord for chord on the pianoforte.

So lost in the flow of Mozart's Fantasy in D Minor was she, that she never heard Hawkes step into the room. It was only after the last chord faded into silence that she became aware of the presence of another.

"Who is there, please?"

Even as she spoke, she knew. There was, ever so faint, a woodsy fragrance in the air. An uncontrollable rush of shy pleasure filled Sarah's chest almost to the bursting point, in anticipation of another encounter with Lord Castleford. They had gotten along so well in the excursion to St. Paul's that she believed all their past confrontations might be forgotten. There was something so full of promise, so in tune with the sunshine that had at last revealed itself after days of rain, that Sarah felt it was inevitable that they should meet here today.

" 'Tis naught but a shadow, my dear."

Sudden heat warmed Sarah's cheeks. It would seem that the Beast intended to continue addressing her most familiarly as "dear." The hand he had kissed trembled on the keys. She dropped it down off the instrument, along with its mate, and clasped them together in her lap.

"My lord!" she said, trying not to sound unseemly pleased, for she was, she reminded herself, promised to Geoffrey and it was cravenly wanton in her to desire kisses of another man.

"Did I frighten you?"

Hawkes's concern struck a chord within her so that her heart sang like a tuning fork. "I did not hear you come in."

"Let's hope no one else did either," he said languidly. "I should like us to have a moment of private speech, without alarming anyone's notion of propriety."

She was flustered by the suggestiveness of his request,

for there was something in his tone that reminded her of that disturbing moment on the terrace when he had pressed his cheek to her hair and whispered with unkindly passion in her burning ear; that moment when she had felt like a mouse caught in the talons of a bird of prey. There had been the same suggestive innuendo in his voice the last time they sat in the garden, when he had described her shadow, and again at St. Paul's when he had kissed her hand. That there was something dangerously flirtatious in his manner whenever they were alone she could not deny, or in fact dislike, but that flirtation might lead to the shame of a seduction alarmed her more than a little, for there was something unrestrainable within her that wanted more than anything for his teasing, seductive ways to continue.

She stood abruptly, overturning the stool in her haste.

He was beside her in an instant, righting it, his voice, his presence, the very scent of him, unsettlingly close.

"So much for no one hearing us." He sounded amused.

Sarah strove to rein in her galloping heart and still the trembling of her fingers. "Why is it that no one must hear us, my lord?"

"I would have private speech with you on a delicate matter. Shall we see if the roses smell as sweet today as they did the last time we took a turn in the garden?"

She would have liked to refuse him, indeed her better judgment told her she must do so, for time spent alone with the earl always upset her equilibrium, but her knees seemed turned to water, while her tongue clove mutely to the roof of her mouth, and there was an overwhelming need within her to discover what private matter he spoke of.

Gently he took one of her hands, and with no indication that he noticed its tremor, tucked it into the disturbing warmth of the crook of his arm. His pace carefully matched to hers, he led her out into the warm smell of roses.

Sarah's thoughts flew like the bees that hummed among the flowers, contemplating any number of topics he might conceivably wish to discuss with her, none of them delicate. Did he meant to seduce her? Could she withstand his advances if he did, or would she succumb, as her mother was rumored to have done, so long ago, to the winning ways of the Baron DeValle?

It was he who broke the silence, his words halting.

"The matter I wish to discuss, is one of the heart."

Sarah stopped dead in the garden path and dropped her hand from his arm. The sun seemed too hot on her head, the air too close. The fact that she was in the company of a man who made her pulse race, her hands clammy, and her temperature higher, did nothing to reduce her discomfort.

"Whose heart, sir?" she managed to ask.

"My—" He paused and for an instant her own heart lifted, but when he went on, his words, faintly mocking, definitely amused, brought it plunging down again. "—my ward, Miss Lyndle, informs me that he is of a mind to discontinue his schooling. He would, it seems, far rather learn at your feet."

"Nate? At my feet?" Sarah's pulse throbbed in her ears. The heat of the day seemed suddenly oppressive, its golden, rain-washed promise turned to brass. "Whatever can have spurred such a nonsensical idea?"

"My ward discussed his reasons at length," Hawkes assured her, his sarcastic languor increasing. "Among them were included, as best I recall, your beauty of person, voice, spirit, and mind, as well as remarkable intelligence and an uncommon understanding of his favorite pasttimes."

The recital of another's compliments, from his lips, sounded decidedly uncomplimentary. Sarah tugged at the high collar of her walking dress. Her stays felt too tight. This was certainly not a seduction. They had reached a corner in the garden. The pressure of Hawkes's hand on her arm to lead her in a new direction seemed as excessive as the humidity that rain and sun had combined to create. His voice droned inexorably on, as latently threatening as the bees.

"In addition, Nate mentioned the obviously adult regard with which you did respond to his affection."

She felt him staring at her, searching her every expression, as clearly as if he reached out and touched her with the look. Her hand stirred on his arm. "Beg pardon?"

His voice was smooth. "Shall I review the entire list, madam, or was there a specific item that you have trouble comprehending?"

A shaky laugh preceded her agitated reply. He called her madam. The word seemed unusually formal. She had, perversely, grown used to his addressing her as his dear.

"Whatever did Nate mean by 'adult regard.'"

"Ah, I too had difficulty understanding that point. So, I begged him to clarify in what manner you responded to his attentions, being of a mind that the boy did but misinterpret some perfectly natural action of your own."

"And his response?" The thought that he believed her capable of seducing his ward, a young man six years her junior, made her dizzy. Did he, like Sylvester Naughtley, know of her mother's folly, and think her cut from the same cloth?

"Well, Miss Lyndle, the rather garbled and red-faced account I received was difficult to credit, but I have never known my ward to be a liar. He states that you did, and I quote, 'caress his face.'"

Sarah sighed. Her hand fluttered on his sleeve again. Her only words were heavy with comprehension. "Oh dear."

The smell of roses seemed suddenly overwhelming. Sarah knew not how to answer. She was suffering the disappointment of discovering that there were limits to the trust and understanding that she and Lord Castleford had established. It had seemed to her that he could read her emotions, feelings, and purpose, to the very core of her being, as clearly as if they were ink and she the page. But she had been wrong in her assumption. Here they stood, as separate in understanding as if the printing on the page she represented were a foreign language to him.

Hawkes's mocking amusement changed. Sarah heard, with a sinking heart, biting sarcasm flood his voice.

"I take it then the account is rooted in reality?"

"As much as your own reputation is rooted in reality."

The arm on which her hand rested grew rigid. "Indeed!"

Feeling faint in her disappointment, for she had hoped to make him understand with her analogy, Sarah let loose a troubled sigh. "I would assure you, sir, that it has by no means been my intention to engage the affections of your ward in passing my hands over his face. I did but wish to see his features. I think of Nathanial much as I would a younger brother. I was under the mistaken impression that he regarded me in much the same way. I will, with all haste and as much delicacy as I can summon, clarify my feelings for him."

"You relieve my mind, madam." He bit the words off.

Sarah could tell that he was anything but relieved. He wounded her with his remark, with his lack of trust. She could not clarify this stupid misunderstanding without bursting into tears of disappointment. Lifting her chin, she said with a touch of asperity, "I have only to tell Nate that my future is firmly fixed . . ."

"Fixed, Miss Lyndle? You are promised?" he rasped.

She nodded, her throat so constricted she found she could not utter a word.

"You have accepted my cousin's offer then?"

"Your cousin's offer?" she repeated. The comment seemed to her a nonsequitur, its meaning incomprehensible. "You cannot mean Stewart wishes . . ."

The earl caught her up as she tripped on an uneven paving stone. When next she realized what she was about, his arms, one like a band of hot iron supporting her back, the other beneath the bend of her knees, were bearing her aloft, out of the penetrating heat of the sun. A scathing remark passed his lips about the folly of poor workmanship as he lowered her onto one of the many shaded benches lining the garden walk.

It was in the unsettling moment that it took for Sarah to regain her faculties, the out-of-control instant when she realized that his face was so close to hers, his breath, warm and musky, bringing heat to her cheeks, that Sarah realized how much she regretted her promised state. Never, in Geoffrey's company, though she had known him all her life, had she felt desire coursing through her body as it did now. Never had she dreamed she might feel content to nestle her head against a gentleman's lapel while he carried her about.

The warmth and scent of him engulfed her, intoxicating as an elixir. Her lips parted to take in more air, and as if drawn to her by the soft inhalation, his mouth came down to brush hers with a gentle tenderness, a hesitantly glancing pressure that startled her as much as the fact that he dared to kiss her.

Her gasp of astonishment was smothered by the second only slightly more demanding descent of his mouth. As hot breath and firm lips danced across the sensitive surface of Sarah's lips, testing her resistance, she felt liquid desire well up within her like a thirst wetted but not quenched. She could not seem to stop herself from responding to the dangerous matching of their mouths with a little moan, a slight arching of her back, and a responsive pressure that had him inhaling abruptly with pleased astonishment. He seemed then to devour her mouth, to taste its every surface with a ferocity of passion that sent a thrill of intense pleasure gliding up the length of her spine.

The power of such passion, the intensity of her own desire, so deftly unleashed, awed Sarah. Her heart crashed about in the cage of her ribs like a terrified bird. Pulling away from Hawkes as quickly as she had pressed herself to him in this illicit embrace, she turned away from the fervently seeking mouth with a little mewl of denial.

"No!" she breathed. "Stop."

His breath coursed raggedly across her lips as he hovered uncertainly, poised to swoop again should she recant such refusal. His shoulders shuddered against the brace of her hands with the pent energy of a horse reined in before a race is run.

Head swimming, heart slamming, pulse throbbing loud in her ears, Sarah pushed herself up out of his arms with such conviction that he exhaled gustily and helped her to rise. His helping hand was a seductive warmth in the small of her back that might have tricked her into succumbing to the comfort of his embrace with only the faintest of pressure.

Heady with the wine of his kisses, Sarah wondered if the thrill this intimate contact brought her might be called love, or if it was merely wanton lust that stirred her pulse to such racing tumult. Pushing herself away from that thought, away from the terrifying unknown of her own feelings, she dabbed at the moisture beading her upper lip with the mortified conviction that she had lost all shreds of dignity in both thought and deed.

Hawkes spoke, his voice so remote and emotionless that she suddenly and irrationally felt like sobbing.

"I beg pardon, madam, for what would seem to be another unpardonable blunder. The beast within me does, on occasion, take possession of my better senses, and lead me to the most reprehensible behavior."

Sarah fanned her face with her hands and sat a little further from him. She would have liked nothing more than to sink her head against his shoulder, just once more, in order to feel some spark of warmth, some hint of comfort from him, for his icy tone did nothing to still the uncomfortable racing of her heart. She mustered up a wan smile.

"You, sir, would seem to be far better informed concerning the affairs of my heart than I am myself. I had no idea Stewart meant to offer for me."

Her valiant attempt to make light of the moment did nothing to ease the rigid formality of his words.

"I am a blundering fool, treading roughshod over your personal affairs. I had no notion that your future was firmly fixed, and then knowing, had no right to compromise you with a kiss. Is the fortunate gentleman to whom you are promised someone of my acquaintance?"

She sighed, wishing with all her heart that they spoke of anything but this, wishing with every aroused fiber of her being that she had delayed her rejection of his ardor. What words might he be whispering to her now, had she continued to respond to his kisses? What imp of mischief had possessed her tongue to blurt out news of Geoffrey to him?

The words could not be unspoken, nor deeds undone, nor promises unmade. She had promised to marry Geoffrey. Marry him she would, dignity intact.

"I do not think you know him, sir. We grew up together. Geoffrey Garvey is a member of Wellington's forces, in the Third Division of heavy cavalry. He has been in Spain . . ."

"I do not know him." He cut her off. His voice seemed to come from far away, for all he sat right next to her. Sarah could think of nothing more to say. In brooding silence, he helped her up from the bench, and led her, pale and equally silent, from the garden.

Sarah burned with a tumult of emotions, chief among them a wildly unstable desire to be held safely in Hawkes's arms. She was shamed by her wanton disregard for her own promised state, shamed by her mishandling of Nate's naive affection for her, surprised to hear of Stewart's intentions, and amazed, beyond belief, to discover that she enjoyed kissing the Beast and wished nothing more than to press her lips to his again.

Hawkes leaned his forehead against the cool window-pane of the study and tried to make some sense of the madness with which he would seem to have become possessed. Was there indeed some uncontrollable beast within him that would seduce an innocent blind girl? Was his passion so ungoverned that he might accuse her of seducing his ward in one breath, and then seduce her himself with the next?

"Whatever did you say to Sarah, Ashley?" his mother demanded with some heat, bustling into the room with an energy that would have pleased him at any other time.

"Is she recovered?" Hawkes pulled his head away from the window. He wanted the girl. That much was clear. Despite all promises to Stewart, despite her promised state, he wanted her.

"No, she is not recovered!" Amelia scolded stoutly. "I have never seen her look so poorly. What have you said or done to distress her so? I could not get a word out of Sarah."

Hawkes scowled out at the roses so blithely lifting their

faces to the sun. His own face felt very stiff, his neck unbending. She was promised. She had told him as much, and
then he had kissed her! Was he completely depraved?
Could passion so completely divest him of pride, and
honor, and moral certitude?

"Did you know, Mother, that Miss Lyndle is promised?"

The dowager blinked in dismay. A strangely hopeful
smile touched her lips. "But of course, dear. She told me
the first day we met. An antiquated notion for her father to
take into his head, do you not agree?"

"Antiquated?" How could he agree with her? He had no
knowledge on which to base his answer.

"Yes, he wishes to tie the girl to a young man she has not
seen in years, on the basis of a friendship shared with his
father. No telling what kind of a nodcock he may be. I must
say, that while my own marriage was an arranged one, I
would not have cared at all for the notion of marriage to
someone I knew only as a childhood chum." She regarded
his reaction with bright-eyed interest.

"Does Miss Lyndle care for the match?" Hawkes braced
himself for the answer, convinced that the afternoon was a
complete and irrefutable fiasco. Sarah had promised herself. It was too much to hope that she did not care for the
match.

"She did tell me it puts her father's mind at ease while
she is away from him. He would not have allowed her to
come to London without the commitment, you know."

He offered no response. There was much he did not
know about Sarah Lyndle. He had made a point of not
knowing. Now he was consumed with a desire to know
everything about her, and his mother was ready to fill his
ears with just that. He made no move to stop her.

"This Geoffrey appears not to have been home above
half a dozen times since he first went away to school. Eton,
I believe Sarah said. Then he took the Grand Tour, and now
he is gallivanting about somewhere in Spain."

Hawkes refused to allow himself to hope. His conduct
did not merit hope. He had dishonored both himself and
Sarah with his attentions.

"I do not think one can qualify serving in Wellington's

Third Horse Division as gallivanting, Mother," he said severely.

Amelia shook her head. "Pish! The point is, Mr. Wellington spends far more time with the boy than Sarah does. She seems to think they will get to know one another again, well enough, when he returns. Such stuff!"

Hawkes fell into a brown study, his jaw working. He must nip his passion in the bud. It must never flower, for it threatened to poison both his own existence, and poor Sarah's. It would be disgraceful in him to stay, for if he did, he would surely end up seducing the girl, and the last thing Sarah needed was to be thrust into the same indefensible position which led her mother to flee London.

"I'm off to Brantley in the morning. Is there aught you would have me bring back to you?"

"You mean to go to Brantley, Ashley?" his mother squeaked. Her plump hand rose to the hollow of her throat.

"Yes. I've a great deal of work to do," he said with a conviction he was far from feeling.

He could not tell her he could no longer bear to be near Sarah, that his feelings for the young lady were grown dangerous; that they threatened to lower him to the despicable level of someone like Bret Preston. He had deceived both himself and Stewart with his selfless promise not to compete for Sarah's affection. It was ridiculous to make promises one could not keep, and he could no longer safely swear to keeping this one. He was hopelessly entangled in a growing concern for Miss Lyndle's welfare and a rising desire for her affections. He teetered on the brink of not only breaking his word of honor, but far worse, of ruining Sarah's chosen future with the very fortunate Mr. Geoffrey Garvey.

Garvey was an obstacle Hawkes had never anticipated. Small wonder though that he should so misjudge the state of Sarah's heart, when he could so little trust his own. Why had he fallen in love with the very woman he had sworn to ignore? It went entirely against his sense of decency and honor to have done so. He must go, while he still possessed the willpower to tear himself away. Hard work, distance, and time would cure the ache in his heart, and still the ache in his loins.

"But, Ashley . . ." His mother twisted her hands as she began, as if she might twist fate, given the right words.

His unyielding look silenced her.

"My mind is made up. I leave in the morning."

Chapter 13

AFTER a night in which Sarah enjoyed little sleep, she rose early, as had been planned, in order that she might squeeze herself into Lady Castleford's landau beside Amelia, who had, some few days past, agreed to convey a party of four to Elise Petersham's statue display. The party included Lady Beale and her daughter Anne, both in high spirits because the weather was perfect for the enjoyment of an outdoor gathering.

Quiet and despondent, Sarah was too focused on the memory of her conversation with Hawkes to notice how quiet and despondent her hostess was. She could not forget the humiliation of having been suspected of seduction, nor could she dismiss the dismay with which Hawkes had met news of her betrothal. But Sarah wallowed in guilt over enjoying the sensation of having been clasped in Hawkes's arms and kissed until she was breathless.

The gossip that flew around her in the carriage could not divert her thoughts. A hitherto unknown wave of desire had swept over her as she lay in Hawkes's arms, which so contradicted her intention to honor her promise of marriage to Geoffrey that for the first time she felt that, like her mother, she should never have come to London.

It was mention of the name Otto DeValle that jerked her from her self-absorbed state.

Lady Beale spoke with the self-important air of one who possesses a juicy bit of gossip. "I hear that both the De-Valles were accidently sent an invitation to today's gathering."

"How dreadful!" exclaimed Lady Castleford, clasping

her bosom. "With Otto dead and poor Sylvia's still in mourning."

"Half-mourning. It has been three weeks since the funeral." Anne Beale was an exactingly precise young lady with an odd taste for gallows humor. "We must hope the baron does not rise to the occasion," she said flatly.

"Really, Anne," her mother shushed her, and then unwittingly added her bit to the morbid joke. "The Petershams were on their way back from Egypt at the time of Otto's death. Elsie had no notion she was inviting a corpse to her statue display."

Lady Castleford clucked her tongue sympathetically. "How very embarrassing for everyone concerned. Well, there is not the slightest possibility we shall see Sylvia. She cannot conceivably feel well enough to participate in anything so lighthearted as an outdoor entertainment."

It crossed Sarah's mind that it was equally unlikely that Hawkes would attend the Petershams' display, and yet there was, oddly enough, despite her feelings of mortification and embarrassment and shame, none with whom she would rather spend the afternoon.

It was not Hawkes's intention to attend the statue display. To the contrary, he began his day with the firm idea that he would be on the post road headed west and away from Sarah Lyndle, as fast as his horses could carry him.

At an early hour, therefore, when most of the young men of his acquaintance were retiring from the activities of the night before, he stopped in at his favorite coffee house for a glance at the morning's news, before quitting town.

He was hailed from a table at the back of the room by a number of bleary-eyed young officers he both knew and liked. Bret Preston was among them. Hawkes was in brooding need of a fight, and if anyone owed him a fight it was Bret. He joined them, half hoping for a confrontation.

All of Hawkes's associates knew how much he abhorred gossip. They knew, too, that he had not so much as flickered an eyelid in Bret Preston's direction since the day he had cast him out of Catherine Stone's bed. Warily, they watched the two, as Bret tried to behave with a nonchalant devil-may-care air, in picking up the thread of a story he had been in the midst of telling when Hawkes joined them.

"You know what it is like in the military . . . well, the clever dog found himself a dark-eyed beauty in Spain."

Bret's eyes flicked nervously to Hawkes's unfocused stare as he remarked with lewd innuendo. "Fool went and married her, though I am told she cannot speak a word of the King's English."

A ripple of subdued amusement circled the table. Bret's were not the only eyes darting speculative glances in Hawkes's direction.

"How good is Garvey's Spanish?" someone asked.

"Apparently, exceptional," was Bret's suggestive reply.

Hawkes's eyes narrowed. "Whose Spanish?" he asked quietly, knowing that his entrance into the conversation would be construed either as a challenge, or tantamount to a public forgiveness of Bret's abuse of their friendship. His words silenced all other chatter at the table.

Bret warily met his gaze.

"Geoffrey Garvey, Third Horse. He's shipping home. Do you know him?"

Everyone at the table breathlessly awaited his answer. Hawkes felt suddenly very foolish. This conversation, of all conversations, should not be so closely followed. He shrugged and made a bored show of examining his nails.

"Perhaps it is best that I do not," he drawled, "for had I the pleasure, I should be forced to search out and deliver a wedding gift." Rising amidst the amused guffaws of those who ringed the table, Hawkes politely inclined his head at an openmouthed Bret Preston, and turning on his heel, headed for the door. Preston's antics no longer mattered to Hawkes. Sarah's reputation superseded his own loss of pride. If what Bret claimed was indeed true, he must needs work fast to save her being labeled an unwanted woman, jilted by her betrothed for the love of a dark-eyed foreigner.

Hope racing to his head like too much liquor, Hawkes went straight to the military offices, to verify if he could the truth as to Lieutenant Geoffrey Garvey's current marital status. His expression as he stalked out again was so forbidding, his stride so purposeful, that none dared stand in his way.

"You will never guess who is here!" Anne Beale fairly squealed with breathless relish as she came scurrying back to the spot in Elsie Petersham's garden where Sarah's party had settled.

Lady Beale, who followed hard on her daughter's heels, had enough breath in her to grunt disapprovingly, "Out and about, before the poor man's even grown cold."

"She looks divine," Anne gushed.

Her mother silenced her. "Decidedly inappropriate, the Widow DeValle appearing here, Amelia, as I'm sure you'll agree, invitation or no invitation. Sylvia cannot suffer an ounce of proper feeling for her husband, to be so cold-hearted. I turned my back on her as soon as ever I saw who it was. But come, you must have a glimpse."

Her daughter agreed. "You must see. She's wearing a fetching little black bonnet with black and white feathers."

"You shall stay here, Anne," Lady Beale insisted.

Anne began to object, but Amelia agreed.

"Oh yes, please do, for Nathanial was just in the midst of telling us all about this statue the Petershams brought back with them, all the way from Rome. It is of, umh . . ."

"The Roman goddess of spring," Sarah prompted gently.

"Chloris." Nate was eager to share his knowledge. "My guess, about 450 B.C. She would have been holding flowers or a budded tree branch in the missing limb."

"Missing what?" Lady Beale inquired in such severe tones Nate was instantly silenced.

Having thus quelled the young scholar's opportunity to further delay the more pressing business of going to stare at a widow whose appearance in public offended her sensibilities as much as any mention of limbs, Lady Beale succeeded in steering Amelia away from the younger members of the party. Her daughter, not at all anxious to be bored by lessons in Roman antiquity, soon made an excuse to take herself off by a different path.

Left alone with Nate, Sarah realized with trepidation that

as she had promised Hawkes, it behooved her to in some way diminish his budding affection for her.

Nate seemed not in the least disappointed that she remained his only audience. "Did you know, Chloris was so beautiful that Boreas, the brutal north wind, and Zephyrus the mild west wind, fought for her favor?"

Sarah would have been alarmed to know that as he spoke he was mentally comparing the cool marble perfection of the statue to what he perceived as the flesh and blood perfection in her person. Feeling far from perfect, she said, "She chose Zephyrus, didn't she? So that her flowers might bloom in his warmth." Her mind could not help but dwell a moment on the unusual warmth that Nate's guardian always managed to generate within her. She wondered what it might be like, to choose one's own husband.

"A romantic conclusion," Nate said, reminding Sarah of her purpose.

"Logical," she said briskly. "Just as logical as the determination of my own proposed husband." And yet, even as she said the words, her mind questioned the logic of marrying Geoffrey Garvey.

Nate would have interrupted her, indeed he spluttered vaguely in an attempt to do so, but she would not allow it.

"When next we sit together, I shall most certainly be married, and you shall be a distinguished scholar." She paused, dreading his reaction.

Into the silence he blurted. "I'd no idea you were promised."

"The commitment has not been made public." She spoke with a calmness she was far from feeling, for she heard pain in his words, and he scrambled up out of his chair with an abruptness that spoke of the blow she had just dealt him. "Banns have not yet been published, but our fathers have planned the whole."

He paced around the statue in stunned silence.

"There is an understanding, you see. We were no more than babes when they put their heads together with the intention of binding not only their names, but their adjacent lands as well by such a move. I thought I had mentioned as much to you." She fanned herself nervously, knowing full well she had not, and for an instant overwhelmed with guilt that this young man should suffer heartache for her sake.

He threw himself down in the grass, the table between them. "No, you never did."

Sarah kept talking, allowing them both time to recover. "Geoffrey used to lead me about when I could no more than toddle. Together we were no end of mischief, I'm told. Quite the best of friends until he turned nine, and took a sudden dislike to all things female." She could hear Nate plucking up blades of grass with unhappy abandon.

"Do you know, I can remember the very day he stopped coming to play with me? He had promised to make paper boats so we could sail them down the stream that runs through our fathers' estates. On his way, he came upon a bunch of boys from the village. Learning his intentions, they poked dreadful fun at him for wasting his time and paper building boats for a little girl who could not even see them. They knew he had to hold my hand to show me where to go and teased him roundly. It was not at all the thing for a boy to be doing at that age. He ended up sailing his paper boats with the lads. The next day they invited him hare hunting, the day after that, fishing. I saw very little of Geoff from that day forward."

The tempo of Nate's work in the grass increased.

"Why do you want to marry such a paltry chap as would go off and do that?" There was anger as well as scorn in the question.

"Oh, Nate," Sarah said softly, wishing she believed her own words. "That was years ago. We were children. I'm sure Geoffrey has matured a great deal since then." She leaned forward to confide. "Do you know, I have never learned to make paper boats."

"No?" Nathanial asked gruffly, nursing his hurt, but no longer bruising the lawn. " 'Tis simple," he scoffed. "Kid stuff."

"Oh," she said, a trifle wistful.

The grass plucking commenced again, a little slower now, while the two of them sat wretched and speechless for a long, awkward moment.

A sound in the pathway distracted her in the instant before Hawkes's silky voice broke the stillness. "A smooth bristol works best, but broadsheets and penny papers do quite well. Easier to lay one's hands on."

"Hawkes!" Nate exclaimed, leaping up.

Sarah would have liked to have leapt up as well. A feeling of relief swelled into her agitated heart.

He was here! Not gone out of town as his mother had informed her he meant to do. The man who had turned her heart and mind upside down with both his accusations and his kisses was here, and speaking to her!

"My lord, you sound quite expert in the particulars of paper boat building," she said, her throat tight. There was much she would communicate to this man, and none of it had to do with the building of paper boats.

"Hawkes used to build the most water-worthy craft a boy could ask for when I was a lad, didn't you, Hawkes?" Nate said stoutly.

Sarah was amazed to hear the low, lazy voice reply, without the least trace of sarcasm, "Perhaps we might beg a few sheets of paper off Lord Petersham's bootblack and teach Miss Lyndle how it is done."

Nate's spirits were on the rise. "Well, I should think him a most inferior bootblack if he did not possess himself of a great stack of odd bits of paper. Shall I pop round and ask him for an armload?"

"An excellent idea," his guardian agreed smoothly, and there was something in the way he said it that made Sarah's heart jump with the certainty that Hawkes wished to be left alone with her.

Chapter 14

SARAH felt as if the very quality of the air had changed in the shadow of the statue of Chloris, goddess of spring, when Lord Castleford sat down opposite her. Like a stone thrown in still water, Hawkes sent little ripples out to rock her; strange, nameless sensations of anticipation, of expectations not yet met. An eerie feeling possessed her most private self, as if she should hold her breath so that she might better feel, hear, and sense what was going on around her, as if, could she but stand still enough and breathe shallowly enough, with her eyes wide open, she might by some miracle get a glimpse of this mysterious individual who shook her to the very core of her being.

Sarah's skin crawled with a sense of impending change. Hair prickled at the nape of her neck. What possibilities did fate and this man, mean to bring her?

"I have spoken to Nate about Geoffrey . . ."

"Ah yes, the inestimable Mr. Garvey," he drawled. "It is with news of that very gentleman that I disturb you. Garvey has, you see, gone and gotten himself . . ."

He was interrupted by a voice Sarah dreaded.

"My Lord Castleford! We had no expectation of seeing you here, did we, my pet, and with none other than Lady Lyndle, who is looking as lovely as ever her mother did," Sylvester Naughtly hailed them with oily obsequiousness.

Sarah refused to be rattled despite the dreadful man's persistence in mentioning her mother.

"Mr. Naughtley," she said with a forced smile, keenly aware of the absolute silence that had taken possession of Hawkes's side of the table. She was glad they had been interrupted, glad she should not be required to discuss Geoffrey with Hawkes, for it occurred to her that he might be bringing news of Geoffrey's death. With a sort of desperate joviality she inquired, "That would not be Lady Petersham's bootblack come with you, would it?"

Her question brought a surprised snort from Sylvester, a feminine gasp, and a low, lazy chuckle from Hawkes.

"Can it be I have the privilege of introducing you to the Baroness DeValle, Lady Lyndle?" Sylvester sounded inordinately pleased by the prospect. "Ironic, if such is the case, for 'twas I introduced your mother to another DeValle not many years ago."

Sarah cringed. He could only mean her mother and the late baron. Feeling ridiculous and scattered, she said, "I am pleased to meet you, Lady DeValle. I am told you wear a fetching hat."

The baroness surprised her with a willingness to be amused, despite the uncomfortable tension in the air.

"My hat is boot black, Miss Lyndle. Will that do, in lieu of the real thing?"

Sarah followed the humorous tact the baronness took.

"I'm afraid your hat will not do, unless it floats," she said lightly as the woman sat in the chair Nate had vacated.

Hawkes surprised Sarah by entering into the conversation. "We mean to build boats to float in the goldfish pond. Your hat will not be required if my ward is successful in his search for paper."

"From the bootblack!" Sylvester crowed. He began to scribble gleefully in his journal, mumbling, "How very droll!"

The baroness admitted with a laugh that it had been many summers since she had enjoyed the pleasure of building boats.

Sarah was dizzied when Hawkes abruptly changed the subject.

"Condolences, Sylvee, on your recent loss."

Naughtley's pencil stopped scratching.

Sarah felt herself caught in the middle of an encounter both strained and uncomfortable.

The widow responded with a hard-edged sort of sadness.

"I'd no idea you had such sentiment within you, Hawkes.

I thank you, for while I do not suffer from Otto's passing, I do find myself strangely sobered. Death serves to point out how short life really is, and how stupid a quarrel with old friends can be."

Hawkes was strangely quiet. The silence stretched thin.

Feeling invisible as well as blind, Sarah wondered if Hawkes cared for Sylvia still, and realized with sinking despair that it should not matter to her one way or the other if he did.

"Life is at best a brief endeavor," he said softly when it seemed the silence could go on no longer. "Shall we call a truce?"

Sylvester's pencil scribbled furiously.

The baroness sighed. "A truce would be lovely," she agreed, and for the first time her voice showed some sign of strain. "Perhaps Stewart will agree to such an arrangement."

Hawkes deliberated over the suggestion. "Perhaps," he agreed.

The boat races, conducted above an openmouthed host of fish, were judged vastly entertaining by most of those who attended the statue display. By the end of the afternoon, there were few of the elegant roster of guests who had not been down upon their knees, gleefully coaxing their own carefully folded craft to float among the lilypads.

There were two guests who took no pleasure in launching the armada, the Baroness DeValle and Sylvester Naughtley. As much as she might have liked to participate, the Widow DeValle showed uncommon good sense in taking her place instead among the more sober matrons who sat and watched the proceedings. In so doing, she succeeded in stilling the clacking tongues that had been busy over the impropriety of her public appearance so close on the heels of her husband's demise. Watching was not half so entertaining as participating. The baroness followed the progress of the boat building with a bored if somewhat petulant expression, and when the activity showed no signs of abating in popularity, she politely took her leave of Lady Petersham and left the party without a backward glance.

Sylvester, having placed himself in the thick of the activity to the muddy ruination of both the knees of his breeches, the tail of his coat, and a number of the pages in the gossip-filled journal he was currently scribbling, went with her.

Undoubtedly Hawkes would have himself enjoyed the activity of boat building much more had he not carried dour thoughts of Geoffrey Garvey and the unpleasant prospect of revealing what he knew of him to Sarah. There were unexpected pleasures in teaching a blind female how to construct paper boats. Unable to watch the folding technique with her eyes, she must needs do so with her hands.

"Like this," Nate directed as he and Sarah sat opposite one another, paper between them, at one of the wrought-iron tables near the goldfish pond. Flighty as butterflies, Sarah's hands hovered above Nate's as he went quickly through the motions of folding a paper boat.

She snatched her hands away again as soon as he had finished, saying brightly, "I think I've got it."

Too restless to settle in a chair, Hawkes circled the table as she folded a bit of paper into something that did not in the least resemble a boat. The results were rather backward, and not at all seaworthy.

"Shall I lead you through it one more time?" he offered before Nate could think to.

"Yes, please, this is all wrong," she said meekly as he leaned in over her shoulder to regard her poor results.

"Perhaps it will be easier for you to follow if we face the same direction. Otherwise your viewpoint is both upside down and backward."

"Sounds logical," she agreed.

"If you will permit me then . . ." Hawkes leaned closer, wrapping himself around her like a cloak, his chest pressed into the curve of her shoulder. Warm and aware in his arms, she stiffened as the plush softness of her cheek grazed his for the briefest of moments. Her breath whispered raggedly through her lips, her chest rose and fell in an arrested rhythm, and her back and shoulders went rigid as ramrods. Their ears bumped. She shied away. He squeezed his eyes shut a moment in order to control the urge to pull her closer still to dip his nose into the fragrant wonder of her curls. The sweet scent of her hair made his head swim. Its softness brushed his chin. He resisted the inclination to trail kisses along the sweep of her neck.

"Splay your hands across the backs of mine, like children riding piggyback." He used the softest, the gentlest of voices.

Nate looked up from his boat folding.

Hawkes winked at him.

Sarah laughed self-consciously, and so close was she pressed to him that Hawkes could feel the rise and fall of her every breath as she did so. Stiffly she complied, her hands stiff as crabs, and just as ready to scuttle away, given provocation.

"Relax," he said brusquely. "You will never grasp what I am doing if you do not more fully grasp my hands."

Slowly, like a flower opening for the sun, her fingers unfurled, settling petal soft on the backs of his own. The weight of trust those small gloved hands embodied as they began to stretch out over his own like a second skin, sent a hair-raising tremor through Hawkes's arms and across the base of his skull. The lengths she was willing to go to in order to learn touched him deeply, for he knew she feared him, and justifiably so, since he had forced his kisses on her in his mother's rose garden.

"Show me," she instructed, her voice unsteady.

Hawkes looked up to find Nate regarding the two of them with dawning comprehension, as if he saw for the first time with incredible clarity how his guardian felt about Miss Sarah Lyndle.

Hawkes hesitated.

Nate's expression seemed suddenly very mature, if a little wounded. "Go ahead," he prompted as he rose from the table. "I can see which way the wind is blowing, but the water is yet to be tested." He had a manfully dignified look about him as he strode down to the pond, paper boat in hand.

Hawkes watched him go as he slowly folded another ship, Sarah's hands following his every move.

"He is a delightful young man," she said softly, enfolded

in the circle of his arms. "You have done an excellent job in the raising of him."

"Have I?" Hawkes wondered, as the boat took shape beneath their tandem hands. "Have I done him a disservice in coming between him and his first love?"

Sarah's hands stopped for a moment. "Surely not, sir. His interest cannot have been a lasting one. And we would not at all suit."

He pressed the finished boat into her palm. "No?" he sighed. "Only time will tell. Has not your love for Geoffrey Garvey endured since childhood?"

She turned the craft they had made together about in her hands with a heavy sigh. "I care for Geoffrey, my lord, but I do not think I love him."

That got his attention! He stared at the calm outline of her cheek, the demure fall of her lashes, the way a curl of her hair kissed the lobe of her ear as she plumped the shape of the boat.

"No?" he breathed.

"No," she smiled and tried to make light of the subject. "How can I, when he never made good on his promise to make something so lovely as this." She held up their boat. "Shall we see if she is water worthy?"

He came very close to telling her then of Garvey's defection, of the threat to her reputation, of his own burgeoning feelings for her. He came so close, the words pressed against his lips, but there was something childlike in her aspect, something so bent on enjoying the moment of their creation, that he refrained.

"Come," he said, "let's launch her."

It was later, when Sarah's interest waned in boat making and the races on the pond, that Hawkes told her.

Sarah had settled herself like a child in the grass, her face turned to catch the breeze. She smiled as he sank down in the grass beside her, and there was something in the curve of her lips so replete with joy, that he wished he had come today with no more purpose than to see her happy. Golden tendrils of hair loosening from the knot at the crown of her head, wafted across her face.

He reached out to catch back a wisp of her hair that would seem bent on caressing her cheek.

"Thank you," she said shyly. "This has been great fun. It is a shame I was robbed of such pleasure as a child."

A burning sadness rose within him. For Sarah's sake, he made an effort to sound cool. "I agree. Will you be glad, I wonder, to know that it is not your destiny to marry the thief?"

She bowed her head, tongue darting out to wet her lips. "Has Geoff been killed?" Her shoulders seemed braced for a blow.

Hawkes had not expected her to leap to such a morbid conclusion. His sadness deepened. "No, my dear. Garvey is very much alive, and very much, I regret to say, married to another."

All color drained from her cheeks. "You are sure?"

"Positive. He has requested transport from Spain for his wife. I have seen the documentation."

Her hand flew to her throat in a protective gesture. "You continue to be better-informed regarding my affairs than I am myself, my lord," she said stiffly. "I stand jilted, and yet you know of it before I have so much as been informed."

He wanted very much to ease her pain, to stroke her hair and comfort her, to return to her the peaceful look his words had so cruelly stolen.

"I take it your plans to marry were not widely known?"

She shook her head.

"Then you need not fear gossip, if you are willing to swallow pride in order to stifle any malicious speculation before it begins."

"What do you suggest?" The words sounded brittle.

"Arrange a celebration."

The knuckles in the hand at her throat were white. "Sir, I fully comprehend that I stand jilted. In addition, the picture of a future most dear to my father's heart is all to pieces, yet you tease me with the suggestion that I celebrate?"

He leaned forward. That she considered him capable of a callous disregard for her feelings when she was already suffering a shattering blow cut him to the heart.

"I am serious," he insisted. "You would do well to invite

Garvey and his new wife to a gathering which includes a number of talkative witnesses. Your joy in an old friend's marriage will be duly noted and talk of a jilting squashed before it is begun."

Sarah listened intently. Her hand fluttered from her throat to her forehead, where she rubbed the knot between her brows with the base of her palm.

He reached out to cage the troubled hand in his own.

"I know this is difficult," he said. "But, I cannot say I am sorry Garvey cried off. You deserve far better, my dear."

She bit down on her lower lip to stop its trembling, turning her hand in his to return the pressure of its clasp.

"You will attend this . . . fete celebrating fate?" She tried to sound jaunty despite the tears that swam in her eyes.

"Bravo, my dear!" he praised her, his voice very tender. "That's the spirit that will see you through this thing. You may count on my attendance. Shall I deliver invitations for this fete when I leave town—to your father perhaps, and the Garveys?"

She let go of his hand and pressed the flat of her palm against her sightless eyes in a tragically poignant gesture. A puzzled, panicked frown knit her brow. "Leave town?"

Hawkes's heart quickened. The disappointment in those two simple words almost decided him against going.

"I regret to say that I shall be gone a few days."

Her lower lip was trembling again. A single tear slid down her cheek.

"Nate means to return to school. I have offered to deliver him, and on the way back to London, I shall stop and speak with your father. His first reaction to Garvey's defection will likely be to order you home. I intend to talk him out of such a move, for if you are bundled into the countryside hot on the heels of Garvey's crying off, there will be no chance at all of stilling the rattle of gossip that must follow. May I call on you as soon as I return, and see how the fete progresses?"

His words, concerned as they were with her happiness, accelerated the tremor in her lower lip. "It is very good of you. . . ." Her voice broke up amongst her words.

He interrupted her, his manner lightly teasing. "I do not do things out of goodness, but because I care to do them."

And then, because he cared to do so, Hawkes cupped Sarah's chin in the palm of his hand, so that he might ever so gently pass the ball of his thumb over her cheek, erasing the damp track of her tear.

"Take heart, my dear," he whispered.

Chapter 15

IT occurred to Hawkes when he dropped by the Turveys' to pick up Sarah's correspondence to her father and the Garveys, that even in this, the most private and heart-wrenching of moments, Miss Lyndle had no means of privately voicing her thoughts. The two letters that were given into his keeping had been written in Lydia Turvey's elegant copperplate. Wishing he might have penned them for Sarah himself, he tucked them into the pocket closest to his heart and drew comfort in knowing Sarah entrusted him with their delivery. He wished he might as safely pocket the whole of her, to carry her away from this mess of Garvey's making.

"Will you stay and breakfast with us? Your cousin means to join us," Sarah asked with an intensity that was hard to refuse.

He paused to consider what her heart held for his kinsman before saying gently, "I think not. Nate is waiting, and I mean to be on the road with all possible haste."

He bowed over her hand and allowed his lips to brush her knuckles with far briefer contact than would have pleased him. A smile trembled on her perfect lips. Hawkes could not remember when Sarah had looked more beautiful than she did now, in parting. He gave her hand a reassuring squeeze, and then, falling prey to impulse, he lightly kissed her pale forehead. "The faster to return to you, my dear."

She blushed furiously, her hand flying up to touch briefly the spot he had pressed lips to, as she said with forced cheerfulness, "Indeed, sir, you must not dally. We are planning a fete for Sunday next, and should be vastly disappointed were you not to participate."

Hawkes trod down the steps in front of Dr. Turvey's house with the strong sensation that he moved in the wrong direction. He wished he might somehow split himself in two, so that half of him might remain here with Sarah while the other half went about the business of averting scandal. One of the more obvious reasons for his reluctance to leave town stood, quizzing glass raised, regarding the crest on the door of his waiting carriage.

"Find you some flaw, cousin?" he inquired.

Stewart looked him over with surprise, his china blue eye very large and round behind his quizzing glass.

"Only in finding you here, Hawkes. You have developed the disconcerting habit of popping up where you are least expected. I understand you went to, of all things, a garden party yesterday, when only last night 'twas Nash, no mayhap Gray, said you were rusticating again. Brantley, he said. Gone for a week."

"One should not rely too heavily on gossip, Stew."

"Speaking of which, have you actually renewed acquaintance with Sylvia DeValle? I was never more shocked than to hear as much at White's. My eyes must still be on stalks."

"White's, cousin? I thought you preferred the stakes at Brook's."

"I do." Stewart smiled broadly. "Happens the stakes were lucky at both clubs yesterday. Extraordinarily so! I must tell you all about it when you have a moment."

Hawkes could think of nothing he might relish less than to stand gossiping in the street at that moment. His lips were urging him to go back and kiss the girl properly, not on the forehead as if he were her uncle, but Sarah's letters burned a hole in his pocket, warming his heart and reminding him of promises that must be kept.

"Love to chat, Stew, but I'm on my way out of town this minute. Nate goes with me to Oxford."

"Kenneling the pup, are you? Splendid!" Stewart crowed. "My luck is indeed changed. Devil's own, I assure you." A small frown clouded his elation. "Only troubling thing . . . Nathanial informs me Miss Lyndle is promised to an old childhood chum."

"Nate is sadly misinformed." Hawkes climbed into his carriage.

"Misinformed? Are you certain?"

"Absolutely!"

"Jove, I should have known better than to credit such a ramshackle tale."

Hawkes could not resist the temptation of teasing Stewart. "I return in time for the fete," he said with a nonchalance he was far from feeling.

"Fête? What fête, Hawkes?"

The famous eyebrows rose. "Why Miss Lyndle's, Stew. Surely you are invited?"

As Stewart's jaw dropped in dismay, Hawkes smiled and signaled his groom to release the leader's heads.

"Come and tell me all about your extraordinary luck"— the vehicle lurched forward— "when I return."

With Nate safely delivered to school, Hawkes barreled through the gateway to Lyndle Hall in the middle of the following afternoon. The distance that separated him from Sarah seemed enormous, and a wrenching fear that something dreadful might happen with himself so far from her side, bedeviled his enjoyment of the excellent time his horses had made.

A lackey carried in his card with aggravating languor, returning at length to divest him of redingote, gloves, and walking stick before ushering him to his master's study.

The study, Hawkes found upon entering the room, was in fact a library. Bookshelves lined the walls, their ranks interrupted by two portraits and a pair of French doors offering a pleasant view of an herb garden. The first of the portraits depicted a breathtaking young woman in a formal setting. Hawkes concluded she had to be Sarah's mother. The resemblance was striking. If rumor was to be believed, the beautiful Lady Lyndle had been a shockingly flirtatious gadfly of a female, with a propensity for losing vast sums of money over a turn of the dice.

The second, smaller portrait drew and held his attention as he crossed the room. It was of Sarah, as a girl. In the moment captured on canvas, the serious child Sarah had once been, held a ball in her hand, an offering to the silky black and white papillon puppy who lived forever at her feet. A pretty child, her hair hung long and soft and curling down her back. There was an avid interest in the perfectly painted sea green eyes that troubled Hawkes. These were sighted eyes, and so believably rendered, they seemed to follow his progress into the room with an expression of loneliness that wrung his heart.

Sarah's looks had improved with maturity. There was a quiet confidence, a strength of purpose to be found in the face of the sightless young woman, that was nowhere to be seen in this portrait of the girl she had once been.

A pale and balding gentleman sat in front of the paintings at a paneled desk, a pair of spectacles shoved onto his forehead, his back to both the portraits and the distraction of the view.

"You surprise me, my lord." He squinted down at the card in his hand, and then up at Hawkes, like a mole that has only just tunneled through to daylight.

"How so, Lord Lyndle?" Hawkes's winged brows rose.

"I had thought you to be a man of greater years."

Not at all dismayed by such a Turkish welcome, Hawkes sketched an abbreviated bow. "Sorry to disappoint, sir, but that will change with time. Perhaps I should come back at a later date."

A grudging twist of amusement lifting the corners of his mouth, Lyndle discovered the spectacles on his forehead and did not hesitate to use them to advantage. "What you lack in years you make up for in audacity."

Hawkes inclined his head. "I do not think we know each other, my lord, certainly not well enough that you might find me lacking, even in something so trifling as age."

Lord Lyndle waved in the direction of the portrait that gazed out over his shoulder. "We are acquainted. After a fashion. My daughter's letters are full of Castlefords."

Hawkes began to say something, thought better of it, and delving into his pocket, pulled forth Sarah's letters.

"Which brings us to why I am here. Knowing I meant to survey an estate in the neighborhood of Lyndle Hall, your daughter sends yet another missive."

Sarah's father took the paper. "In the neighborhood you say? By my estimation your closest property would be Brantley Manor, and that cannot be less than thirty miles. You came so far, just to play postboy?"

Hawkes's gaze strayed once more to the portrait of Sarah. "I am fond . . . of my mother, sir. Your daughter has been instrumental in bringing her out of a lengthy period of mourning. The distance was not so great."

"I see." Lord Lyndle said, squinting from Sarah's letter to Hawkes and back again. "Do you know that I was quite prepared, on first hearing of your friendship with my daughter, to forbid her the association of your person?"

Hawkes stiffened perceptibly and spoke with a dangerously icy politeness. "How so, sir?"

"Gossip has it you are referred to as the Beast."

"Gossip has, sir, a tendency to tell only part of any given story, and is generally sordidly inaccurate."

Lord Lyndle seemed to be aware that his words had overstepped the bounds of etiquette, and that he had been answered in kind. "Young man, I am not known for my tact." He spoke brusquely, nothing apologetic in his tone.

"Understandable." Hawkes's gaze flickered to the portrait of Sarah's mother. "Gossip has been no more kind to you, sir, than to myself."

The old lord looked with growing approval at his guest. "It has not," he agreed. "Far from it."

Steadily Hawkes regarded him, the veriest hint of amusement warming his sarcasm. "Circumlocution is greatly admired these days, sir. I prefer a direct hit. Is there any particular piece of gossip with regard to my name that you would care to have verified, for I have every intention of continuing to see your daughter."

Lord Lyndle laughed outright, as if Hawkes had passed through some sort of verbal fusillade with flying colors.

"Sarah said you always come briskly to the point."

Hawkes gaze flew again to the portrait above the desk.

What else, he wondered, had Sarah found to write about him?

Lord Lyndle waved her most recent missive. "She has written to me on more then one occasion of your profound kindness."

"You confuse me with my mother, sir, and my cousin, Stewart."

Edward Lyndle's tone brooked no argument. "I am not confused, sir. My daughter considers your friendship and favor a remarkable honor. She has mentioned your arrangements for her riding pleasure, your kindness in assuring she was not reduced to the roll of wallflower at her first ball, and her pleasure in a specially arranged tour of St. Paul's."

At a loss for words, Hawkes's gaze flew to the portrait, and as swiftly nodded to the floor. "Ah."

Lord Lyndle nodded. "I am indebted, sir. I was concerned, because of her affliction, that Sarah's visit to London would prove a mistake. Is she happy, as she says?"

"Your daughter has the greater gift of bringing happiness to those around her, sir, than that of pleasing herself," Hawkes hedged, wishing more attention had been paid to Sarah's letter, for surely the question of her happiness was answered therein.

Whatever else either of them might have said was cut short by the unexpected and quite breathless entrance of a stout old gentleman, clutching a gun and clad in hunting attire. He was closely followed by a large foxhound, a slender gray whippet, and Lord Lyndle's dismayed butler.

"Sir Garvey was most insistent that he see you imme—" began the butler.

"Oh, begone, Hackers. Lyndie can see I've bust my way in without you being able to stop me." The blustery gentleman in topboots and buckskin seemed quite at home in the library, as did his dogs, who sat themselves down to scratch. He extended a large gloved hand to Hawkes.

"So you're Henry Castleford's brat. Name's Garvey, Garth Garvey. Was acquainted with your father some years back, your brother, too. Bruising rider, shame he took a toss. Hackers said you was here. Wouldn't normally interrupt. In very poor taste I know, but I've news Lyndie must be told. Won't have him finding out from anyone else."

Hawkes had every reason to believe the news that Garvey came to divulge had to do with his son Geoffrey. "I am sure what you have come to say is indeed urgent. I take my leave of you."

"Nonsense! You're not going, my lord." Sarah's father contradicted him. "There is more I would say to you, and Hackers is just now gone to fetch our refreshment, haven't you, Hackers?"

The butler clapped shut his mouth, bowed hastily, and left the room.

"I shall leave you to kick your heels here but a moment, my lord," Lord Lyndle insisted. With a decisive nod, he opened the French doors so that he, the dogs, and the garrulous Garvey, whose color seemed unnaturally heightened, might step outside.

A few moments later, the draft of the inner door opening to allow Hackers to enter with the tea tray, sucked open the improperly closed French doors. The heady perfume of mint and lavender permeated the room, and the breeze blew some paper from the desk, but it was an exclamation from the garden, in which a name he recognized was mentioned, that brought Hawkes languidly to his feet.

"Leave it," he ordered, and before the butler could so much as think of bending down to restore the disarranged papers to the desk, he found himself being escorted rather smartly from the library, encouraged by a firm grasp upon his elbow.

"As if he were lord and master of the place," Hackers complained with sorely affronted dignity to the upstairs maid.

Hawkes closed the door on the back of the offended manservant, of a mind that whatever was being discussed in the garden was not for a servant's quick ears and ready tongue. He stepped to the French doors with every intention of clicking them fast.

"Poor, dear Sarah!" Sir Garvey railed in a voice that knew not how to whisper. "It's all to pieces, Lyndie."

Hawkes found any admirable intentions he had originally felt regarding the disposition of the open door, overthrown.

"Clumsy of Geoffrey, not letting us know sooner. I had best fetch Sarah home from London." Lord Lyndle's voice possessed a stunned finality.

Sir Garvey let loose a sympathetic snort. "By all means, but for the moment, get rid of Castleford. Think of the scandal should the truth get about, devil take it. Go in now for tea, Lyndie, else the earl is sure to think us both country turnips, completely devoid of manners."

"Join us," Lord Lyndle begged. "I am in no condition to face the man alone."

"For tea? And me in topboots?" Garvey snorted. "Best not. Make my excuses. I shall come over later, once he is gone, so that we might decide what is to be done."

Leaving the French doors ajar, Hawkes removed himself to the tea tray, poured out two cups of the steaming brown liquid, and sat, chin in hand, contemplating the painted likeness of Sarah. How could Garvey be so addlepated as to callously place Sarah's name and reputation in peril of being labeled forever with jilt?

"Do you take your tea white, sir?" he inquired placidly when Lord Lyndle came in through the door. "Or do you prefer a dollop of something stronger?"

"Brandy would be just the thing."

Presenting a generously laced cup to his distracted host, Hawkes felt compelled to say, in a pleasantly nonchalant manner, as the china, once taken, chattered nervously in its saucer, "She did not love him, you know."

"What?" Lord Lyndle jerked his attention back to his guest with dawning comprehension.

"Geoffrey Garvey. She does not love him."

With hushed horror Lord Lyndle exclaimed, "You know?"

Hawkes shrugged, as if his knowing were no great thing. "Perhaps it would be best if I sat here quietly while you read your daughter's letter."

Blinking as from a blow, Lord Lyndle brought his spectacles down from his forehead and began to read. When he had finished, his color began to return.

"This fete . . . ," His look was piercing. "Your idea?"

Hawkes nodded.

"I see what you're about."

"Excellent. You will come then? Together we may be able to scotch this scandal before it's begun."

Lord Lyndle nodded emphatically. "There's no keeping me away!"

Chapter 16

A knock sounded on the door to the library at Brantley. Annoyed, Hawkes raised his eyes from the papers he studied. He did not appreciate interruption while he conducted business, and at present he was reviewing four months of affairs at Brantley Hall with his overseer, Tom Creer. It was a job that normally took several days, but he intended on this particular occasion, to complete the task in the length of an afternoon, barring unnecessary interruption. He was bound and determined to return to Sarah Lyndle's side by morning.

"Enter!" His voice displayed his displeasure.

It was Jasper Nibbs who dared impose. "A visitor, sir," the butler related, face expressionless, tone polite.

Hawkes frowned. "I made it quite clear that I am not at home to visitors, Nibbs."

"You did, sir. The lady insists, however, that you will see her, my lord. She would not be turned away."

"Lady?" Hawkes put down his pen.

The woman sat with her back to the sitting room door, her features hidden in the cowl of a somber, hooded cloak. For one insanely delirious moment, Hawkes dared hope this might be Sarah, unable to face alone the devastation of having been jilted.

"Madam?"

It was Sylvia DeValle who turned to regard him, a frosty look of hauteur in possession of her features. She was still beautiful, this woman who had scorned his love. There was no scorn in the determined set of her jaw, now, no animosity either. It occurred to Hawkes as they faced each other for only the second time in more than five years, that the woman before him was a stranger. The wise, worldly, impatient eyes that met his without flinching, and the beautiful but bitterly compressed mouth had very little to do with the carefree young lady who had once captured his heart.

He had imagined this day, a day when they would face one another without the baron between them, but now the day had come, and his feelings were not at all what he had anticipated.

"You are changed," she said. "I did expect that in the very least you would keep me waiting for intruding unannounced."

"That would be beastly behavior," he said with sarcastic languor. "At present I keep my overseer waiting."

"He need not," she offered stiffly. "You have but to show me the door." She rose regally, with the intention of making her way past him.

"You have come a great distance to be heard, Sylvee." His use of the pet name stopped her, but her lips remained firmly locked, as if she were cognizant of how strange they were to one another and no longer wished to speak to him.

"I am obliged to listen," he insisted.

Reluctantly, she sank onto her seat, with the look about her of a woman without options.

Burning with curiosity as to the reason for her driving all the way to Brantley to speak to him, he strode to the door, summoned Nibbs, and desired him first to dismiss Tom Creer, and then to bring refreshments. Then, choosing a straight-backed chair in which to seat himself quite formally opposite her, Hawkes announced with purring sarcasm, "You have my full attention, Baroness."

With unhurried hand Sylvia DeValle pushed back her hood. "I come seeking a favor," she said, chin held high.

Eyelids drooping down to hide genuine surprise, for he would have thought Sylvia too proud to come to him on such an errand, Hawkes stood and walked to the window, allowing both space and silence to stretch between them.

"I am at a loss to understand why, of your many acquaintances, you should come to me."

Sylvia went white about the lips. "I am aware there is no

love lost between us, Hawkes, but I am willing to find you candid rather than rude, will you only allow it."

He returned to his chair and bent a wary, waiting look on her. "Touché."

She sighed. "I am faced with a dilemma. It requires keen knowledge of horseflesh and property, as well as discretion and honesty. Of all my acquaintances, friendly or not, it is in you that I find the greatest abundance of those qualities."

"You flatter me, Sylvee. Why me, and not my cousin? I was of the opinion that your feelings were far more strongly involved with Stewart," Hawkes said dryly.

She accepted his assessment without demur. "It is for that very reason that I find myself unable to approach Stewart," she offered paradoxically.

He frowned, trying to make sense of such backwardness. "What is this favor you would have of me?"

A single tear slipped down the widow's cheek. Ignoring the moisture, she said, "I intend to sell the baron's stable, and I would like you to handle the details."

Hawkes was interested, but leery of tears. The baron's stable was a vast one. It was logical enough to assume that Sylvia would no longer care to own racing or breeding stock. He saw nothing worthy of even a single tear in the widow's plan to rid herself of the burden of so many highly strung thoroughbreds, all eating their heads off. What defied logic, in his estimation, was why the sale of said animals should require discretion and honesty above and beyond what one might expect from the baron's solicitor.

The baroness went on in a businesslike manner. "I would have the horses and vehicles auctioned gradually, to increase the possibility of obtaining full value."

"Vehicles? You mean to liquidate vehicles as well?"

"I intend to keep only the team of chestnuts, my riding mare, and my curricle," she said steadily.

"I see." Hawkes said slowly, but there was something in his tone that gave lie to those two simple words. He did not see. Selling off everything was more than extreme, it smacked of desperation.

"There are debts to be paid," she said lamely, as if some

sort of explanation was warranted, no matter how inadequate.

Hawkes frowned, watching her closely. "Debts not honored in the settling of the estate?"

Sylvia would not meet his questioning look. She stared out the window and plucked the edge of her sleeve.

"Personal debts, of a sensitive nature," she said at last, her voice very low. "The baron's brother must never learn the nature of these debts."

It occurred to Hawkes that the marriage of Sylvia Hupton to Baron Otto DeValle had not been the glittering match it was purported to be. Simple gaming debts warranted no such clandestine arrangements. Only debts of a most dishonorable nature would spur Sylvia to such secretive heroics. She seemed willing to sacrifice her financial security to honor this debt. She had already sacrificed her pride, in turning to him for help.

Struck again by the sensation that he faced a stranger, Hawkes's frown deepened. "Tell me, Sylvia, for I have always wondered, why did you not see fit to squash the rumors that began to circulate the day before your wedding, that I had taken advantage of you?"

The widow shifted uncomfortably under his intense scrutiny. "I . . . I am dreadfully sorry about that, Hawkes, but you see it better suited my purposes to let the rumors fly. I cannot tell you why, only that my object was not to ruin your good standing." She sounded defeated. "Perhaps I was in error, coming here."

"Perhaps, perhaps not." He pinned her with an especially intense look. "Only tell me, Sylvee, were you happy with the baron?"

She flinched as if he slapped her with the words, and then answered with a vehemence that made her voice shake. "Not for a single moment, Hawkes. I had no idea what perfidy the man was capable of. Will you believe me, I wonder, if I tell you there lurked a monster behind the baron's polished veneer? My husband was a man who ruined the lives of those he came into contact with. I would not allow him to ruin mine while he lived. I have no intention of allowing his actions to trouble me further, now that he is dead."

Hawkes executed a courtly bow. "I cannot quarrel with such sentiments. If it is in my power to assist you, Sylvee, I will."

Less than a quarter of an hour later, Hawkes handed Sylvia into her coach, marveling over the absence of feeling he had assumed would be rekindled by the renewal of their acquaintance. Even now, with her hand warm in his, he realized that his only desire was to be of assistance to someone he had once held very dear. He puzzled for a moment over the fact that he felt no greater sense of loss. As he did so, he chanced to look up. Trotting up the sweeping drive on a lathered and blown sorrel came the now familiar figure of Lord Edward Lyndle.

In that instant, as his entire being was jolted by the terrifying concern that some disaster had befallen Sarah in his absence, Hawkes realized that his desires were too exclusively focused to include Sylvia. He had room in his heart, in his thoughts, for only one woman—dear, blind, beautiful Sarah.

As the coach would in all likelihood have bowled over Lord Lyndle and his wheezing mount, the width of the drive being not enough to encompass both vehicle and rider, Hawkes waited unblinking to welcome his second unexpected guest.

"My lord," he called out when the older man was within hailing distance. "Is aught amiss?"

"Yes." The word seemed to echo as it came back to him. A cold wave of fear dashed Hawkes's skin with the same light sweat that he had felt on the day his father fell dead of an apoplectic fit. His chest tightened.

"Sarah?" he blurted.

"Sarah is fine."

The baroness, whose gaze bounced between them as though she were watching shuttlecocks, said nothing, but the interest in her eyes spoke volumes.

Too late realizing how much the state of his heart he revealed with his concern, Hawkes greeted Sarah's father and introduced his guests to one another.

Oddly enough, the two had never met. They regarded one another for a moment with sad and curious understanding. The situation seemed suddenly far too complicated to Hawkes. Just how did one go about introducing the woman one had once thought to marry, to a man whose wife her husband had ruined?

The baroness solved his dilemma by leaning out of her carriage window with a faint smile. "Lyndle is it? My husband wronged many people, sir, but none, I think, so greatly as you. I cannot right the baron's wrongs, but I hope you will not hold that against me."

Lord Lyndle's weary voice was strained. He had the nervous, wide-eyed look about him of a man caught in the midst of a social gaffe of incredible proportion.

"I've no quarrel with you, my lady, but I come unannounced, and clearly at a bad time. I'd no idea you had guests, my lord. Perhaps it would be more convenient if I returned another day."

He bowed stiffly to the baroness and would have turned his blown horse had not Hawkes, who suffered the uneasy impression that Sarah's father believed he had ridden not only into the midst of his own painful past, but a romantic tryst as well, stopped him.

"What nonsense, sir. Anyone can see you are near to falling from the back of that creature you ride."

The baroness watched both men with a look about her of complete understanding, as if she read the nuances of what had been said, and left unsaid, with absolute clarity.

"I am just leaving, sir." She graciously added her own voice to the convincing of Lord Lyndle. "Hawkes and I have been talking horseflesh. I am of a mind to sell off some of my stable, and he has graciously agreed to handle the business of it." She eyed Lyndle's blowing mount with disfavor. "Perhaps you would be in the market, sir? If so, drop a word in Castleford's ear. He'll vouch for the quality of my cattle. Won't you, Hawkes?"

Hawkes nodded, and as Sylvia leaned back inside, she said by way of parting, "I have met your daughter, sir. At a garden party," she said by way of parting with Lord Lyndle. "She is lovely. A quiet, contained young woman with excellent manners."

Lord Lyndle nodded. "Not at all like her mother," he said softly, and without malice.

Sylvia shrugged. "I would not know. I never had the pleasure of an introduction to Lady Lyndle." She indicated with a nod that Hawkes might gesture for the coachman to whip up the waiting team.

Both gentlemen watched the coach in its passage to the gate. Lord Lyndle gave a little jump when Hawkes spoke.

"Would you care to have one of the animals off her, sir? I've never seen a more sadly blown creature than the one you're astride. Step down," he invited. "We'll see this poor fellow gets a rubdown while you join me for a glass of port."

"I did not come for a glass of port, my lord," Lord Lyndle said dourly. "I came to inform you that Geoffrey Garvey refuses to go to London!"

Hawkes's head snapped up. "Won't go?" he demanded.

Sarah's father nodded grimly.

"Says he's mortified. Too embarrassed to face her." He scowled as his gaze strayed once more in the direction of the departing coach. "Dumgudgeon! Hasn't any concept of the true depths of mortification and embarrassment that a man can feel."

Hawkes's eyes narrowed down, and his tone was deadly serious. "We shall see about that, my lord!"

Chapter 17

SARAH was miserable in knowing it was possible she was soon to become an object of pity and ridicule to her new friends and acquaintances. There was something shameful, wounding, and terribly disappointing in being jilted.

Despite the lowering of her spirits, however, she possessed no desire to be seen as despondent and unhappy in the wake of having been cast aside. She threw herself into a frenzy of activity; both in planning her fete, and in accepting as many of the invitations she received, as time and Lydia's patience allowed. Routs and balls, drums and nuncheons, concerts and plays, all saw their share of her. She kept a smile plastered to her lips and the thought that Hawkes must soon return with news, foremost in her mind. No one guessed her torment.

The only opportunity she gave herself to consider the plans for her future and the unexpected potential of her alternatives, was late at night, tucked safely between the sheets, with a goosedown pillow clasped tight in her arms. It was then Sarah's thoughts vaulted from mountain top flights of sublime fancy to the deepest valleys of despair.

No longer required to marry Geoffrey, Sarah was free to contemplate an entirely different future for herself, with possibilities both exhilarating and debilitating. She might, she realized, end her days a lonely spinster. Yet she could not resign herself to such hopelessness. Hawkes had said that his cousin meant to ask for her hand. Such a future held no more appeal than spinsterhood. She hugged her pillow to her breast, her imagination transforming the bag of goosedown and ticking into a shadowy figure she embraced with passionate abandon. The pillow-man brought her comfort, but it was the Beast, not the Beauty he resembled in her mind's eye.

Was she a fool to contemplate a miracle, to dream of a future with Lord Ashley Hawkes Castleford, Earl of Henley? Sarah prayed she was not, and clutched her pillow more desperately to her bosom, and dropped into a dream-tossed sleep that neither rested nor refreshed.

Hawkes's first thought, when he sought her out upon his return, was that he had never seen Sarah Lyndle look so worn.

She was alone in his mother's vast, echoing music room, practicing on the pianoforte, and even before he passed through the doorway he could tell the music was not conducted in Sarah's normally sweeping manner. False starts and a fumbling in the more difficult passages, spoke quite eloquently of an unsettled state of nerves.

Her head tilted as he walked into the room, and her hands crashed down on the keys in a discordantly jarring manner. "You are returned," she exclaimed with undisguised joy and started up from the bench with a fervor that would have carried her straight into his arms had he not stopped her.

Hawkes felt he had not the right to sweep her into his embrace, not while his promise to Stewart hung between them like an invisible barrier. His word, the measure of his ethical worth, bound him from her. He was diminished if he could not hold steadfast to promises, just as Bret Preston and Geoffrey Garvey had diminished themselves in his eyes.

His voice, when he spoke, was pointedly formal. "As promised, Miss Lyndle, I return in good time for your fete, and bring you tidings of your father, who also promises to attend."

His tone stopped her headlong rush to approach him.

"I am relieved," she said uncertainly, sinking back onto the bench. "I have been miserable with waiting. Father is well?"

"In fine form. He sends his love and a letter."

"Will you read it to me?"

He settled beside her on the music bench and was pleased to find that she did not shrink away from contact with his person, but seemed quite content to sit shoulder to shoulder with him, so that the warmth of their bodies reached out and intermingled. It was, he thought as his sleeve kissed hers, as if a part of his physical self dared to renege on the promise to Stewart after all, and reached out to touch her, despite his best intentions.

"My dearest Sarah . . ." he began reading, and paused. It was the first time her given name had passed his lips, and that, coupled with the license he had been given to call her his dearest, caused him to turn his head, that he might see if she was as affected by those few words as he.

Both her heightened color, and the clasping and unclasping of her hands upon her lap, triggered in Hawkes a strange, light-headed sensation of elation. Selfish of the feeling, he repeated the letter's introduction, as if the words welled up, unchecked, from the very heart of him.

"My dearest Sarah . . ."

She heard the difference. He saw her head jerk, as if to negate what her ears had taken in, while the warm contact of her shoulder shied away.

He continued reading, his voice carefully devoid of emotion, its steadiness in no way an indication of the true state of his sensibilities. As he read, Hawkes's gaze flew often from the white foolscap in his hand to the more telling page of Sarah's expressive face.

The letter dealt primarily with Lord Lyndle's concern for his daughter's well-being and happiness. It reiterated his intention to attend her birthday fete, and ended with an expression of a father's love and affection that once more gave Hawkes leave to address Sarah with the feelings buried in the depths of his heart out of respect for his cousin.

When he had finished, the clock in the corner of the room was the only voice that spoke. Sarah sighed, and in splaying her fingers discordantly across the keys of the pianoforte, brought the length of her arm in heated contact with his.

"I do not look forward to this fete I am planning, with any feeling other than dread," she said softly.

Forgetting for a moment promises, Hawkes lifted her hand away from the keys on the back of his own, and fit his fingers between hers. Shyly, she pulled her hand away from his, to explore the bit of tape that bound his knuckles.

"Are you injured, my lord?"

"Yes, my dear, to the very core of my heart, for you do not seem to care in the least for comforting."

She laughed, which had been his object, and gently fingered his bandage. "The wound is not fatal, I trust?"

"No, my dear, not fatal."

Lightly taking her face between the palms of his hands, he planted a kiss in the middle of her forehead. She blushed furiously, but did not pull away, and thoroughly astounded him by first reaching out to clutch at his lapel, following which she dipped her fair head down to nestle it for a moment against his shoulder.

"I have missed your teasing ways, my lord," she whispered into his chest, testing his resolve not to gather her into his arms. "I am glad you are returned," she sighed. "I do not think I could have faced this thing alone."

He cupped the crown of her silken head in one hand, and patted her back in what he considered an avuncular manner, while heart and body and soul cried out with such force for a greater hold upon her, that he was compelled to shut his eyes and lean into the lush mass of her hair.

"There is great strength within you, my dear," he said firmly, as much for his own benefit as hers. Gently, he disengaged her hold on him. "You have but to call on it to make your way through the most trying of times. I have every faith you will manage your coming encounter with Mr. Garvey with aplomb."

It was with equally graceful aplomb that Hawkes received a call from Stewart on the following morning, despite the bitter reminder said visit served of the gross injustice Hawkes did himself in too blindly promising his cousin that he posed no competition for Sarah's heart or hand.

Stewart brought with him his best friend, Mortimer Sailles, and a music box, the latest prize he had won at cards, which he said he thought Sarah might like. Hawkes would have preferred his cousin came alone, for he meant to discuss Sarah with Stewart, but with no show of his chagrin, he waved his guests into his study.

Stewart leveled his quizzing glass at his neatly bandaged knuckles. "What's toward?"

With an enigmatic smile and hooded eyes, Hawkes shrugged off the question. "Banged into something."

Stewart lowered his monocle. "Some poor bloke's nose, mayhap?"

Hawkes arched one formidable brow and shook his head. "No, not a nose. But, never mind that. Show me this contraption you mean to give Miss Lyndle."

The music box was exquisite, and Stewart did not need prodding to show it off. A brass songbird with crystal eyes, it sat upon a wire nest, wherein a metal music reel that played "The Magic Flute," was hidden. The bird opened and closed its silver beak to the tinkling tune, occasionally spreading its metal wings as if to fly away.

As Hawkes bent over the clever toy, imagining Sarah's delight in it, Mortimer Sailles took himself off by the window.

"Your little man's down at the end of the street," he said presently, and both of the Castlefords looked up.

"Blast! Is he really?" Monocle raised, Stewart stepped to the window and peered down into the street. "Cheeky fellow. Not content with driving me out of my club, he must needs follow me here as well."

"Money problems with your tailor again, Stew?" Hawkes drawled sarcastically.

"Can't be that. Paid off all my debts, you know."

Hawkes did not know. His eyes widened in ill-concealed astonishment. A wild rush of hope surged through him. If

Stewart's debts were gone, so was his cousin's most compelling reason to marry Sarah Lyndle.

Stewart was looking rather pleased with himself. "Cards, boxing, horses. I cannot seem to lose." He waved his hands in airy disdain.

"Coming this way, he is." Mortimer forecast gloomily from his vantage point at the window. "He'll be banging on the door before the cat can lick its ear."

"Never!" Stewart scoffed, but he was disappointed in this conjecture by the banging of the door knocker below. "Hawkes's man will turn him away," he prophesied blithely, convinced, it would seem, that his luck held in all things.

Curiosity aroused, Hawkes stepped to the window to see the persistent little man for himself. "'He will not be turned away," he said smoothly. "Silverman comes at my request."

"Silverman?" Stewart looked dumbly at Mortimer, who said stolidly, "Knew he looked familiar."

Stewart squinted irritably through his monocle. "Well, I must say your solicitor looks rather changed from the only other time I've clapped eyes on the bloke."

Hawkes was mystified. "How so?"

Mortimer was nodding. "Chap was wearing red flannel and a nightcap at the time."

"It was three o'clock in the morning, I'm ashamed to admit," Stewart said.

Hawkes's eyebrows shot up. "Why so early?"

"I was in a mood to invest."

Mortimer laughed. "Bet him a monkey he would never go to your solicitor and invest half his winnings responsibly."

"Three o'clock in the morning is responsible?"

Stewart shrugged. "I had won every other wager made that evening. It seemed irresponsible not to take Morty up on the bet."

"We were both foxed. . . ."

A knock upon the door preceded the entrance of the butler, who announced Mr. Norton Silverman.

A short, dapper, bearded gentleman with inquisitive green eyes stepped into the room. To the combined astonishment of all concerned, his gaze locked on Stewart as he crowed, "At last, I have run you to ground."

"To ground?" Stewart repeated, lifting his quizzing glass to direct a withering look at the smaller man. "I'd no idea you were a Melton man, Mr. Silverman."

Hawkes shot his relation a black look, effectively stilling his tongue. "Have you been chasing after my cousin, Norton?"

The solicitor bobbed his head, and delving into his leather case, fetched out a sheaf of paper. "Your cousin, my lord, has come into a bit of wealth, sir."

"Wealth?" Mortimer Sailles winked at Stewart. "Jove, that's a clever jest. Whoever put him up to such a Banbury tale?"

As if convinced he spoke to the only man in the room in full possession of his wits, Silverman continued to address Hawkes.

" 'Tis true, sir. At his express request, I invested all that he gave me."

"This investment? It does well?" Hawkes asked.

"Indeed, sir. Beyond all expectation. The venture has increased in value six times. There is a rage to trade shares in 'Change Alley these past few days, and while I had hoped for as much, I am myself astonished by this frenzy. It cannot last."

"So, you come to encourage my cousin to sell?"

A nod. "Just so, sir. There's a tidy profit to be made."

Stewart, who had sat down abruptly on hearing that his shares were worth six times his original investment, said jovially, "Sell, by all means, Silverman. Sell the lot!"

The solicitor could not conceal his relief. "Of course, sir. And what would you have me do with the money?"

"Why, give it back to me, of course. I've a mind to buy a house, and perhaps some horses."

Hawkes was surprised. "A house, Stew? I'd no idea you wished to number yourself among the landed gentry. What property interests you?"

"Brantley."

"Brantley!" Hawkes was shocked. However, given a moment, in which he brooded, dark eyes sweeping the room, he focused on the now-silent metal bird that glittered upon its wire nest. In that object he discovered Stewart's motive. His eyebrows lifted.

"Why Brantley?" His voice was soft as velvet.

Stewart, too, focused on the music box, his mouth fixed in a tight smile. "I shall soon be needing my own nest. Brantley is in close proximity to Lyndle Hall. It has occurred to me that a blind bird would be far happier were it an easy matter to flutter off home to visit with her father."

Hawkes's mouth twisted as he rubbed at his bandaged knuckles. "Touching, Stewart."

Mortimer Sailles's chest swelled out with delight. "We shall see you both safely buckled soon, eh, Castleford?"

"Both?" Hawkes bent a catlike look of curiosity in Mortimer's direction, the twinge in his hand forgotten.

"Hisst, Morty." Stewart wrinkled his nose irritably. "Hawkes has no plans to be hitched."

"No?" Morty rubbed his brow, perplexed. "Ah yes, now that you mind me of it, that bit about the baroness was only a bit of Bret's idle gossip."

Stewart frowned.

Hawkes's clouded mood grew darker. "It is rumored then that I intend to marry the baroness?" he surmised, ignoring for a moment the presence of Silverman, whose head swiveled from one speaker to the next with bright-eyed interest. It was Stewart's reaction that most interested him, for he was sure that his cousin still carried a torch for Sylvia.

"No, no." Morty clarified, blind to Stewart's silencing scowl and noisy clearing of his throat. "Boot's on the other leg. Flummery has it that the baroness has set her cap for you."

Stewart made a bored show of taking out his ormolu snuffbox when Morty refused to take his hint. Hawkes could not see his cousin's hand shake, but the first pinch of snuff rained down on the rug.

"When do you mean to bend knee to her, Stew?" he asked with deliberately muted intensity. Hawkes had yet to be convinced that Stewart cared more for Sarah than for Sylvia.

Stewart jumped. The second pinch of snuff, so carefully placed on the back of his hand, ready for inhaling, joined the first on the Aubusson. "Do you mean Miss Lyndle?"

"There is some other lady you mean to bend knee to?" Hawkes drawled. "Or has solvency cooled your fever to be married?"

Stewart frowned. "Of course not." He snapped the snuff-box shut and irritably tucked it away in his pocket. "I mean to ask her on her birthday, should the moment arise."

Despair rose into the back of Hawkes's throat. He choked it down. The idea of honoring his stupid, ill-fated promise was totally repugnant to him if Stewart was not truly devoted to Sarah; it was as repugnant as the idea of continuing to visit Brantley, should Stewart marry her.

"Well, cousin . . ." Hawkes said cynically, the look he directed at Stewart a piercing one, his tongue like a lead weight between his teeth, "if you do indeed commit yourself to loving and honoring Sarah Lyndle above all others, and succeed in winning her heart and hand, I shall deed Brantley over to you as a wedding gift."

His words drew stunned, openmouthed expressions on the faces of each of the three men who listened. Mortimer was first to recover. His words exploded in the stillness of the room.

"Gad, Hawkes! Damnably good of you, old man."

Hawkes knew his promise had little to do with goodness. His promise was an empty one. He could not believe Stewart capable of committing himself completely to Sarah, just as he did not believe it possible Sarah's heart and hand were to be won by Stewart.

His cousin's china blue eyes locked on his.

"Are you bloody sure about this?"

Hawkes closed his eyes. His hand was throbbing beneath the bandage. Brantley, so close to Lyndle Hall, would be both a sore reminder and uneasy temptation to him, should his cousin succeed where he was sure he must not. He nodded.

"Absolutely sure." His firmness brooked no argument. He turned his back to Stewart, his bandaged fingers playing absently with the metal songbird so that a few bars of "The Magic Flute" tinkled, with grating cheerfulness, into the silence.

Impatiently, he shut the thing off.

Chapter 18

H AWKES passed an indifferent night's sleep, his mind busily engaged in the task of discovering the perfect argument with which to dissuade Stewart from his pursuit of Sarah Lyndle. He had promised to convey his cousin and his musical bird to the fete, in order that he might explain the problem of his own growing feelings for Sarah. But the words in which to do so would not come, and Hawkes could think of little reason, other than her blindness, that any man would abandon pursuit of Miss Lyndle, once acquainted with her.

Stewart settled himself and his parcel and trained his quizzing glass unerringly on the slight swelling that disturbed the line of stitching across the knuckles of Hawkes's buff gloves.

"Will you tell me today how the other fellow looks?"

Hawkes smiled enigmatically.

Stewart sighed. "You were not always such a button-lip."

Hawkes considered explaining. There had been a time when he would have. But Sarah Lyndle stood in the way and this was not the topic with which to begin to explain to Stewart his feelings for her. He shrugged. "You know I abhor gossip."

Stewart's laugh had an injured sound. "I know you hate to be the subject of gossip, but you are, I regret to say, the centerpiece of a rather farfetched, faradiddle of late."

"Really?" Hawkes could not have evidenced less interest.

"Yes, you will laugh, but I was told that the baroness DeValle has asked you to help her in selling off Baron DeValle's stable."

Hawkes regarded Stewart with profound interest. Was this jealousy? "From whom did you garner this jewel of information?"

Stewart returned his keen look. "That gossip monger Bret, of course." He chuckled. "Did you know that Catherine Stone has dumped him already, in order that she might pursue Montague?"

Hawkes eyed his cousin steadily beneath lowered brows. This conversation had nothing to do with Bret, or Catherine Stone. Stewart was most concerned with the issue of Sylvia DeValle. His lips had a pinched look.

"Has he got it right, then? She came to you?"

"You object to my helping Sylvee with the sale of her nags?"

"Object?" Stewart's voice was as thin as his smile. "But . . . no, absolutely not. Why should I? I am only startled that it is through gossip that I should hear such a thing, and not by your lips."

"I know how mention of Sylvia DeValle pains you."

His cousin scowled, an expression unusual for Stewart, who professed frowning gave one unsightly lines. "Your silence pains me more, as does her reluctance to seek assistance of one who would have at one time readily chopped off his right arm, did it but please her."

Hawkes eyed him in frustration. What was it Sylvia had said? That it was for that very reason she could not bring herself to approach Stewart. They seemed, he thought, to warily circle truth here, without ever touching on the root of it. Stewart was jealous of his renewed communication with Sylvia, an emotion that seemed in direct contradiction to Stewart's professed intention to tie himself for life, to Sarah.

"There was a moment yesterday when it did occur to me to tell you, but I dismissed the notion." Hawkes watched every nuance of expression that clouded Stewart's visage. "At the time, your thoughts were happily filled with the prospect of marriage and solvency."

"Next you will be telling me that you mean to marry Sylvia," Stewart stated coolly.

Hawkes's brooding gaze raked over him. "Should it mat-

ter so much to you if I did, when you mean to troth yourself
to another? You would seem to have forgotten Sarah Lyndle, cousin."

Stewart stared out at the passing street. "Forget?" He
sounded offended. "In no way do I forget."

With a twisting stab of regret, Hawkes observed that it
would appear his cousin spoke the truth. Stewart behaved
in an oppressively attentive manner toward the object of his
professed desire that afternoon. It was he who chose the
chair in which Sarah must seat herself, and it was on his
arm that she made her way there. Stewart plumped up the
cushion for the small of her back and stationed himself at
her elbow, amusing her with some jest that brought her musical laughter rippling forth.

Hawkes observed with expressionless stoicism as Stewart fetched Miss Lyndle's punch and filled her plate. At
Stewart's insistence a small firescreen was placed beside
Sarah's chair, so that the sunlight might not fade the brilliance of her sprig muslin. Stewart too made a grand pro-
duction of presenting to Sarah his musical bird, an object
that arguably validated his cousin's constancy.

The mechanical bird had the misfortune to be unwrapped
at the very moment when several tensely awaited guests
made their appearance. On hearing her father's voice, Sarah
forgot the box in her lap and jumped up, with the intention
of racing to the door. Had it not been for Stewart's close
proximity and hasty response in rescuing it from such a
fate, the pretty music box might have ended in a smashed
heap on the marble floor.

Hawkes stood with equal alacrity to stay Sarah's mad
flight. "May I escort you to the door?" he asked. Bending
low to whisper, his dark locks mingled with golden curl as
he warned her, "Your father does not come alone. Sir Garvey and his wife follow, and behind them Geoffrey and his
bride."

Her fingers tightened on his sleeve, and her cheeks
blanched white, but with nothing more than a slight catch
in her voice to betray the state of her sensibilities, Sarah
bade him take her to welcome them. Halfway to the door,

she spoke three words, very softly; three words that plucked at the Earl of Henley's heart much as her fingers plucked at his sleeve.

"Stay by me," she begged.

Stay by her Hawkes did, much to Sarah's relief. Throughout the smiling ordeal of welcoming their guests, it was from the Beast's strong arm that she drew support. Hawkes gave her fingers a bracing squeeze as she spoke, and she was pleased and heartened and relieved beyond words by this small show of his concern as she said, "Geoffrey, is that you? I am told you are happily wed, old friend."

A rush of relief that more than equaled her own, was evident in Geoffrey Garvey's voice, a voice so changed in its tenor from the last time they had shared conversation, that it was as if she spoke to a complete stranger. The new Mrs. Garvey was introduced.

Sarah smiled, and extending her hand with an enthusiastic warmth that surprised herself as much as those around her, she said, without hypocrisy, "I am pleased to meet you."

In halting English, the new Mrs. Garvey indicated her pleasure as well.

Secure and untroubled on Hawkes's shielding arm, Sarah felt there was something very right about no longer being obligated to marry the stranger Geoffrey Garvey had become. She was moved to say to her guide, in a voice so low that no one else could hear, "You lead me through the dance again, sir, without my crushing anyone's toes. This is not so difficult as I had imagined."

"You are quite light on your feet," he said with the drawl she had begun to think more whimsical than biting. "My cousin would step in, if you will have him."

"Please, my lord, I would not have you leave me, just yet." She clutched a little desperately at his hand and was surprised when he flinched.

"As you wish, my dear," he said as he pried loose the stranglehold of her fingers. "But you must promise to avoid mangling my knuckles."

"Nasty eye you're wearing," Sarah heard Stewart remark to Geoffrey as they were introduced, and would have paid little attention to Geoff's answer had it not been for the unusual stiffness that seemed to take possession of Hawkes's arm in that moment, a stiffness unbending until Geoffrey responded tersely.

"Battle wound."

Making the connection between the black eye and Lord Castleford's bruised knuckles, Sarah slid her gloved hand down to touch upon Hawkes's hand and said with playful gratitude, so that only he might hear, "Thank you again, my lord, for convincing Geoffrey to attend."

"My pleasure," he drawled with ill-concealed satisfaction.

A little while later, as the party of newcomers mixed with those already settled in the little drawing room, Stewart sought to regain what he had lost in the possession of Sarah Lyndle's attention. He spoke from his place beside his aunt at the far end of the room, saying in a cheerful voice, in which none but Sarah might detect a note of petulance, "Miss Lyndle! How is it that I am the last to learn of your uncanny ability to 'see' faces? I find myself quite done in with self-pity. From what my aunt tells me, I perceive it to be a most delightful experience."

Sarah knew her words might wound Hawkes, but with no other explanation to offer, she said, "My mode of vision, which has been described as a caress to the face, has been judged too intimate for mixed company. I no longer endeavor to see in this manner, lest my motives be misinterpreted."

An exhalation of air slipped through Hawkes's teeth, as if he had been struck in the stomach.

"Ah, cousin," Stewart said, "I can see by the cloud upon your brow that you are confused."

"I am most anxious to be enlightened." Sarah was sure Hawkes addressed her with the words, as much as his cousin.

Stewart patted the empty chair beside his. "Here is a

comfortable spot, Miss Lyndle. Perhaps you will be so kind
as to enlighten us all."

She was relinquished to the chair.

Hawkes took his own place next to Mrs. Turvey across
from Sarah, the better to observe her countenance. She had
never seemed more lovely, no, nor more unattainable to
him. Her face showed some signs of strain, but there was
something indefinably moving about her expression. It was
as if her thoughts, even in the most pressing of circumstances, added an extra dimension to her beauty. He was
filled with remorse. His shortsighted acceptance of a
lovesick young man's unschooled definition of "adult regard" had hemmed this fine creature in. That had never
been his intention. Blindness would seem to hem her in
enough without any interference on his part. Sunk in self-
recrimination, it was some few moments before it became
clear to Hawkes that the doctor's wife had addressed herself to him.

Correctly interpreting his blank stare, Lydia was good
enough to repeat what would seem to be a very ill-timed
non sequitur. "Have you ever played blindman's bluff, my
lord?"

Hawkes's blinked at her, confused. "Many years ago."

Across the room, his mother clapped her hands together.
"What a lovely explanation for the way Sarah goes about
seeing. 'Tis very much like blindman's bluff."

Lady Garvey, who had until this moment, hovered
silently beside her husband, spoke, her tone fondly reminiscent. "Sarah and Geoffrey spent hours in games such as
that, as children." And then, as if the words had slipped
from her tongue unguardedly, she looked across at her son,
her face stricken. "Is that not so, Geoff?"

Geoffrey pulled his attention away from interpreting the
conversation into Spanish for his wife's benefit, and a little
smile, as from a pleasant memory, lifted the corners of his
mouth. "We did have some fun at games did we not,
Sarah?"

The words were tentatively apologetic and Hawkes could
see that their unvoiced question did not escape Sarah's

keen ear. Her mouth was soft and forgiving when she replied, and her hand flew out in Garvey's direction, as though in supplication. "You were always very patient with your clumsy playmate, Geoff."

It occurred to Hawkes as he observed the exchange that never had he been so moved by the gesture of any young lady as he was moved by that outflung hand.

"Shall we play?" His mother's question surprised them all. There followed a moment of confused silence. Lady Castleford's plucked brows rose in the same slightly sardonic manner her son's were wont to do. "Blindman's bluff. Shall we play?"

The suggestion was a daring one, but Dr. Turvey seconded her farfetched notion. "Excellent idea! We shall all, if only for a few moments, know what it is like to 'see' as Sarah does."

Two spots of color flared up in Sarah's pale cheeks. Hawkes watched in speechless awe. His mother loosened the square of Norwich silk from her shoulders, and bound it around her head so that she could not see.

"How's that for a blindfold?" came the muffled question.

The rest of the party, eyes locked with rapt attention on the dowager countess—who stood before them, rather like a demented highwayman in paisley mask—could not after their first moment of tongue-biting silence find reason to demur. Chairs were placed appropriately, and the game began.

In his turn, Stewart was immensely pleased to identify Sarah before he had so much as laid hands on her. "None could mistake the scent of heliotrope," he murmured suavely, too late realizing his error in tipping his hand before it was played.

"Your nose outsmarts you, nevie," Amelia clucked sadly, as she zealously whipped the blindfold from his eyes. Hawkes thought his mother looked enormously pleased with herself as she handed the shawl, unthinking, to Sarah, who had no need of the blindfold. She sat patiently, the scarf in her lap, as the others, in pantomime, recommended first Sir Garth Garvey, and then with more enthusiasm, Hawkes himself, as Sarah's subject.

Presently, Sarah was informed that all was ready, and Hawkes, taking the seat opposite hers, steeled himself for what was to come.

A smile lifted Sarah's lips as Hawkes settled into the chair. Nostrils flaring, ever so slightly, she seemed to read some clue in the air as to who he was. Hesitantly she reached out to find his shoulders. For an instant, she seemed to brace herself there.

Her touch, when she reached out to trace the contours of his face, was bittersweet agony. Ice and fire, her fingers left a brand on Hawkes, physically and emotionally. Like trembling butterfly wings they traveled the perimeter of his face, spanning his forehead, his cheekbones, his chin. Her every agitated inhalation whispered like a promise in his waiting ears, and the unsteady trail of her touch unbridled in him, desires long held in check.

She traced the bushy line of his brows, both hands moving outward, twice, as if one time were not enough to fathom their width and depth. Then her fingers passed down each side of the monstrosity he considered his bent beak of a nose. She acknowledged its size with an expression so alive with discovery that he felt it take on new and admirable shape beneath the magic of her touch.

Like a rabbit transfixed by torchlight, Hawkes remained perfectly still, but for his eyes, and these moved slowly, intently lingering on every detail of Sarah's countenance, so close before him. There were none who saw how focused was his regard, save Sir Garvey, who from his vantage point had a direct view of him. A knowing smile soon lifted his lips, as if that gentleman found something to please him in Hawkes's expression.

Sarah's hands, the palms like warm coals, her fingertips unnaturally chill, settled on the planes of Hawkes's cheeks, and the Earl of Henley thought with regret that the incredibly moving exploration of his features must be at an end.

He was too hasty in that assumption. Sarah meant to see all of his face, every inch of it. This was no cursory glance. She had been granted an opportunity to stare at him. Stare at him she did. The cool, scented hands moved with deliberate intent along the clean-shaven bone of his jawline, searching out his earlobes, which proved unusually sensitive to her touch, and then his eyes, which he closed. She shocked them open again by caressing the sensitive line of his mouth.

A shudder racked him, so intense was this contact between them. It was understandable that Nate should misinterpret such an examination. Sarah's mouth was lifted in uncensored delight. Her lips cried out to be kissed, and Hawkes would have liked nothing better than to oblige them. It took every ounce of cool restraint he could muster to resist kissing her soft fingertips, to resist wetting them with his tongue and nibbling each length with craven teeth, right there in front of a room full of witnesses. No one had ever touched him as Sarah touched him. It was as if she reached beneath his skin, into the heart of him. A wrenching sensation of incredible loss welled up in Hawkes's heart, showing itself briefly in the depths of his eyes. He had promised not to pursue his feelings for this young woman and the hold she had on him. Today, Stewart meant to ask for these hands. There was tragedy in such a twist of fate.

Finished with him, Sarah sighed deeply, as if she had been holding her breath. Hawkes swayed forward to drink in the sweet, intoxicating odor of tea and peppermint that mingled with the heliotrope she pressed to temple and wrist.

"My lord." Her pleasant, throaty voice trembled with amused surprise. "Yours is a handsome face. Not at all beastly."

Laughter met her startled syllables.

She flushed, discomfitted by her own bold statement.

Hawkes could not bring himself to smile, but he sent the entire company into whoops, saying with irresistible sarcasm, "You turn my head, Miss Lyndle. I am unaccustomed to such flattery."

Chapter 19

S ARAH could still feel the warmth of Hawkes's flesh like a fire in her fingertips when, at the close of the afternoon's festivities, her father stayed behind, for a moment of private conversation. There was something reminiscent of the waltz in the floating lilt of her tread as she serenely led the way to the back parlor, her mind turning over the information her hands had gathered. The face of the Beast had begun to take shape in her mind like a piece of clay beneath the hands of a potter. She now knew what contours made up his forehead, his chin, and the nose that was not quite straight. She knew the thick, mobile texture of his eyebrows, the lean, tautness of the skin across his cheekbones, the soft fullness of his lips. Like a child tasting something sweet for the first time, Sarah reveled in her knowledge. Something in the knowing made her very happy she was not to marry Geoffrey Garvey, and more concerned than ever by the suggestion that it was Stewart who meant to ask for her hand.

"You choose your acquaintances well, Sarah." Her father's voice swelled with paternal pride as she settled in one of the many chairs in the parlor. "I cannot help but think that your mother would have been most pleased by the obvious affection with which you are received."

Sarah nodded absentmindedly, her attention focused in the tips of her fingers, which still pulsed in a most disconcerting manner. She marveled that her father, who knew her so well, saw no evidence, no outward sign of this burning rhythm in her hands. Was there not visible proof of the sparking heat that had leapt from the earl's flesh to hers, branding her in some way, for all to see? She leaned her cheek upon the palm of a hand still warm from its contact with Hawkes's cheek.

"Mr. Castleford is a very polished young man. He seems quite fond of you."

Pressing her palms together, Sarah pushed away thoughts of Hawkes, that she might concentrate on what her father was saying.

Her father was laughing. "Do you know," he said, "I had once thought it was the 'Beast', and not the 'Beauty', who sought your favor?"

Sarah's happiness, like a fly caught in amber, was suspended by the remark. One hot hand flew to her throat. "Indeed, Father? And now?" It seemed her very future hung on his answer.

"It is quite clear, my love, that it is Stewart Castleford who is most taken with you."

"And not Lord Castleford?" she prodded gently as her trembling hand, its warmth fading, fell away from her throat. She did her best to subdue the hysterical impulse to tell him he was wrong, must be wrong, that the Beast did care for her. She could not be so terribly mistaken in her own feelings, could she?

"Why, as to that, I daresay it was on his cousin's behalf that he made such a push."

"Push, Father? Whatever do you mean?" A seed of doubt had begun to sprout.

"Well, you know, it would be in the family's best interest to smooth the way, as it were, if Stewart meant to ask for you."

"Do you mean Geoffrey's black eye, Father?" Sarah leaned forward, clasping and unclasping her hands. His answer was important to her.

He laughed. "You guessed that, did you?"

"Has Lord Castleford made a push in other ways?"

Her father, pressed by her questions, answered irritably, "Well, of course he has, Sarah, in any number of ways. You should but see the neat little bay he has fixed me up with, so that I might put old Sampson out to pasture."

Sarah tried not to read too much into what he said. She strove to calm her voice. "Has he so? How very kind. Lord

Castleford is a tremendous judge of horseflesh. I think you may rest easy with any cattle he recommends to you."

"He's a knowing one all right. The bay is excellent! One of the Baroness DeValle's animals."

"DeValle?" Sarah was surprised.

"Yes. Beautiful woman. Mentioned she had met you. Means to sell all her cattle. Castleford is handling the details."

"Is he?" Sarah's voice plummeted, along with her spirits. It would appear that the renewed relationship between Hawkes and the Widow DeValle, went well. That in itself might not have completely shaken her confidence in the escalating esteem she had imagined existed between herself and Hawkes, but coupled as it was with her father's conviction that Stewart and not his cousin was enamored with her, her confidence suffered a tremor of devastating magnitude. Sarah could not deny that she was in a fair way to falling in love with Hawkes, and to discover that he shared no such feelings, indeed that he felt drawn to another, was lowering to the extreme.

She clasped and unclasped her hands, which had begun to feel strangely bloodless, and wondered if she must resign herself after all to the prospect of becoming an old maid, for how could she agree to marry Stewart when it was his cousin she cared for?

The Beauty and the Beast rode away from Sarah's fete in a silence that was not broken until, with a sigh, Stewart blurted, "Do you aspire to marriage, cousin?"

"Marriage?" Hawkes repeated from the dark corner of the carriage, into which he had wedged both his shoulders and his thoughts of Sarah Lyndle. "Yes, I have aspirations," he drawled with hopeless irony.

Stewart raised his quizzing glass, to peer into the corner where he sat.

"Do you find yourself in love then?"

Hawkes considered a moment how he should answer, and then admitted without any hint of his customary sarcasm, "There is one I have met. I think she could make me very happy"—the sarcasm had returned—"gives she not her heart to another."

"Aye, there's the rub." Stewart mused. "Might I ask who?"

"You might, but I do not think I would answer."

Stewart contemplated the tassels on his gleaming Hessians. "I would have you happy, cousin."

"As you are, Stew?" Hawkes purred. His look, from the depths of his corner, was far more probing than the question would seem to merit.

Stewart frowned down at his boots and then produced a handkerchief to wipe away the dust that marred their toes. "Precisely, Hawkes. Precisely so," he said lightly. "I have no right to be dismayed that Sylvia DeValle places her trust in you. As you pointed out, my future lies down a different pathway." He paused a moment, looking out the window, and then with a poignant smile said, "If you should, now or at some future date, wish to take Sylvia to wife, then I wish you both happy."

Hawkes blinked in dismay. "I am overwhelmed, Stew," he said. "I thought perhaps you loved her still. I have reason to believe she still cares for you."

Stewart pursed his lips. "Be that as it may, I will ask you no more concerning your relationship with her, and expect you to divulge no more than you find suitable. I have heard that she and Otto were husband and wife in name only. It would seem the rumor she started so long ago may yet come true."

"Rumor? What mean you?"

Stewart sighed, impatient with his ignorance. "Why the rumor that you had ruined her."

Hawkes stared at him, dumbfounded. "She started the rumor? You are sure?"

Stewart tried manfully to hide his displeasure as he nodded.

"That's odd." Hope still hanging by a thread, Hawkes thrust his hands into the pockets of his coat with an impatient grunt. "I do no more than assist Sylvia in a business matter."

Stewart did not look convinced. The two young men sat

in weighty silence as the horses were drawn up before his apartments. A footman jumped down to open the door with the alacrity Lord Castleford insisted upon. Hawkes felt opportunity slipping through his fingers.

"I wonder if you might help me," he said. The footman, assuming his assistance was required, peered around the door.

Stewart froze, his leg halfway out of the carriage. "Help? In what way?"

Hawkes hesitated, for never before had he chosen to gossip about another's misfortune. "You are far better informed than I with regard to the goings-on in this town. Have you any idea why the baroness would want to sell almost every horse she and her late husband owned, and all but one of the vehicles?"

Intrigued, Stewart retrieved his too-hasty limb, and much to the consternation of the footman, pulled the door shut. "All of them? How odd! You did of course ask her why such extreme measures were to be taken?"

"Of course. She mentioned debts of a sensitive nature. To whom, I do not know, but Sylvester Naughtley shadows her every move, and I cannot think Sylvia so lacking in good sense as to have any real affection for one such as he."

"Hmm." Stewart tapped his front tooth with the rim of his quizzing glass. "You checked out the possibility of real encumbrances on the estate then?"

"Yes, nothing out of the ordinary. All paid off. The estate stands free and clear."

The drumming on the tooth ceased. "Smacks of blackmail. Shall I nose around? See what's on the wind?"

Genuinely relieved, Hawkes smiled. "That would be splendid. You know how much I should hate to go chasing gossip."

Stewart chuckled and rapped briskly on the door panel. "Happy to oblige. Naughtley has been making himself a pest to Miss Lyndle of late."

"Has he?" Hawkes drawled with interest as the door was opened by the footman, who wore the dubious expression of a man who expected the door to snap shut in his face yet again.

The Castlefords were not alone in their concentration on matters involving the Widow DeValle at that moment. Sarah could not dismiss her concern that Hawkes still loved the woman. She allowed herself to be disrobed by Susan, the housekeeper, who clucked contentedly over the success of the day, despite the ladies' maid having taken ill. Sarah paid scant attention as she stepped obediently into the hip bath prepared for her. It would seem she had, as naively as Nathanial, inappropriately fixed her affections. She sank down into the water, feeling exposed and vulnerable.

In light of the information concerning Lord Castleford's renewed interest in the beautiful Widow DeValle, every moment that Sarah held precious because of its having been shared with him seemed changed. Every kind word, every gentle gesture that Sarah had dared hope gave evidence of Hawkes's growing affection for her seemed suddenly less certain, less substantive. Had she exaggerated reality, somehow distorted it, so that what she thought was a burgeoning love, equal to her own, was in fact nothing but shadow? Deep in her heart, she had to admit that it must be so, that in her blindness she had somehow missed seeing the truth. The revelation brought a tightness to her throat and weighed down her joy in the day. A tear added its warm bite to the bathwater.

"Is summat the matter, love?" Susan, her voice motherly with concern, came laden with the final bucket of bathwater.

"Oh, nothing really, Susan. Today was wonderful. Everyone so kind." A few more tears joined the first.

"Now, now, ducks. What's toward? Tell old Suz'." The housekeeper's kind voice sluiced warm and comfortable over Sarah, like the water that she added to the bath.

Sarah responded with a question of her own. "How does one know when one is in love, Suz?"

"Oh so, it's love is it? Well, that's one as will always keep the eyes wet." Susan shook the last of the water from the bucket, handle clanking, and then sat herself gingerly down, with the bucket for a chair. "As to how one knows, well . . . that's not an easy question you would have me answer. You must ask your heart, and you must ask your head, I suppose, but rely not on just one or t'other."

Sarah fished up the soap cake. It proved as slippery as Susan's advice. What did her heart and head agree upon when it came to her feelings for Hawkes?

Susan lifted herself, creaking, off the bucket.

"And what must one do, Susan, if the one whom one loves, loves another?"

"Well then," Susan sighed. "One must find another to care for, ducks. There's nothing else for it."

"Nothing else for it," Sarah repeated slowly.

"That's right. There's a many as has done as much before you, dearie, and lived, content with compromise."

Sarah lathered her burning cheeks with soap as she relived the moments she had, as the Beast himself would say, "caressed his face." Her heart hammered in a most disturbing way at the memory. It would be compromise indeed to settle for something other than love now that she knew its power.

Chapter 20

Hawkes found he could not stop his hopes and thoughts from straying to Sarah the next morning when he and his solicitor met with the Baroness DeValle in order that they might sign and deliver the bill of sale for the bay horse to Sarah's father at his hotel.

Stewart had not yet proposed, that was certain. There had been little opportunity for declarations of love, with Geoffrey Garvey on the premises the previous day. Hawkes found cause for hope in the delay, until they were met at the door to Lord Lyndle's suite by none by none other than his cousin, on his way out, walking stick and hat in hand.

Stewart seemed no less dismayed to see him. His jaw dropped, along with his amber-headed walking stick when he came face-to-face with Hawkes and Sylvia, arm in arm. The stick bounced off the door Stewart had just come through and rolled to a halt at the edge of Sylvia's skirts. Stewart blinked and knelt to pick it up. He was thus, kneeling at the baroness's feet when Sarah's father popped his head out the door.

Lord Lyndle chuckled. "On your knees already, my boy?" He winked at Stewart as if the two of them shared some private jest. "I laud your enthusiasm lad, but question your eyesight."

Stewart, ever the cool one, lifted his lips in a brittle grin. "Just practicing, my lord," he said.

Hawkes felt his heart stop beating. He knew in an instant what happened here. Stewart had done the proper thing. Stewart generally did. He had come here this morning to ask Sarah's father for Sarah's hand.

"Practicing?" Hawkes repeated, wishing his cousin to the

very devil. "I thought you might be offering up a prayer, Stew."

Stewart stood, his face mottled with color, poise lost, but walking stick recovered. He shot an embarrassed look at the baroness. "I haven't a prayer to offer. Never did."

Lord Lyndle laughed. "There's other business than praying that's conducted on one's knees, isn't there, Lady De-Valle?" He winked at the baroness.

Sylvia nodded, a strange, wistful smile on her lips. "All kinds of commerce," she agreed, "even the business of begging forgiveness."

Hawkes thought Stewart looked much struck by her words, but Lord Lyndle interrupted whatever he might have meant to say by addressing the baroness.

"Shall we sign those papers on the bay now, my lady?"

Sylvia nodded, and as her gaze fell away from Stewart, so, too, did Hawkes's hopes fall. It had seemed to him, for a moment, that the air between Sylvia and Stewart hummed with possibility.

Sylvia, too, would seem to have felt the charged quality of the air, for she was reluctant to break off her conversation. "Stewart?" She seemed struck by an idea.

"Yes?" There was little hope in Stewart's expression.

Sylvia seemed determined to enchant with her smile. "Are you in the market for a horse? Would you care to ride out this afternoon and take a look at the creatures I have for sale?"

"Capital idea," Lord Lyndle seconded, and clapping Stewart on the back, he had no idea what consternation he gave rise to in the breast of more than one of those gathered when he insisted with a twinkle in his eye, "For now, we must not keep you, eh, my boy?"

Sarah would not have minded had Stewart been kept from her entirely. She sat in Lady Castleford's arbor, her hands caressing the amazing pages of Valentine Huay's strange book for the blind, while her mind ran back and forth over the question of love. So sunk in contemplation was she that when the sound of booted footsteps first assailed her ears, her heart leapt into her throat with anticipation. This must be Hawkes, come again to this special place of roses and shadows, drawn by the intensity of her thoughts and feelings with regard to him.

But it was not Hawkes. The boots were tassled ones, and the scent, sandalwood. Stewart was the gentleman who spoke. "Miss Lyndle," he said. She was struck by the queer notion that the utterance of her own name held for him a sort of uncertainty.

The newly broken stem of a rose was thrust between her fingers. To hide her disappointment, she dipped her nose into the petals with a sigh. "How lovely, Stewart," she said politely, even as she decided that the odor of roses could never fail to remind her of the hot afternoon she had been swept into Hawkes's arms. She heard Stewart as he took a handkerchief out with a snap and felt the movement of the air in front of her as he dropped the square of linen into the grass so that he might sink one knee upon it.

Startled, she lifted her face away from the rose.

"I think it can come as no surprise to you, Miss Lyndle, that I hold your person in the highest esteem," he said, the words as labored as his breathing.

His words did come as a surprise, for Sarah had not in her heart of hearts believed that her father could be right. Her fingers, closing fast on the stem of the rose, found a thorn. The pain was nothing compared to the anguish in her heart as her hopes were dashed. She bit down on her lower lip to stop from crying out.

"I have just been housed with your father," Stewart said pensively. "He has no objection to my addressing you on this subject."

Letting go of the rose so that it sat upon the open pages of her book, Sarah began first to stroke the velvet petals, and then, absently, to pluck them free from their thorny stem. She did not want to believe that Stewart was proposing to her. To admit that was his purpose, was to admit it was the Beauty who would have her, and not the Beast.

She could not pluck the words from Stewart's mouth as easily as she plucked petals. The rose rained into her lap, like a flower that has dissolved itself into pale pink tears.

Stewart kept on talking, and what he said sounded very like a proposal.

"Your father went so far as to say that he should be pleased to call me his son . . ." he told her, "should you find the notion to your liking."

Sarah paused in the systematic destruction of the rose. "Notion, Mr. Castleford?" She would not believe his purpose until the words were said.

Stewart loosened his cravat and went on hesitantly. "Will you do me the great honor, Miss Lyndle, of accepting this poor hand of mine in marriage?"

He spoke smoothly and reached out until the hand he referred to lightly brushed against hers. She was shocked to discover that his hand not only shook, it was quite damp with perspiration as well. She sat as if frozen, remembering when they had been introduced and Stewart had taken her hand with cool formality in a kiss exemplifying social perfection. Nervously scattering rose petals, her hand went out to lightly cover his, for she was touched by his rattled condition and took it as a sign of his feeling for her.

As if embarrassed by the disgusting dampness of his hand, Stewart swiftly withdrew from her clasp.

"Dear Mr. Castleford . . ." She was both distressed and moved and completely at a loss as to how one went about saying no in such circumstances. "You do me great honor with your proposal. My heart, indeed my mind, are quite overthrown with the enormity of your question. . . ."

He stopped her by standing abruptly to brush off the knees of his pantaloons. "Do not feel you must answer me now," he said. "I neither require, nor expect it in this moment."

She knew he searched the blankness of her eyes for some indication of what her response might be.

"I do but beg you to consider the idea. I have a selfish desire to see you happily settled. I have the means at hand to fulfill that desire. Humbly, I offer you my"—he seemed reluctant to remind her of his hand—"my respect and affection."

Her voice trembled. She hoped he would not realize it

was despair that made it warble so. "You are very kind, Stewart."

"Not at all," he protested. "I realize my question comes hard on the heels of a most grueling time, in which all plans for your future have been overset. This can be but compromise. . . ."

It was the word compromise that kept her from refusing him outright. Was compromise not better than a life of loneliness and dashed hopes? She could not say, not without giving the matter further consideration. "Perhaps you would do me the honor of meeting me here, at this same time, tomorrow. I will know my mind by then," she said, and hoped that her tangle of thoughts might in fact unravel in so little time.

His heels clicked together. "Until tomorrow then, Miss Lyndle, I leave you with all hope of a positive reply."

When he had gone, Sarah sat in a deep, changed silence that seemed to press in on her ears as uncomfortably as any noise might. It occurred to her that Stewart had never once told her that he loved her. She sighed as she got up from the bench. Wilting rose petals, like lost dreams, fell from her lap.

Chapter 21

HAWKES studied Stewart as he approached the gate at the end of the mews the late Baron DeValle had made into stables. Hawkes was certain that Stewart came straight from having proposed to Sarah, and it was his intention to deduce the success or failure of that proposal without ever having to ask outright. His cousin had not the look about him of a man who had met with acceptance. Neither posture nor expression were swelled with the pride of having been granted one's heart's desire. Hope rose in Hawkes's heart, like a bubble on the wind, but like a bubble, it was fragile. Stewart did not appear buoyed up by good fortune, but then again, neither did he appear cast down by rejection. He had not the dragging steps or dejected mien of a man who has seen a dream shattered and hope denied. He wore instead the dazed look of a sleepwalker, the unpained, dreamy slackness of the patient given laudanum for the toothache. It was the same look Hawkes had witnessed in boxers who suffered one blow too many to the head; a dazed, uncentered lack of focus.

Stewart's gaze did not alter until a horse whinnied and leaned an eager nose as far as he could stretch in his direction. The sound jerked Stewart out of his daydream like a marionette whose string is pulled too suddenly. The frozen immobility of his facial features sprang to life, and it suddenly became clear to Hawkes why his cousin's demeanor unsettled him. The disturbing thought pressed forward from the back of his mind that his cousin loved horses more than the woman he had just proposed to. There was a joyously contented light in Stewart's eyes as he stroked the animal's nose. Hawkes had never witnessed such a look in Stewart's eyes for Sarah.

"Where's Syl . . . Lady DeValle?" Stewart asked him.

Hawkes raised an eyebrow. "Rather formal aren't we? Since when have you taken to calling Sylvee, Lady DeValle, even in her absence?"

Stewart's mouth twisted. "Since I proposed to the Lyndle, this morning."

Hawkes froze, tensing for the emotional blow that might follow. He drew no breath for an instant. Stewart lifted his chin and looked quizzically at him, gaging his reaction. The horse nudged his hand, demanding attention.

"She accepted your offer?" Hawkes managed to ask.

Stewart shoved the eager nose out of his way. "She gives me her answer tomorrow." He slid a wry look at his cousin and pursed his lips. "It was damnably difficult to propose, but what an interminable bit of hell to have to wait for an answer."

Hawkes nodded. "I can imagine," he said heavily. "You shall be forced to wait for Sylvia as well, I'm afraid. She's gone riding with Sylvester."

"You let her go off alone with that spider?" Stewart looked as if he might like to set off in pursuit.

"Yes," Hawkes drawled. "I was pleased to be left behind. Sylvee can look after herself. I have in the meantime been chatting up the stable lads for information with regard to why she is in such haste to sell her horses."

"You?" Stewart exclaimed. "Encouraging gossip with stable hands? I should have liked to have seen that."

Hawkes's mouth twisted. He could not tell Stewart that he was driven by his concern for Sarah more than any feeling of sympathy for Sylvia's dilemma. What he had discovered had proven most enlightening. "I am convinced that the spider, as you call him, has woven an intricate web in which to snare not only the baroness, but anyone else whose reputation can be threatened by the sordid tales he has chronicled in his omnipresent journals."

Stewart bristled. "What did the lads say?"

Hawkes's voice sank into a fiercely sardonic drawl. "Grimsby, the head lad, tells me that our Mr. Naughtley brought out the worst in the baron while they were friends."

"The worst? And what worst is that?"

"Wouldn't say precisely"—Hawkes's eyebrows rose a fraction of an inch—"but he did go on to accuse Naughtley of pestering his younger stable lads. Said he had to warn him away after he heard they'd been offered riches beyond their ken."

"Wouldn't take much to be beyond a stableboy's ken," Stewart pointed out. "What did these offered riches hope to purchase?"

Hawkes's lip curled. "Unspeakable acts."

There was a pregnant pause.

"My, my," Stewart murmured. "I'd no idea! But with the baron dead, how does Sylvester hope to use this against Sylvia?"

"You know the Huptons. They believed Otto was above reproach, else they would never have allowed Sylvia to marry him. They take more pride in their lineage than they ever have in the family's fortunes."

Stewart frowned. "No one would believe Sylvester's gossip."

"Oh yes they would. It was widely believed I had succeeded in seducing Sylvia, and that was no more than words on the wind. They would believe this, especially if it was published in tantalizing detail."

Comprehension dawned. "The black books?"

Hawkes nodded. "The black books."

"So, it is blackmail. Sylvester means to sponge off Sylvia for as long as she has funds to pay him." Stewart's voice dropped. "One cannot help but wonder what vices are worthy of such dearly bought silence." His china blue eyes narrowed. "It might be worth our while to lay hands on these journals."

There was no time for further discussion. Sylvia DeValle rode a spirited gray thoroughbred into the mews, followed by Sylvester Naughtley, the leggy spider come after the fly, mounted on a swaybacked, spavined creature that Hawkes identified as a rented hack. The baron would never have allowed such an equine atrocity to chew hay amongst his prime bits of blood and bone. Naughtley and the horse were both breathing hard, as though unaccustomed to exertion, and while that might have accounted for the animal's drooping lip, Hawkes did not think it fully explained Sylvester's gaping mouth as he caught sight of Stewart. Sylvia, on the other hand, looked both beautiful and unruffled as she urged her horse to a smart trot across the yard in a fitted black velvet riding habit with a crisp, white lace jabot to relieve its severity. The ample skirt of the habit swept almost to the ground, rippling along the gray's belly, like waves behind a clipper ship. She welcomed Stewart with a breathtaking smile.

"Do you mean to have one of my horses, Mr. Castleford?" she asked. "Shall I have the lads up to show you their paces?"

"I like the look of him, madam." Stewart had his monocle trained on Sylvester and not the horse, but when Naughtley at last thought to clap shut his gaping mouth and draw offended breath through his needle-thin nose, Stewart swung the glass back in the direction of the horses. "I'm amazed you can bear to part with them."

Sylvia's eyes were bright. There was a look in their depths, meant only for Stewart; a warm look of suppressed mirth, for Sylvia knew Stewart well enough to appreciate the subtlety of his insult to her companion.

Sylvester, who watched the couple as intensely as Hawkes, fished from his pocket the ever-present calf-bound book, along with a stub of a pencil.

"There are times when one must part with even that which one loves, Mr. Castleford." Sylvia said with slow emphasis, as if each word was of vital importance.

Hawkes's eyes narrowed as Naughtley licked the lead of his pencil and scribbled in his black book.

"Must one cut up happiness in order to stay out of Dun Territory?" Stewart seemed to challenge both Sylvia's words, and the look in her eyes. There was, Hawkes decided, more being discussed here than the sale of a horse.

"Debts must be paid." Sylvia said firmly, but for all its strength, the statement sounded like an apology. Hawkes realized, as if a clock had just struck the hour, that these two, with mutual understanding, spoke of debts long since due, debts that had dramatically changed their lives. Debt was the only reason Sylvia had married DeValle. She had sacrificed her happiness and her love for Stewart to settle debts. There were women all over London, a few more every Season, who wished for, who were in fact groomed for, nothing more than what Sylvia had so far accomplished with her life. Now she seemed prepared to give it all away in an effort to avoid scandal.

It was cruel irony that Sylvia should reveal such a change of heart on the very day that Stewart asked Sarah to marry him. In the space of a breath taken, Hawkes pondered the enormity of this commonly accepted form of commerce; the commerce of love and title and money. He had accepted the business of marriage, as just that, a business transaction, for most of his adult life. Now that he might lose Sarah to the system, it stunned him. Why did he persist in honoring a promise that perpetuated such a mockery of emotion? The miserable fact that he had done nothing to stand in Stewart's bloody way, before it had reached the point of his having asked Sarah Lyndle to barter her own way into the marriage market, sickened him.

Without excusing himself, without a word, he turned on his heel and left the yard.

Sarah wept. The tears washed softly down her cheeks to drop without heed onto the Brussels lace bodice of her gown and into the bamboo cage she leaned her cheek against. Lydia's parakeet seemed not to notice that its seed was a trifle salt and damp, any more than it seemed to care for her distress, but Mrs. Turvey, coming quietly in to find Sarah in tears, did.

"Has the naughty creature pecked your hand?"

"No." Sarah's reply was muted, and she passed a hand across the dampness on her cheek in an effort to regain her composure. "I depend on this little fellow to sing me out of the mopes." Her attempt to sound cheerful was gallant, but a sad, shuddering hiccup interrupted her final word, quite spoiling the effect.

"My dear," Lydia began, but those particular words coupled with her heartfelt concern, provoked a fresh outburst of tears.

Sarah wondered if Hawkes would still call her his dear were she to marry his cousin. She thought not.

"Now, now, my love." Mrs. Turvey gathered Sarah into her ample arms and allowed her outburst to wet one very comfortable shoulder. "Come now, pet. Is it that silly business with Geoffrey Garvey and his new wife that has you in a pucker?"

Sarah gave a watery chuckle and pulled herself away from the warm comfort of Mrs. Turvey's embrace to blow her nose. "No, no," she said, mopping her wet face. "I know you will think it quite heartless in me, but I'd quite forgot about Geoff, Lydia."

"Then what is it, Sarah? What upsets you so?"

"Mr. Castleford has asked me to be his wife." The pitiful wavering of her own voice moved Sarah to tears again.

Lydia did not understand her distress in the least. With a breathless squeezing hug she chortled, "How wonderful! No wonder you are quite overset, coming as this does higgledy-piggledy after your disappointment with Garvey. To be first visited by the young man who saw fit to leave you standing in the lurch as he did, and then the very next day to have your hand solicited by another young man. Why, it must be quite unsettling."

Sarah managed a nod. "I know not what I shall say."

"Say? You have only to say yes or no. Have you not already done so?"

"No. Stewart said under the circumstances, that he understood I should require some time to consider his request."

"How very thoughtful of Stewart. He shall make you a very considerate husband, you know."

Therein lies the dilemma, Sarah thought. She didn't

know. She clasped her palms to her temples. "Oh, my head does ache."

"But of course it does," Lydia said comfortingly. " 'Tis not an easy thing to decide if one can bear to spend the rest of one's days beside a body. I think you should be very happy. Stewart's proposal rescues you from all potential of an unsettling reaction to Garvey's putting you off. It could not be better timed. The Castleford name will shield you from any unpleasantness, and the Castleford family will be pleased to welcome you into their fold."

Sarah's attention was arrested enough to pull her throbbing head up out of the cradle of her hands. "Think you so?"

"But of course, love. Lady Castleford dotes on you, and the earl would certainly squash any nasty gossip in a trice."

"Yes, he would do that," she agreed as sadness again overwhelmed her. He had already done that.

"Yes, of course he would. Did he not see to it that you have Button to ride, and convince you to dance when no one else could, and buy you that lovely book with the raised letters?"

"The book?" Sarah breathed the words as if afraid Lydia might unsay the thing should she speak any louder. "I'd no idea it was he gave it to me."

"Oh dear me, yes, and I've broken my promise to him in letting that slip. He was most particular in wishing the gift to be an anonymous one. Although why a man who is called Beast should wish to hide any kindness is beyond me."

Sarah did not say so, but she agreed with Lydia. Why should Hawkes have wished to keep his gift to her a secret, unless, and her sadness increased at the thought, he had not wanted her to get the wrong impression as to his intentions.

"Will you have him, then?" Sarah's father asked as a hackney cab delivered them to the Beales' for dinner.

Sarah was not attending. Her thoughts were on the

prospect of a life as the Beauty's wife, with the Beast a member of her newly extended family. Such a future seemed unbearable. Every sensibility must be offended. There would be no avoiding coming into contact with Hawkes and such contact would prove painful.

Her father tapped her arm. "Well, will you have him?"

"What?" Sarah jerked away from her bleak thoughts.

"Castleford. What say you to his offer?"

"Castleford?" she repeated, confused for a moment. "Oh, you mean Stewart."

"I'll not stand in your way if you mean to have him. Seemed a pleasant enough fellow. He obviously means to provide for your happiness in all ways. I cannot say that I quite like the manner in which he has so recently turned his fortune, but I cannot fault him for his readiness to spend it all in making you comfortable. I was much struck when he revealed his intentions to purchase Brantley. . . ."

"Brantley?" Sarah's voice sounded shrill to her own ears. She lowered her pitch. "You are certain he means to do so?"

"So the lad told me himself. His cousin means to deed the place over to him on your wedding day. Pleased me no end to think you'd be settled so near to Lyndle Hall."

"On my wedding day?" Sarah said breathlessly. Her spirits, which had begun to recover, took another plunge. It would appear that Hawkes approved of his cousin's intentions.

Her father went on as if the matter were decided. "I wish you very happy."

Sighing, Sarah allowed a wistful smile to turn up her lips. "I have yet to say yes, Father," she reminded him gently.

Her father demanded with asperity, "You will say yes, will you not?"

Sarah rubbed the bridge of her nose. She was getting the headache again. "I have not quite made up my mind."

Her father patted her hand as though she were no more than a child and he knew what was best for her. "Well, miss, don't dillydally around too long, or you may find yourself not only the center of gossip, but upon the shelf as well. A young man with Castleford's polished air and good looks will be snapped up in a trice, now he's swimming in the ready."

"Yes, I'm sure you're right," murmured Sarah with the thought that she could not imagine marriage to any Castleford save one.

Chapter 22

SARAH'S head was throbbing in earnest by the time she and her father reached Lord and Lady Beale's house. She could not stop thinking about her promise to answer Stewart's proposal in the morning. Could a future with some contact with Hawkes, as his cousin's wife, be preferable to a future without him at all? She thought not, but in the end could not be certain.

As she and Lord Lyndle were ushered to the drawing room where the gathered company waited for dinner to be served, she begged her father, "Please be so good as to find me an out-of-the-way place to sit and nurse my head. I am not feeling at all the thing, and would not make very good conversation."

He obligingly led her to one of the three windowseats that graced the room and went off to fetch a curative for her head. It was not her father, however, who returned with the remedy. Sarah knew it was Hawkes before he uttered a word, and she faced him as if confronting danger. Indeed he was troublesome, when it came to the state of both head and heart, which began to pound in furiously painful harmony.

"How are you, my dear? Your father tells me you have the headache."

So kind was his voice, so gentle his inquiry, that Sarah found herself hard-pressed not to burst into tears. She would have liked nothing more than to rest her aching head upon his shoulder with a weepy explanation of how dreadfully confusing the affairs of her heart had become. She would have liked to have told him everything; that she could not stop thinking of him, of the way his voice vibrated in her ear, of how her hands burned at his touch and her senses seemed to come to life whenever he was near. She wanted him to know that she listened for his step, his voice, his laughter. She wished him to comprehend that he was the throb in her head, the ache in her heart, the tears on her pillow, but common sense and her burgeoning doubts over his approval of Stewart's suit and his feelings for the baroness made her mum.

"I am a little off color, my lord," she managed to respond without abandoning her composure.

"Perhaps this will help," he said softly, and pressed a vial of hartshorn and a glass of water into her hands.

She took the noxious drink and sipped, all the while wishing he would go away and leave her to her suffering, for his presence only served to intensify the pain in her head.

"You are troubled by something?" He sank down before her on one knee, his movement stirring the fabric of her skirt, as much as his question, his very presence, stirred an abject despair in her heart.

"It is kind of you to ask," she said, and the words caught in her throat, for it suddenly occurred to Sarah that kindness was at the heart of all that the earl had done for her. It was kindness that had moved him to ask her to dance, kindness that led her up the ladder at St. Paul's, kindness that saw to it a book for the blind should fall into her hands anonymously, and kindness that helped to stifle cruel gossip of Garvey's jilt. It was all kindness, only kindness. She had been blind to that. She had mistaken kindness for love. Kindness, and a kiss in the heat of a rose garden.

The words he had quoted to her in the Whispering Gallery sounded in her memory. "Love does not alter when it alteration finds." It was true. Her own love for him did not diminish, though she now believed he looked upon her only with the kindness of a potential relative. She had not thought that fate could be so cruel. The intensity of her feelings, unreciprocated, seemed a harsh sort of punishment—a hell of her own making. She almost wished him cruel, a beast in fact as well as in name, so that she might not have made such a heartbreaking error in judgment.

She could feel his eyes searching her face.

"You look pale in this light, my dear."

He seemed determined to cut through her facade of control. That he should tease her so, with a concern so profound one might mistake it for emotion of a more intimate degree, made her a little angry. She had no intention of giving in, either to his kindness or to the turmoil of her emotions. She swallowed the headache potion, though it made not a drop's worth of difference in her suffering, and fanned herself, to cool both forehead and feelings.

His voice was soft and low and infinitely moving. "This week has been rather wearing, has it not?"

Why did he persist in addressing her as his dear? Why did he speak to her of the very thing she least wished to discuss? Could he not see how unable she was to respond to his inquiry?

"I am feeling rather pulled," she agreed.

"Like a Catherine Wheel, I'll be bound."

He did not mistake her distress. The very fondness in his voice pulled tortuously the frayed ends of her nerves. It was kindness, nothing more, she reminded herself.

"There is something I have to say, better discussed in private. Do you mind if I call on you in the morning?"

She wanted to weep, or shout, or beat her fists against his breast. What good did talking do? And what, pray tell, did they have to discuss? The affairs of her heart? Could it be he meant to encourage her to accept his cousin's suit, just as her father and Mrs. Turvey had? Had he been informed, so soon, of his cousin's intentions?

"I shall not be at home for callers in the morning. I have an appointment that I must keep. Perhaps another day would be better?"

"No. I do not think it would."

"Would it not?" She tried to sound quelling.

He was not cowed. "I had rather hoped that we might converse before you give Stewart his answer."

Her breath hitched in her throat. She felt foolish. Of course, Stewart would have told him of his proposal. They were best friends as well as cousins. She made a valiant effort to sound lighthearted. "You were right, of course, about Stewart asking me to marry him."

He was silent a moment. She could feel him studying her face. He shifted his position, and it occurred to her he could not be very comfortable there, down upon one knee.

"You are to meet him tomorrow, with an answer?"

She pressed a palm to her forehead. It had begun to feel as if her brain were being squeezed by some giant fist. Impatient with the pain, and his questions, and the decision she must make by morning, she dropped her hand back down again and tried to extricate herself from this discussion. It annoyed her that he should be so aware of all that transpired in her life, and so ignorant of her yearning for him. Something childish within her was tempted to test the limitations of his infinite kindness, for perhaps, were he but cruel to her, or sarcastic, or mocking, she might find the absence of his love easier to bear.

"You would seem, once again, to be far better informed regarding the affairs of my heart than I am myself," she said, borrowing some of the ironic sarcasm with which he was so fond of instilling his words.

A silence stretched between them, a silence so heavy as he knelt gazing into her pained face that her neck began to ache with the weight of it. She wished he would go away. She had begun to sound waspish, and she could not like that in herself.

The dinner gong sounded. Before she could make a move to rise, he had sprung up from his kneeling stance and stood ready to assist.

"May I take you in to dinner, my dear?" he said, little knowing how much it wounded her to hear him call her that.

She felt the movement in the air before her, heard the hushing sound of fabric as he held out his hand to her. She could not take it. There was the heat of too much yearning within her aching heart already, without the added fuel of his burning hand on hers. There was no getting around him without his permitting it, and it would seem he had no intention of making such an allowance. She stood without accepting his assistance, expecting him to step back, but he did not do so immediately. Neither did he reach for her, though. As if he sensed her resistance, his hand fell.

Face-to-face the narrow space between them vibrated, like the space vibrates between a magnet and metal, distanced just enough not to fly together. There was a force, an intensity in his very voice, that lured her.

"I must speak to you," he insisted, leaning closer.

The hair at the nape of her neck rose, as the scent of him washed over her, filling her nostrils, turning her head.

"Will you not come a little early in the morning?" he breathed, the heat of his question rifling the surface of her lips. "Will you not agree to meet me in my mother's music room? There is something vitally important I must ask you."

She swayed toward him, irresistibly drawn, overpowered in her better sense by the need to know what it was he considered so important, caught up in a spell of hope and desire. She wanted him to kiss her in that instant, to draw her into the comfortable haven of his arms. She wanted his assurance that it was not only kindness that he felt for her, but love.

The powerful magic of the moment was broken by the intrusion of a servant, come to inform Hawkes that a gentleman, a Mr. Bret Preston, had come to the door asking to speak to him.

"Preston?" Hawkes heaved an angry, impatient sigh. "What the devil does he want?"

The messenger shifted uncomfortably. "He said, my lord, seeing as it pertained to your cousin, that he was sure you might spare him a minute. Shall I send him on his way?"

Hawkes stepped away from Sarah, staggering her, for his presence, like a prop, did seem to have been holding her up.

"Where have you put him?" Hawkes asked, and even as he spoke his hand shot out, both to steady her, and to detain her flight, for it was her intention to slip by him.

Sarah did not think he sounded at all pleased. The servant was sent on his way with the instruction that he would join Mr. Preston momentarily.

"You were about to tell me whether or not I might have the opportunity to speak with you tomorrow," he reminded her as he tucked her arm through his and walked with her into the dining room. Headachy and sad, Sarah felt certain she knew what it was Hawkes wished to discuss. Like everyone else, he meant to champion his cousin's cause, and she was heartily sick of other people deciding what was best for her life.

"You must not keep Mr. Preston waiting," she said, settling into her chair.

He sank into the chair beside her, and as if he could read her very thoughts, said softly, "I have no intention of leaving your side until I have obtained your promise to meet me."

Sarah wished nothing more in that instant than to make him go away and knew instinctively that the fastest way in which to do so was to agree. "I will come early," she said leadenly.

"Excellent," he said, and only then did he do as she wished in leaving her alone with her headache.

Hawkes was feeling as though his life teetered on the brink of disaster when he burst rudely into Lord Beale's smoking closet in search of the annoyingly intrusive Bret Preston. Never had Sarah so distanced herself from him as she had this evening. She had seemed suddenly as cold and detached as her gaze. It shook him that he had to pull a promise of speech with her with the reluctance one might expect in the extraction of a tooth. He knew she was suffering, and not just from the headache. It pained him that she had not seen fit to confide in him her trouble and it irritated him that Bret Preston, of all people, should be the one to pull him from her side as dinner began.

"Mr. Preston, you would seem to have the habit of turning up where you are neither wanted nor expected," Hawkes said, brutally sarcastic as he stepped into the smoking room.

Bret looked up from the large wooden elephant humidor where he had been making a selection from the cigars stored within. "I can see how you might have gathered such an impression," he admitted, unprovoked. Choosing one of the cigars, he rolled it between finger and thumb to test its crackle. "But I interrupt your dinner with every expectation of making up for the past." He passed the cigar beneath his nose with an approving sniff. "You see," he said, "I believe I owe you an odd favor or two."

"And this one involves Stewart?"

Bret struck a match with the intention of lighting up his chosen cigar. "Yes. Tell me, is it true, that he is still pining after Sylvia DeValle?"

"Stewart proposed to Sarah Lyndle this morning." Hawkes said levelly, holding his rising anger in tight check.

Bret lipped the end of the cigar, the lit match forgotten between his fingers until heat reminded him and he shook it out. "The blind girl? How very odd," he said thoughtfully and struck up another match.

"Odd?" Hawkes prodded, wishing Bret would get on with what he had come to say.

Bret took his time, however, his brow still puckered in thought. He lit the cigar and sucked in until the end was burning nicely. Exhaling heavily, he said through the cloud of his own making, "Yes odd. I was really quite convinced it was Sylvia Stew meant to have."

"What convinced you? Last I heard, you were telling the world that I should soon find myself tied to the widow's apron strings."

Bret gave him a penetrating look. "Well, I have been known to fall down in my judgment, on occasion," he admitted.

Hawkes frowned and thought of Catherine Stone.

Bret saw the frown and nervously flicked ash into a bone china tray. "Forgive me. . . ."

Hawkes looked up swiftly, unwilling to suffer through an apology, but all Bret said was, ". . . I wonder. You see, I have just this evening seen your cousin at a club he is not in the habit of frequenting, engaged in a rather heated game of hazard. I was sure it must have something to do with the Widow DeValle."

"What has Sylvia to do with a game of hazard?"

Bret blew a cloud. He wore a puzzled expression as he watched it disperse. "Well, it is Sylvester Naughtley Stew seems quite happily bent on losing the majority of his recent winnings to."

"Losing?" Hawkes protested. "At hazard? Not Stewart."

Bret shrugged and gave Hawkes a sliding, sideways glance. "I tell you truly, my lord, he shall not have enough left to buy so much as a junkman's nag by morning, at the rate he's going. Lad seems bent on winning possession of all of Naughtley's little black books, or ending up in Dunn Street with the effort."

Hawkes's eyes narrowed. "At what club will I chance to find my cousin?"

"He is at the Two Sevens," Bret said as he languidly blew smoke-rings at the ceiling. And then, softly came the question. "Care for some company?"

Hawkes had turned to go. He paused, considering the request, and without turning said, "Care to come along? I am in the mood for gossip."

Bret stubbed out his cigar as he rose. "You, Hawkes? Hungry for gossip? Something about Naughtley, perhaps?"

"Naughtley, and his connection with the late Baron De-Valle."

Bret gave a devilish chuckle. "Ah, juicy stuff!"

The patrons of the gaming hall in Jermyn Street were too interested in watching the game of hazard Hawkes had come to see to spare him or Bret so much as a glance when they entered, even though they broke house rules in bringing two young stable lads with them. The crowd was four deep around the dicing table, murmuring in hushed awe like a crowd of relatives gathered outside the door of a dying man, where they waited to hear the last gasp, the last rites, and the disbursement of the will.

Stewart, it appeared, was the dying man, or at the very least, the beaten one. His sleeves had been folded neatly out of the way for an unfettered casting of the dice, and every golden hair was in place, but a dwindling pile of counters was to be observed to his right, a wide-eyed Mortimer Saile to his left.

"May we go now, Stew," Morty was saying, "or do you intend to lose it all?"

"Main," Stewart called out, ignoring his friend, and made his cast. "Six," he announced, examining his throw with composure, through his monocle.

Morty looked around a little wildly, as if for help, spotted Hawkes and Bret just come in together, and pushed through the crowd toward them.

"Chance," Stewart called evenly, and casting again, drew a murmur, as if of sympathetic pain, from the crowd.

Hawkes did not have to look to see that Stewart had thrown out, but he was surprised to see how well his cousin bore the loss. Stewart still looked as cool as a cucumber, and no less enthused for the game as he passed two more of his counters down the table toward Sylvester Naughtley.

Sylvester announced with unsportsmanly glee, "Crabs! My throw," and greedily added the counters to a gluttonous pile that had been heaped atop three small, black, calf-bound books at the end of the table. Hawkes concentrated a moment on the books, and then with narrowing eyes, turned his attention to the man they belonged to.

In direct contrast to Stewart, Sylvester looked as if he had combed his fly-away hair with a gardening rake. His mouth twisted upward in slightly dazed glee whenever his bulging eyes chanced to fall on his pile of winnings. His voice shook as he took up the dice to make his throw.

"Main nine," he warbled, a man caught in the fever of winning. And then, casting quick again, as if afraid his luck would run away from him, the crowd once more forecast the results of the throw, with an excited little outburst of "knicked it, he's knicked it again, the lucky bastard."

Mortimer Sailes, his eyes wide and alive with concern, had pressed through the crowd, and he tugged now at Hawkes's sleeve.

"Can you stop this madness?" he gasped. He's been at it all evening, and no end in sight till the last halfpenny is gone."

Hawkes drew Morty with him away from the table as the dice were passed back to Stewart. Bret Preston, a stable lad from Sylvia's yard at each elbow, politely refrained from crowding them.

"Quick now, for he loses even as we speak. Has my cousin been drinking overmuch this evening?"

"No," Mortimer assured him, his eyes darting over Hawkes's shoulder to the crowd. "Not a drop."

"Main." They heard. "Seven."

"Did he choose to come here to play?"

"Insisted upon it," Morty said, and then winced as Sylvester cackled behind them. "Crabs again!"

"Said he knew that elbow-shaker frequented the place." Morty jerked a thumb at Naughtley.

Hawkes nodded. "Stewart set out to find Naughtley then?"

"Aye, more's the pity."

"The dice? Are they Fullhams? Can it be Naughtley is cheating?"

"Dispatchers? Can't be. They're Stewart's own. He brought a set with him and insisted they be used in the play."

Hawkes eyed the black books again. "Did he tell you why he wanted to play Naughtley?"

Mortimer sighed. "Well, he did ramble on as to how he had decided at last just what it was he wanted to buy with his investment money, but it made no sense at all to me."

"What did he say?" Hawkes demanded. "Can you remember?"

Mortimer nodded, his mouth sagging. "Said he meant to

buy back a piece of the past, for an old friend. I've no idea what he meant by it."

"I see," Hawkes said, and he did see with a clarity that took his breath away. Stewart meant to risk everything he owned to buy back a piece of the past for Sylvia.

"Ha! I have won all you have to offer," Sylvester crowed, raking in his markers.

As if Stewart felt his cousin's presence, the china blue eyes turned for a moment and locked on Hawkes. The monocle was calmly raised. Stewart dipped his head regally, acknowledging his cousin's presence. There was something in the stunned blankness of his look that reminded Hawkes of the night Sylvia had told them she meant to marry DeValle. The crowd parted that Hawkes might make his way to the table.

"This is a dangerous game you play, Stew," he said, deceptively mild as he scanned the table. "Has he indeed won everything?"

Stewart's china blue eye looked watery behind the monocle.

"Not all," he protested, undaunted. He tipped his head toward the table. "I have one marker yet to win with."

"One marker?" Naughtley chuckled, all of his attention focused on the gathering of his riches. "I leave it to you, Castleford. I would not have it said I completely paupered a man."

"Such chivalry, Naughtley! You restore my faith in mankind," Hawkes purred smoothly, something dangerous in his voice, something predatory in his gaze.

Naughtley looked up. The gleeful grin slid awkwardly from his thin lips. Behind the spectacles, his close-set eyes narrowed.

Hawkes carefully shifted his position, that Sylvester might catch sight of Bret behind him, as well as the stable lads he had gone out of his way to bring with them. "One must assume, Naughtley, that even you have some concern for what the gossip mongers make of you," he drawled.

A ripple of amusement passed through the waiting crowd of gamesters. Sylvester's reputation for gossip collecting was widespread.

The color drained from Sylvester's face. "You are mistaken," he spat. His eyes flinched away from the stable lads. Belligerence fired his face in a rush.

There were those among the crowd who had observed the direction of Naughtley's distracted looks, if not their object. Like a soft wind, whispered speculation began.

Hawkes made a point of looking anywhere than at the boys behind him. He picked up the dice, and carefully balanced them in his palm, as though balancing fate. His gaze rose then to fix unwaveringly on Naughtley's troubled countenance. "A man who lives in a glass house should not throw stones, Mr. Naughtley." The ivory cubes clicked together as he closed his hand around them. "Else it undoubtedly comes crashing down around his ears."

"Do you threaten me?" Sylvester leaned across the table to hiss.

"By no means, Naughtley," Hawkes purred. "This is, to my mind, a promise. No more. I should like to think it was a promise I shall never have to keep." The dice rattled again as Hawkes dropped them in the casting cup. "You have been inordinately lucky today, sir. Pray, do not forget how easily luck turns." To emphasize the point, Hawkes inverted the casting cup onto the center of the table, with a flick of his wrist, and left it sitting, the dice hidden beneath it.

Sylvester's hand snapped out, thumb and forefinger poised to flick away the cup.

"Uh-uh-uh," Stewart playfully slapped his wrist. "There is still one marker left to chance. This game is not over yet."

Sylvester fairly salivated in angry anticipation of a confrontation he could win. "I'll take every penny you've got if you are set on losing it," he blustered, "and so confident am I that luck is mine tonight, that I offer you all or nothing, based on what sits beneath that cup."

The crowd buzzed their approval that the play might yet commence, and at such a stake. Hawkes turned his back on the table and made his way to the door as odds and money began to fly among the spectators.

"Wha—Where are you going?" Mortimer asked desperately, trailing after him.

"Do you not mean to stay and see what you have thrown?" Bret demanded. "Stewart is paupered if he loses this bet."

"And Sylvester will be livid if he does not. A sight I have no desire to witness." Hawkes placed his hat on his head. In truth, he could not bear to witness Stewart's downfall, should it come.

He herded the sleepy stable lads out of the door to the club. Behind him, the crowd roared. Luck, it would seem, had changed.

Chapter 23

SARAH'S heart was dark and lonely and heavy as stone. For the first time in her life, she felt that her blindness was complete. A curtain had been drawn down upon self-certainty. She was physically, emotionally, and mentally plunged into the shadow of darkness. Her beliefs and feelings and purpose were become suddenly suspect, her confident ability to see the intangible, despite her handicap, shaken.

Need and desire and wishful thinking had blinded her to reality, she decided. The hungry yearning that had driven her here to London in the first place had devoured her common sense, clouded all vision, and led her in a merry, dizzying dance. And while she danced, life had crept up on her, changing all that was familiar and plunging her in a darkness so complete, she recognized neither shape, nor sound, nor smell. Reality had gone awry. Her fate, her future, her hopes and dreams had lost substance and direction, like smoke in a changing wind.

It was not Hawkes who loved her, it was his cousin, Stewart. The slow spin of that singular thought left her unsteady on her feet, as if she went one direction, while life went the other. Restless and unrested, Sarah came early, as she had promised, to a music room that echoed with emptiness, a place possessed of a stillness so complete that her presence was an intrusion on its peace. In this stillness, Sarah was assailed by a premonition of change, so all-encompassing it slowed her footsteps. The sensation convinced her she had best feel her way slowly, lest she run into some rearrangement of the furniture.

It was her life that had been rearranged, and not the fur-

niture. Feeling clumsy and awkward, Sarah sat herself
down on the bench before the pianoforte and sought to rec-
oncile herself not only with the room and the space she occupied within it, but with her place in life itself, through the
healing flow of music. She broke the silence that surrounded her gently, with the soft, sad strains of Corelli and
Vivaldi, and then attacked the stillness more vigorously
with Mozart, but the whirl of thought and emotion that
troubled her seemed only to intensify as her fingers flew
over the keys. In the end, her hands crashed down with
frustration in the middle of a particularly heart-wrenching
passage.

She let the notes bounce off the walls, let stillness fall
around her like a presence, until its very thickness must
needs be broken, and she reached for the musical bird that
Stewart had given her, and wound it up and let its tinny tinkling fill the room with something less lonely than silence,
and less passionate than Mozart.

She decided that the noise the bird made suited her
mood.

There was something so flatly devoid of emotion in the
sound that she felt compelled to pick out the same stilted
pattern of notes on the pianoforte. The tinny song was
oddly appropriate, almost comforting, as it resounded hol-
lowly in the echoing proportions of the still room, and she
might have gone on indefinitely plinking at it had not the
drifting scent of vertivert stilled her fingers and sent her
heart lurching into her suddenly dry mouth.

"Lord Castleford," she said, and she could not contain
her frustration even in this, the utterance of his name. "How
long have you been here listening, my lord, without so
much as announcing your presence?"

"Long enough to know that you are troubled, my dear."

His voice was warm and lazy and human, and so infinitely dear to her, as the music box continued to spin out its
coldly mechanical tune, that her back stiffened with anxi-
ety. Was this moment, she wondered, all that was left of a
lovely dream in which the earl cared for and desired her as
much as she did he?

She shivered, gooseflesh prickling her arms as he

stepped out of the doorway where he leaned and crossed the room. She wished him closer and she wished him gone forever, all in the same instant. She felt as though at some level he reached out to change the space between them—touching her with something other than his physical presence. She was troubled by a breathless fear as he approached, as if he might mow her down, leaving her crushed and broken in his wake.

He sank down beside her on the bench, his back to the instrument, so that they seemed, in stance as well as in purpose, to be headed in opposite directions. It was not a large bench. His shoulder brushed the fullness of her sleeve. She felt a whisper of his breath, warm on her ear. Her lips parted with the sensation. Her mouth and nostrils filled with his scent. She swayed toward him, not away.

"I wish, my dear . . ."

He had called her his dear again, and as he said it, she could smell the sweet essence of bergamot on his breath. Her own mouth felt dry and tasteless. She wished, quite irrationally, to wet her lips, her tongue, with the hot, sweet taste of bergamot tea.

". . . I wish to discuss with you, a matter of the heart."

Those words, of all the words he might have chosen to address her, were guaranteed to send a wave of anger coursing through Sarah's breast. The last time he had begun a conversation with those words he had been referring to the condition of his ward's heart. This morning she was sure he referred to that of his cousin, and Sarah could not imagine accepting advice from Hawkes in any decision to marry Stewart. She could not, would not listen to him suggest such a future. It contradicted her every feeling.

She lifted her chin, and there was anger, pride, and pain in the words she chose to interrupt him. She wielded them like a knife, to cut away her yearning for him before it ruined her. "Lord Castleford, I have a good idea of what it is you have come to say to me this morning and would beg of you to say no more."

Hawkes drew back from her as though stung. There was nothing lazy in his tone. "What's this?"

She stood abruptly, before courage deserted her, and

paced away from him with the aid of her walking stick—away from her dangerous desire for him. The music box had stopped spinning its mechanical tune. It was an echoing silence that she broke with her vibrating anger.

"I know that you have come to think of yourself as more closely acquainted with the affairs of my heart than I am myself, my lord, but in this matter, sir, you are sadly mistaken. I cannot repeat the mistake I made in so blindly promising to marry Geoffrey. Marriage is too important an undertaking to base on a fear of remaining unmarried, or on what one does or does not have in name and property. I may be blind, but I am not stupid, and as a woman grown, I am quite capable of making up my own mind with regard to either the acceptance or refusal of a proposal of marriage, a proposal that determines my fate and happiness for years to come. I will not be swayed, either by your kindness, or your landholdings, I promise you."

She offended him. She could hear it in the sarcasm with which he laced his response. "Make me no such promises, my dear. I am, you see, half sick of promises that ought not to be kept, for I have myself made one too many of them."

Sick at heart, Hawkes sat staring at Sarah as she stood stiffly in the middle of the room, her color high, her chest rising and falling, as if she had just run a race that took her out of his reach. He was amazed by the vehemence of her outburst and at a loss as to what he might say to make things right between them.

It had never occurred to Hawkes that he might be refused, before ever he had the chance to state his case. There was a sense of unreality to the moment, as though a wall of misunderstanding had been thrown up between them. Every fiber in his being urged him to tear down that wall, or in the very least, to scale it, so that he might fathom what made it stand.

Clearing his throat, he rose, and taking Stewart's music box in shaking hands, wound its key. Then, without a word, as it tinkled thinly into the room, he crossed the distance that separated him from Sarah and made a formal bow.

"Would you care to dance with a shadow, my dear?"

She stood very still for a moment, her back stiff and

straight as a pike-staff. He thought she sounded very close to tears when she replied, "You are very kind to ask, my lord, but surely this is not the time or the place for dancing."

He gazed down at the dear face he longed to cover with kisses, and unable to define the expression with which he was met, took her hand and drew it into the curve of his arm.

"You forget, my dear. I do not do things out of kindness, but because I enjoy doing them. And, of all things, I enjoy dancing with you excessively."

He swayed suggestively in time with their pitiful music, and to his surprise she fell into step, as perfectly, comfortably, and gracefully as though they had practiced together for years. There was a feeling of completeness within Hawkes as he secured her waist within his grasp, as he leaned into the caress of her hair on his cheek. Wordless, and yet sharing of a communication that transcended speech, they whirled down the room in tandem, their steps in complete accord, their bodies drawn together by forces undeniable. A soaring sense of light and hope and promise lifted Hawkes's spirits. The fluid, graceful oneness that they so singularly shared filled him with happy wonder.

They danced until the music ran down.

"The music has stopped, my lord," she pointed out to him as he continued to sweep her about the floor.

He paused beside the French doors that led out onto the terrace and leaning into the delicious golden mass of her hair, he said, "Nonsense, I hear it playing still. Listen, can't you hear it?"

She shook her head, confused, but with the pressure of his hand at her waist and a gentle humming in her hair, he had her moving again, out the door and around the expanse of the terrace.

"Hush," he whispered when she lifted her chin and tried to speak. Softly he said it, gently, so as not to offend, and then he lowered his head and said the word again, his lips moving within a hair's breadth of hers, his breath an intentional caress. "Hush," he insisted. "Listen closely, my dear. Listen for the drum."

She stopped dead still and pulled back from the dangerous proximity of his mouth. "I hear no drumming other than that of my heart. . . ." she said heatedly.

"Ah, but there are two drums pounding," he insisted, and drew her close again. "Listen! It is the sweetest music I have ever heard, the music our two hearts make together."

She froze, her breath fast and shallow on his cheek. "I am confused, my lord," she said warily. "Do you mean to tease me?"

Hawkes drew back in surprise and cupped her chin in his palm so that he might tip up her face and study its expression. "Tease you?" he said, somewhat offended she should ask. "No, dearest Sarah. I have no desire to tease you. I mean however, to break a promise, and that is something I have prided myself in never having cause to do before."

He kissed her then, and while she did not pull away from him, neither did she respond to his ardor with anything other than a startled intake of breath. Her back and neck, even her lips were hard and unyielding. He kissed her again, the hand beneath her chin stretching out to lightly stroke the smooth softness of her neck and jaw and earlobe, and as if in touching her thus he had touched upon a trigger, she moaned, and seemed to sink a little deeper into his embrace, and her lips, now soft, parted sweetly beneath his. Joy flooded Hawkes, and with a moan to match hers, his lips, his tongue, his very breath sought to intermingle with hers. There was something very like the dance in this meeting of their mouths, for they came together in perfect, passionate accord, and moved and swayed and glided with the matching rhythm of their desire.

Heart singing, Hawkes gathered her to him, so that her breast heaved against the resistance of his chest, and their hips and thighs and legs pressed one against the other in tandem need.

She thrust her hands against his chest, and pulled away from his questing lips, to ask breathlessly, "This promise you have broken. What is it?"

Hawkes closed his eyes, and dipped his nose into the sweetness of her hair. "It was a promise to my cousin," he said gruffly. "A promise I find impossible to keep."

He sighed, opened his eyes, and caught his breath.

Fate had caught up with him. There in the lawn, monocle raised, stood Stewart.

"Is something wrong?" Sarah murmured.

His gaze fixed on a pair of china blue eyes, which met his unblinking, Hawkes hugged her more tightly to him and said sadly, "Yes, dreadfully wrong, for long ago I promised Stewart, who has now asked for your hand, that I would not vie for your affection. I find myself unable to honor that promise, and that pains me, for I cannot deny the love I hold for my cousin any more than I can deny that I have fallen head over ears in love with you, my dear."

Stewart blinked, and might have spoken had not Sarah sighed contentedly, and said with great certainty, "Stewart will understand." She lifted her head and inquired softly in Stewart's direction, "You do understand, don't you, Stewart?"

The monocle popped from Stewart's abruptly widened eye.

"I begin to think I do," he said.

"Good," Sarah said contentedly, "for while I value your friendship above all things, Stewart, I do not think we would be happy together."

"Certainly not. His heart belongs to another, my dear." Hawkes returned the focus of his attention to her lips, which were, he felt, in dire need of kissing yet again. "We will not keep you, cousin."

Stewart lifted his monocle, "No, I can see you will not."

"You're off then?" Hawkes suggested wryly.

Stewart turned on his heel with a chuckle. "Yes, I mean to see a lady about her horses. I have a proposal I do not think she will refuse."

"Splendid idea, proposals!" Hawkes said softly as he bent his lips to Sarah's yet again.

"And what do you propose, my lord," she wondered.

"I would lead you in a dance, my dear, a merry dance that will keep us whirling for the rest of our lives."

"I should love to dance, sir," she said softly, leaning her head against his chest and swaying in his arms. "I hear the sweetest music."